Pure and Untouched
AND
Love at the Helm

BARBARA CARTLAND

Pure and Untouched

AND

Love at the Helm

inspired and helped by
ADMIRAL OF THE FLEET
EARL MOUNTBATTEN OF BURMA

New York EVEREST HOUSE *Publishers*

Pure and Untouched

AUTHOR'S NOTE

The fear engendered by the cruel, eccentric, tyrannical Nicholas I, 1825–1855, undoubtably the most alarming Sovereign who ever reigned, changed the lives of his fifty million subjects.

There was nothing with which he did not interfere and nobody was safe from his jurisdiction.

If the firebells rang in St. Petersburg, he ran out and told the firemen what to do about it. He banished Prince Yusupov to the Caucasus because he was having a love-affair of which his mother did not approve.

When the daughter of a Courtier was treated badly by her husband, he had the marriage annulled and wrote majestically: "This young person shall be considered a virgin."

The Tsar's Secret Police, known as The Third Section, were terrifying, merciless, and inescapable. All Russia lived under the shadow of fear which continued even after Nicholas's death.

CHAPTER ONE

1889

THE DOOR of the Library opened and Mr. Matthews, Private Secretary and Comptroller to the Duke of Ravenstock, crossed the room quietly to where his employer was writing at a desk in the window.

He stood respectfully waiting to be noticed, and after several seconds the Duke raised his head to ask impatiently:

"What do you want, Matthews?"

"I thought I would inform Your Grace that a present has just arrived from Marlborough House from Their Royal Highnesses the Prince and Princess of Wales."

The Duke appeared momentarily interested.

"What is it?"

"A rose bowl, Your Grace."

The Duke groaned.

"Not another?"

"This is a very fine example, Your Grace, of early Georgian silver."

"That means another letter that I shall have to write personally."

"I am afraid so, Your Grace."

"Well, put it on the list and make it short. I do not intend to spend my honeymoon writing letters."

"I feel sure, Your Grace, that those who have to wait for your expressions of gratitude will understand the reason."

The Duke smiled, and it brought such an expression of charm to his face that Mr. Matthews thought it was understandable that so many women found the Duke irresistible.

Tall, broad-shouldered, and outstandingly handsome, he was not only the most attractive man in London but also the most raffish.

His exploits on the Turf, the stories of his escapades which when they reached the ears of the Queen at Windsor incurred her displeasure, and most of all the gossip about his innumerable love-affairs, lost nothing in the telling, being both printed in the more disreputable newspapers and passed in whispers from mouth to mouth from the Drawing-Rooms of Mayfair to the Parlours of Suburbia.

There was no doubt that the Duke was amused by his notoriety and paid no attention to his critics.

He played up the implication of his name by choosing black not only as the predominant colouring of his carriages but also as his racing-colours.

At every race-meeting, as the Duke's horse, which was almost invariably the favourite in its race, came galloping towards the winning-post, there would be shouts of: "Raven Black!" "Raven Black!" echoing down the course.

The Duke was known as a seducer of women who were only too eager to be seduced by him.

This was further evidence of what his detractors called his "shocking wickedness," but his friends called it his irresistible "fascination."

Now at last, when those who loved the Duke, including all his relations, had given up hope of his ever settling down and being married, he had fallen in love.

For years everybody had expected that his wife would be one of the few available beauties belonging to the exclusive circle in which he himself moved.

The likely candidates were almost invariably widows, because at the age of thirty-four it was not likely that the Duke would be interested in young girls, for the simple reason that he never met any.

The Prince of Wales had set the pace with love-affairs which included the beautiful Lily Langtry, and it was now well known that he was head-over-heels in love with the alluring Lady Brooke.

The Duke's love-affairs ran the gamut from the more spectacular actresses to the Queen's Ladies-in-Waiting, and each liaison surpassed the last in causing raised eye-brows and disapproving exclamations.

The Duke, however, sailed serenely through life, finding that he was easily bored with the women who surrendered far too quickly, and making those who pursued him not only frustrated but extremely unhappy.

"I like to be the hunter," he said to himself, but it appeared that few women were content to watch him pass by without giving chase.

He had only to look at them with that quizzical questioning in his eyes for them to reach out their white hands to touch him and, almost before he knew their names, to throw their arms round his neck.

"What the devil have you got, Ravenstock," the Prince of Wales had asked him once, "that I do not have?"

"Impertinence, Sir!" the Duke had replied.

The Prince had laughed uproariously.

"I believe that really is the answer!" he had said between guffaws.

Even so, when the Duke's love-affairs seemed to be lasting a shorter and shorter time, and the lines on his face were becoming a little more cynical, those amongst his friends who were genuinely fond of him wondered what could be done.

The answer to their question appeared in the shape of Lady Cleo-del Wick.

The Duke met her quite by chance when he was staying in a house-party which included the Prince of Wales at Warwick Castle, which was not far from the Castle owned by the Earl of Sedgewick.

The Earl and Countess and their daughter Lady Cleodel had come over for dinner, and the Duke, who was sitting next to the nineteen-year-old, found himself astounded by her beauty and fascinated in a way he had not experienced for many years.

Mourning had prevented Lady Cleodel from appearing before in the Social World, and now she was a year older than the other débutantes who were being presented at Court at the beginning of April.

The Duke knew that if he had ever before seen the golden-haired, blue-eyed beauty in the crowded Throne-Room at Buckingham Palace, he would have remembered her.

Looking at her now in the light of the silver candelabra on the table, he thought it would be impossible for any woman to be so lovely.

While her hair was the shining gold of a sovereign, it was extraordinary that her blue eyes should be fringed with dark lashes.

When he had enthused about them, she had explained that she owed them to some Irish ancestor.

When she spoke it was with a soft, hesitating little voice which he would have found extremely seductive if he had not realised how young and pure she was.

He talked to her all through the meal, to the palpable annoyance of the lady on his other side, and when the gentlemen joined the ladies in the Drawing-Room, he had gone straight to Lady Cleodel's side to say that he would call on her the following day.

She had not been fulsomely grateful as any other woman would have been. Instead she had said:

"I must ask Mama if we will be at home. We have many engagements in the afternoons, even though we are in the country."

The Duke had made certain that the Countess would receive him, and when he returned to London he had called at Sedgewick House, where he had found to his surprise that Lady Cleodel was not always readily available.

On several occasions, when she must have been aware that he was coming, she had gone out.

He had danced with her at every Ball they had both attended, but the Duke for the first time in his life had to wait his turn to partner Lady Cleodel, and one night, to his astonishment, he was unable to obtain a single dance, owing to the fact that her programme was already full.

When two weeks later he proposed and was accepted, he had found that even then she was elusive.

The kisses which other women had been all too eager to give him, even before he asked for them, he thought sometimes were not exactly refused by Lady Cleodel but were undoubtedly avoided.

The Duke seized every possible chance of being alone with his fiancée, but she always kept him at arm's length.

"No, no, you must not touch me," she said when he tried to take her in his arms. "You know Mama would not approve of our being alone together if she knew of it."

"Why should she know?" the Duke asked.

"If my hair was ruffled and my lips looked—kissed, she would be—angry with me!"

"But I want to kiss you," he insisted.

"I want it too," Cleodel said softly, glancing up at him from under her dark eye-lashes, "but Mama would be cross, and then she would prevent us from being alone again."

This was something new in the Duke's experience, and he had to be content, even while he mocked at his own self-control, with kissing Cleodel's fingers instead of her lips.

He told himself that because she was so young he must have both patience and understanding.

At the same time, the grace with which she moved, and the things she said in her soft little voice which told him how much he had to teach her about life and love, made him become more and more infatuated.

The Sedgewicks made no pretence about not being delighted at the prospect of having such a distinguished and wealthy son-in-law.

Although the Earl had a large Estate, he was not a rich man. But he had indeed expected, because of her beauty, that his daughter would marry well.

What he and his wife had not anticipated was that she would catch the most eligible bachelor in the County, whose social position ranked only just below that of a Royal Prince.

If the Sedgewicks were surprised, it was nothing compared to the astonishment of everybody else. But it was only the Duke's most intimate friend, Harry Carrington, who was brave enough to say so to the prospective bridegroom.

He had just returned from Scotland where he had been salmon-fishing on the Spey, and at first he had thought it must be a joke.

"You always told me you would remain a bachelor until you were on your last legs!" he had said to the Duke when he found him alone at Ravenstock House.

"That is what I fully intended," the Duke had replied, "until I met Cleodel."

"I have already been told that she is very beautiful," Harry said tentatively, "but at nineteen, how will she cope with you?"

"There will be nothing to cope with," the Duke replied.

He saw the smile of incredulity on his friend's face.

"I know I said that I would not marry, because not only did I think I would never find a woman who would not bore me after a short time, but also because I had no intention of having a wife who would be kissing my best friend as soon as my back was turned."

"Are you insulting me?" Harry asked.

"No, merely stating facts," the Duke said. "The wives of all my best friends have been eager for me to make love to them, and while I am not prepared to refuse the favours that come my way, I am not going to pretend to you that I think it is a particularly desirable way of living."

Harry stared at him as if he had taken leave of his senses.

"My dear Raven," he said at length, "I had no idea you felt like that."

The Duke's eyes twinkled.

"To be frank, it was not something that particularly worried me until I met Cleodel."

"Worried you?" Harry exclaimed. "When I think of all those gorgeous creatures. . . ."

The Duke put up his hand.

"Spare me the reminiscences for, as you know, I never talk about my *affaires de coeur.*"

"Which is a good thing," Harry agreed. "But tell me how Lady Cleodel is different."

"You will see for yourself," the Duke had said evasively.

When Harry met Cleodel later in the day, he had understood.

Besides being beautiful, her face had what he supposed was a look of purity, and she was certainly very different from the sophisticated, experienced women with whom the Duke had associated in the past.

As he watched them together he told himself that the Duke would be alert to protect her against the advances of other men like himself, and it would indeed be a case of the poacher turned game-keeper.

That would keep him out of mischief, Harry thought with satisfaction, and because he really had a deep affection for his friend he was delighted that he had found happiness.

Since there was no reason for a long engagement and the Sedgewicks were terrified that they might lose the Duke, the wedding was fixed for late in June, before the Season came to an end.

It had to take place after Royal Ascot since the Duke had several horses running at that meeting, and, because it would have been very inconvenient to have it in the country during the Season, it was decided that the ceremony should be held at St. George's Hanover Square.

Cleodel was so busy buying her trousseau that the Duke found it hard to see very much of her, but occasionally he asserted himself and, because he was in love, complained that he was being neglected.

"I have no wish to do anything so—unkind," Cleodel said gently, "but I must have gowns in which to look—beautiful for—you."

"Are you really buying them for me?" the Duke asked.

"But of course!" she replied. "Everybody has told me how fastidious you are, so I am very—afraid of—failing you."

"You are perfect just as you are," the Duke said, "and all I want is for us to be married so that I can take you away alone and tell you how lovely you are."

"That will be very—exciting."

"I will make you excited," the Duke said, "and it will be the most thrilling thing I have ever done in my life!"

He spoke with a sincerity in his voice that surprised himself.

Then he put his arms round Cleodel and kissed her very gently, for he was aware that if he was in the least passionate or demanding, she would be frightened.

On one occasion she had held him at arm's length, saying:

"Please—please—"

"I do not mean to frighten you, my darling," the Duke said quickly.

"It is not that I am really—frightened," Cleodel said. "But as I have never been—kissed before, I feel—almost as if you are making me your—captive, and I am no longer—myself."

"It is I who am the captive," the Duke said. "Forgive me, my sweet, and I will not be rough with you again."

He kissed her hands, turning them over to kiss their soft pink palms, and as he did so he thought that no woman could be more attractive and at the same time more difficult to capture.

The women who had loved him in the past had found his behaviour not only incomprehensible but infuriating.

"Raven is the most fascinating devil who ever stalked London," one of them said, "but in the guise of a Saint I find him depressing."

"I agree with you," another of the Duke's loves said, "but make no mistake, that chit straight out of the School-Room will have lost him before Christmas."

"I am willing to wager that it will not last even as long as that," was the spiteful reply.

Strangely enough, the only person who did not admire Cleodel was Harry, but he was far too tactful to say anything to the Duke or to his other friends, who he was certain would repeat any criticism he made about the future Duchess.

But to himself he thought there was something about her that was not entirely natural.

He could not put his finger on it, but with her innocent little ways it was as if she was really too good to be true.

The Duke, however, was carried away on the wings of bliss, counting the hours until he could see his future bride again like any boy with his first love.

Because Ravenstock House in Park Lane was so much larger than the house the Earl owned in Green Street, it was decided that the Reception should be held in the former, and the Duke with his usual passion for perfection was organising every detail.

The guests were to be received in the Ball-Room which opened out into the garden.

The presents were to be displayed in the Picture-Gallery, and the Duke planned that the whole house should be decorated with flowers brought from his country Estate and arranged by his own gardeners.

It would be impossible to accommodate in London all his Estate workers, tenants, and farmers, and he therefore gave orders that only the heads of each department should sit in the Gallery of St. George's.

In the country, a huge marquee was to be erected on the lawn where all the others would start their celebrations late in the afternoon.

This meant that if after the Reception the Duke and his wife travelled from Park Lane straight to Ravenstock by his private train, they would arrive in time to receive their congratulations and good wishes.

He would make a short speech thanking them, after which there would be an enormous display of fireworks.

The bride and bridegroom would have to spend the first night of their honeymoon at Ravenstock, but to the Duke it was somehow very fitting that he should take his bride home on their wedding-night to the house of his ancestors.

It had never troubled him before that he had not an heir to succeed him, but now he told himself that nothing could be better or more perfect than that his son should be born to two people who loved each other as he and Cleodel did.

"Tell me you love me," he had said to her insistently the previous evening as they sat in the garden of Devonshire House, where they were attending a Ball.

"I have—given you my—heart," Cleodel replied.

"It is something which I shall treasure forever!"

He had even contemplated writing a poem to her, but instead he was writing her a letter extolling her perfections, which he intended to send round to Sedgewick House with a large bouquet of lilies-of-the-valley.

He thought that that particular flower best typified her with its delicacy and its fragrance, and there was something very young about it, because it never became full-blown like a rose.

He was just finishing his letter when Mr. Matthews appeared again.

"What is it now, Matthews?" the Duke asked.

"I am sorry to disturb Your Grace again," Mr. Matthews replied, "but the Dowager Countess of Glastonbury has arrived, and I know you will wish to see Her Ladyship."

The Duke rose from the desk immediately.

"Of course! But I had no idea my grandmother was coming to London."

Leaving the letter unfinished, he walked from the Library to the Drawing-Room, where his maternal grandmother was waiting to see him.

Now in her eighties, the Dowager Countess still held herself as straight as a ramrod, and it was impossible not to realise that she had been a great beauty in her youth.

Her hair was dead white, her face was lined, but her features were classical and had remained unchanged.

When the Duke appeared she held out her hands with a little cry of delight.

"Grandmama!" the Duke exclaimed. "I had no idea that you were well enough to come to London. Why did you not let me know?"

"I did not make up my mind until the last moment," the Dowager Countess replied. "But when I had an invitation from the Queen to stay at Windsor, for the races at Ascot, I could not resist accepting it."

The Duke, having kissed her cheek, sat down beside her, holding one of her hands in his.

He looked at her with laughter in his eyes. Then he said:

"That is a very lame excuse, Grandmama! I have a feeling that the real reason why you have come to London is to look at my future wife."

The Dowager chuckled.

"I confess that is the truth! I could not believe that any young girl would catch 'Casanova' after he had resisted every bait and hook cast over him for so many years!"

"I was a very willing catch."

"That is what is impossible to believe!" the Dowager Countess flashed.

The Duke laughed.

"Let me say, Grandmama, how delighted I am that you are here, and of course you are staying with me."

"Of course!" she replied. "I do not know of anybody else with such an attentive staff or another house that is as comfortable as this."

"I am flattered."

The Dowager Countess looked at him with her eyes that were still shrewd despite her age.

"Is it true that you have definitely lost your heart?" she asked.

The Duke smiled.

"Wait until you see Cleodel, then you will understand."

"I doubt it," the Dowager Countess said, "and I think, like all the other women you have loved, I am going to miss the Buccaneer who was invincible and the Pirate who invariably captured the prize."

The Duke's laughter rang out.

"Grandmama, you are priceless! Nobody else ever talks to me as you do, and in such amusing language. But this Pirate has struck his flag, and now I am going to settle down to domesticity."

"Fiddlesticks!" the Dowager Countess declared. "And you will certainly have to find something to take the place of the women in your life."

"That will be Cleodel," the Duke said.

The Dowager Countess did not reply, because at that moment servants came in carrying the tea.

By the time they had set the table with silver and produced every form of delicacy to eat, the Duke was talking not of himself but of the presents they had received and the places they were to visit on their honeymoon.

His grandmother listened attentively, and she thought, as Harry had done, that it seemed incredible that after all the glamorous, brilliant, spectacular women who had attracted him, the Duke should have succumbed to the fascination of a young girl who, however lovely, had nothing much to offer him except youth.

If he had been much older, the Dowager Countess thought to herself, she would have been able to say "there is no fool like an old fool," but the Duke was still young, except perhaps by comparison with the girl he was to marry.

Then she told herself that all that mattered was that he was happy.

She had always loved "Raven," as he had been called since he was a very small boy, more than her other grandchildren.

It was his naughtiness which had started almost from the time he was in the cradle that had amused her, and, having herself been brought up in the Regency period, she found the prim solemnity of the Victorians extremely boring.

She had always thought that the Duke would have felt far more at home with George IV, and when she heard him criticised she excused him for bringing amusement and a sense of adventure to an age that was not only prudish but hypocritical in its outlook.

One of her other grandchildren had told her that he was shocked at his cousin's way of life and his innumerable love-affairs, but the Dowager Countess had merely looked him up and down and said contemptuously:

"The trouble with you is that you are jealous! If you had the looks or the guts to behave like Raven, you would do so! As it is, you can only grind your teeth and wish you were in his shoes."

Because the Duke had so much to say to his grandmother he did not leave her until she retired to her own room, and because they had been talking until the last moment he had to dress in a hurry.

He was dining at Marlborough House, and it was only as he was going downstairs, resplendent in knee-breeches and wearing his decorations on his evening-coat, that he remembered he had not finished his letter to Cleodel.

It had been left in the Library with his bouquet of lilies-of-the-valley, which he had intended to send with it.

Quickly he hurried to his desk, added to the letter a last expression of his love and put it in an envelope.

Then as he picked up the bouquet, which he intended to tell his coachman to leave for Cleodel after taking him to Marlborough House, a thought came to him.

It brought a smile to his lips and he wondered why he had not thought of it before.

*

Carrying the lilies-of-the-valley, the Duke stepped into his carriage, and as he turned towards Marlborough House he was thinking of Cleodel and how he had been unable to see her all day.

Yesterday they had met for a brief drive in the Park, then again at a Ball, but on neither of those occasions had he been able to kiss her.

He found himself yearning for her with an intensity which actually surprised him.

He had kissed so many women and had always felt that one kiss was very much like another, but with Cleodel it was different.

He thought perhaps it was because as she was so young and so innocent she never completely surrendered herself to him.

Because she was unawakened and perhaps a little fearful, there was always a barrier between them.

It was a barrier which he had every intention of removing as soon as they were married, and again he thought how thrilling it would be to awaken her to womanhood.

"I want her! God knows I want her!" he told himself, and he was still thinking of her as the carriage drew up at Marlborough House.

As he alighted he said to his footman:

"I have left some flowers and a note in the carriage. Do not touch them, but come back in three hours' time."

"Very good, Your Grace."

The Duke was greeted by the Prince of Wales and several of his friends, and a number of beautiful women who in the past had aroused his interest for a short time.

As always, the party at Marlborough House was amusing and the conversation glittered and sparkled like a jewel in a crown.

The Duke had one of his "old flames" sitting beside him at dinner, and almost immediately the meal started she asked:

"Is it true, Raven, that you are a reformed character and that your horns are turning white?"

"Will it surprise you if I tell you the answer is 'yes'?" the Duke replied.

"I have always heard that 'a leopard never changes his spots'!"

"You have your metaphors a little mixed, Kitty," the Duke said with a smile, "and in this instance you are wrong."

"Nonsense, Raven! And think how bored we shall all be if you take to psalm-singing and supporting waifs and strays."

The Duke laughed before he replied:

"In the past I have usually been accused of contributing to the latter!"

"That would not surprise me," Kitty remarked, "and it would certainly be in character."

"Now you are being unkind!" the Duke protested. "As far as I know, I have no love-children on my conscience."

"I am sure that is wishful thinking," Kitty said. "And what has this paragon to whom you are engaged got that we who have loved you for years have not?"

"Cleodel is the most adorable person I have ever known."

Kitty groaned.

"That is no consolation when another woman has succeeded where I have failed."

They sparred until the meal was over, then because the Princess was present there was no gambling and before midnight the guests began to leave.

"Are you going to win the Gold Cup, Raven?" the Prince asked as the Duke said good night.

"I hope so, Sir."

"Dammit! That means that my own horse has no chance," the Prince grumbled.

"It is always a question of luck."

"And yours has never failed you yet, so if you meant to console me there is no point in my listening to you."

Then, because the Prince of Wales was in fact very fond of the Duke, he put his arm through his and walked with him towards the door saying:

"When you are married, Raven, I cannot lose you, and I want you and your wife to stay at Sandringham for my first shoot."

"We shall be very honoured, Sir."

"Which means that you will mark up the biggest bag," the Prince said. "I am a fool to ask you."

"I will do my best not to be obtrusive, Sir," the Duke said humbly.

But both men laughed, knowing that such a thing where the Duke was concerned was impossible.

He left Marlborough House and told his coachman to carry him to Green Street.

When the carriage stopped, he got out, carrying the lilies-of-the-valley and the note for Cleodel.

"Go home," he said to the footman. "I will walk from here."

The man was at first surprised, then amused, but many years of training prevented him from showing what he felt, and he managed to keep his expression impersonal until he was back on the box and the horses were moving away.

The Duke waited until his conveyance was out of sight, then he walked down a mews which brought him to the back of Sedgewick House.

He knew that behind the houses on Green Street there was quite a large garden, in which he had often sat out when there were dances and invariably kissed his partners in discreet little arbours or in the shelter of a leafy tree.

There was a door from the garden into the mews, but this was locked and each householder kept a key to it.

The Duke was extremely athletic, and the exercise he took riding, fencing, and boxing kept him in the peak of condition.

Despite being slightly constricted by his tight-fitting evening-coat, he swung himself lithely up onto the top of the wall which bordered the mews and dropped down on the other side.

He thought with satisfaction that he had not even laddered his silk stockings in doing so, and now he moved through the shrubs that hid this part of the garden from the green lawn and Sedgewick House directly ahead of him.

It was the last house on the street and rather different from the others, being older and more rambling.

On the ground floor was a Dining-Room, a rather ugly, elongated room, an attractive Drawing-Room with three French windows which opened onto the garden, and beyond that the small Sitting-Room where he had sometimes been allowed to be alone with Cleodel.

Above this was her bedroom, with a balcony that was matched by one at the other end of the house, where her mother slept.

The Duke had actually teased her about the balcony, saying that one night like Romeo he would serenade her from the garden.

Cleodel had looked at him apprehensively.

"If you did—that," she had said, "Mama would hear you and she would think it was an—extremely improper—way to—behave!"

"Perhaps," the Duke had agreed, "but it would be very romantic, my darling, and that is what you make me feel."

Cleodel had looked up at him from under her long eye-lashes.

"I like you to be romantic," she had said, "like a Knight in a fairy-story who fights a dragon for me."

"Of course," the Duke had agreed, "and you know I would slay all the dragons, however ferocious they might be."

"That is how I want you to feel," Cleodel had said softly.

The Duke thought now that it would seem very romantic to Cleodel when tomorrow morning she found the bouquet of lilies-of-the-valley and his note on her balcony.

He knew from the way the house was built that he would not find it difficult to climb up the wall of the Sitting-Room and pull himself up onto the balcony so that he could leave the flowers where he wished them to be.

He thought it would be difficult for any woman not to appreciate the trouble he had taken to please her, and he knew that if he had done anything like this in the past, the lady in question would not only have been thrilled by his attention but would undoubtedly have invited him in.

He found himself wondering if it would be too outrageous if, having reached the balcony, he called and awakened Cleodel, who would be asleep.

He was certain that any apprehension she had about her mother overhearing them was unnecessary.

The Countess was slightly deaf and the two bedrooms were separated by the whole width of the house, so that even if he shouted at Cleodel her mother would be unlikely to hear him.

The Duke walked through the shrubs holding his bouquet carefully, and by the light of the stars and a young moon climbing up the sky he saw the house ahead clearly.

Then he stopped dead.

For a moment he thought it must be an illusion, a trick of the light.

But he soon saw unmistakably that there was a man climbing up a ladder which was propped against the side of the balcony.

The top of the ladder just reached the bottom of the stone balustrade with which the balcony was surrounded.

Because of the way it was placed, the man was sideways to the Duke and slightly in shadow.

He supposed it was a burglar who intended to rob Cleodel, and it flashed through his mind that nothing could be more fortunate than that he should have come here at this very moment to prevent such an outrage.

Moreover, it would give him the opportunity of proving that he was in fact a Knight protecting the woman he loved against a very unpleasant dragon.

Then as he quietly moved forward he became aware that the burglar was in evening-dress, which seemed strange, and as the man reached the top of the ladder and pulled himself up onto the stone balustrade, the Duke could see his face.

Once again he stopped abruptly, unable to believe his eyes.

The man whom he'd thought was a burglar was in fact a friend, a member of his Club, and only last evening when they were having a drink together Jimmy Hudson had lifted his glass.

"Good luck, Raven!" he had said. "May you always be as successful as you are today!"

The Duke had thanked him, and now as he watched Jimmy throwing his leg over the balcony he felt he must be dreaming.

Then through the bedroom window came somebody in white.

It was Cleodel, and the Duke was sure that she would be appalled and shocked by Jimmy's intrusion.

He waited for her to scream, then decided that he would appear and tell Jimmy what he thought of him and make him sorry he had ever attempted to do anything so outrageous.

Then as the Duke planned to climb the ladder to confront Jimmy unless he retreated at once before Cleodel's wrath, he saw that they were suddenly and unexpectedly clasped in each other's arms.

Cleodel's face was lifted to Jimmy's and he was kissing her, kissing her passionately in a way that the Duke had been unable to do himself, because of her protests and because he was afraid of frightening her.

Their kiss took a long time, while the Duke stood as if turned to stone, unable to breathe.

Then almost reluctantly, as it seemed to him, Cleodel moved from Jimmy's arms and put out her hand to draw him into the darkness of her bedroom.

As she did so she smiled, and the moonlight seemed to light her face with a sudden radiance which made her appear even more beautiful than he had ever seen her before.

Then the balcony was empty, and there was only the ladder standing at one side of it, to make the Duke quite certain of what he had seen and what she had done.

CHAPTER TWO

FOR WHAT seemed to him a very long time, though it could have been only a few minutes, the Duke stood staring at the empty balcony, and as he did so, like a puzzle falling into place he saw how he had been deceived and tricked.

The Duke was not only extremely intelligent, but he had a very retentive memory.

It had stood him in good stead both at Eton and at Oxford, where he had found that by doing only the minimum amount of work he could win prizes and awards.

Now seeing his past flash before his eyes as if through a magic lantern, he saw Jimmy Hudson telling him when they were staying at Warwick Castle that the Earl of Sedgewick had good horses and he was borrowing one to ride in the local Steeple-Chase.

"Be a good friend, Raven, and do not enter for it," he had begged. "I want to win."

The Duke had smiled.

"What is the prize?" he had enquired.

"One thousand pounds, a Silver Cup, and a pulsating young heart," Jimmy had replied blithely.

The Duke had laughed and agreed not to enter the Steeple-Chase, knowing that while the "pulsating young heart" might be an allurement, the thousand pounds was far more important to Jimmy.

Jimmy Hudson, with whom he had been at Eton, was the son of a country Squire who had a Manor House and a very small Estate in the Shires.

On leaving School, when the Duke went to Oxford, Jimmy had served for four years in the Brigade of Guards, and then had realised he could not afford to stay in the Regiment, nor was it getting him anywhere.

He decided that if he was to live the life he enjoyed, the only possible thing for him to do was to marry an heiress.

He contrived to get an introduction to one of London's most renowned hostesses who had two rather plain but definitely rich daughters.

What James Hudson had done was to underrate his own attractions.

He was extremely good-looking in the rather conventional English manner, and he had, when he wished to use it, a charm which, combined with good manners, women found very attractive.

It was not the daughters who were attracted to him in this particular house, but the mother!

After he had squired her from party to party and was invited to her very exclusive house-parties in the country where the guests included the Prince of Wales, Jimmy found a place in Society to which even in his wildest flights of imagination he had never aspired.

Because he was prepared to make himself pleasant not only to attractive women but to everybody else, and also because he was a good card-player, an excellent rider, and an amusing raconteur of after-dinner stories, he became one of the Marlborough House Set.

The Prince of Wales had extended the boundaries of Society to include any man or woman who amused him, and as Jimmy definitely kept him laughing, hostesses soon realised his worth. As the invitations piled up on the mantelpiece in his lodgings, he often complained of how little time he had to answer them.

His winnings at cards paid some of his tailor's bills and provided him with enough money to tip the servants in the houses in which he stayed. But everything else he desired was free.

The ladies who found him a compelling and ardent lover provided him with gold cuff-links and a great many other luxuries that could certainly not be furnished from his meagre Bank-balance.

Like the Duke until he had met Cleodel, Jimmy had had no intention of becoming a married man.

To be confined to one woman when he could find a welcome in almost every Mayfair *Boudoir* would be unpleasantly restrictive when he was riding on the crest of the social wave in a manner which amazed not only his friends but himself.

Thinking back, the Duke knew that it must have been before he had arranged to ride the Earl of Sedgewick's horses to compete in the Steeple-Chase that Jimmy had met Cleodel.

It would have been unlike Jimmy's usual technique to pay any attention to such a young girl, but Cleodel, as the Duke was well aware, was different, and the year which she had lost in mourning would have made her eager for excitement.

It would, he thought savagely, have been Jimmy who had taught her how to attract and capture the most glittering social *parti* in the whole country.

He had often discussed with Jimmy the way women made the love-affairs in which they both indulged far too easy, and in doing so they eliminated the thrill of the chase and the excitement of being the victor in what had been a difficult contest.

The Duke never mentioned any woman by name or indicated that he was talking of anybody in whom he was or had been particularly interested, but generalising he had said to Jimmy:

"Dammit all, I like a run for my money!"

He remembered now how Jimmy had agreed with him, saying:

"I often feel I am a fox with the whole pack of hounds after me and the field thundering behind."

They both had laughed.

Other conversations they had had on much the same theme were now coming back to the Duke.

He could see, almost as if it were a picture forming in front of his eyes, how Jimmy had understood exactly what he was wanting and what would be alluring because it was a new experience.

When Cleodel had held off his advances and had never seemed over-eager to see him again, and the times when he had felt frustrated by her indifference and her refusal to dance with him, it had all been a challenge which he had found irresistible.

He thought it must have been Jimmy who had told her even when they were engaged to keep him almost at arm's length, although of course he now suspected that she was in love with Jimmy and found no other man as desirable as he.

The fact that he had been humiliated and made a fool of made the Duke want to climb the ladder and confront Cleodel and Jimmy in a way which would leave them embarrassed and ashamed.

Then he told himself that that would be too easy a revenge. Moreover, it would spark off an almighty row, and since he did not want the whole world to learn how he had been cuckolded by one of his closest friends, it seemed he must go on with the marriage and make Cleodel his wife.

Then the Duke's lips set in a hard line, and he told himself that he would be damned if he would marry any woman who was behaving as Cleodel was at this moment. The mere thought of it made him so angry that he seemed to see the whole house and especially the balcony crimson as if with blood.

Then as he took an impulsive step forward, he told himself that he must be more subtle and hurt Cleodel and Jimmy as they had hurt him.

A plan came to his mind and he turned slowly and walked back to the door which led from the garden into a sidestreet.

As he expected, it was possible to open it from the inside, and he let himself out and started to walk slowly down the deserted road.

It was only as he came to a dust-bin that he was aware that he was still holding the bouquet of lilies-of-the-valley and the letter he had written to Cleodel telling her how much he loved her.

He stared at both things as if he had never seen them before.

Then slowly and deliberately he crushed the delicate flowers into a pulp before he flung them into the bin, and tore the letter he had written with its passionate expressions of love into small pieces and scattered them over the garbage.

As he walked on, his face was set in hard, cynical lines that made him look much older than his years.

*

The Duke crossed the Channel the following morning in his yacht, which was always kept in Dover harbour, ready to sail at an hour's notice.

Because a Courier had arrived long before the Duke, the Captain could actually weigh anchor immediately after His Grace had come aboard.

The efficiency which the Duke expected from his staff and which resulted in the almost perfect organisation of his houses and Estates had been put to the test when, on arriving back at Ravenstock House after midnight, he had sent for Mr. Matthews.

The night-footman had hurried upstairs and in under ten minutes

Mr. Matthews, conventionally dressed, had joined his employer in the Library.

The Duke's orders were given sharply and briefly, with the result that a number of the servants spent most of the night packing, a Courier left for Dover at dawn, and the Duke's private railway-carriage was attached to one of the early trains leaving for Dover.

Having issued his commands like a General going into battle, the Duke had then retired to his own bedroom.

The next morning he appeared downstairs for breakfast dressed elegantly but with, his servants thought apprehensively, a scowl on his face which they had not seen since he had fallen in love.

When Mr. Matthews handed the Duke his passport and a very large sum of money, he said quietly:

"May I ask, Your Grace, what I am to say to any enquirers as to your whereabouts?"

"After you have sent the notice to *The Gazette, The Times,* and *The Morning Post,* as I instructed you," the Duke replied coldly, "stating that my marriage to Lady Cleodel has been postponed, you will have nothing else to impart."

"Nothing, Your Grace?" Mr. Matthews asked nervously.

"Nothing!" the Duke answered firmly.

"If Lady Cleodel and the Earl . . ." Mr. Matthews began.

"You heard what I said, Matthews!" the Duke interrupted.

"Very good, Your Grace, I will carry out your orders and see that everybody else in the house does the same."

The Duke did not reply. He merely walked away to step into the closed carriage that was waiting to convey him to the station.

The Channel-crossing was smooth. His Courier met him at Dover and he was escorted by several high-ranking railway-officials to a private carriage which had been attached to the Express to Paris.

His house in the Champs Élysées was ready for his arrival, and the next morning a carriage driven by four finely bred horses was ready to take him out of Paris on a road which led in the direction of Versailles.

The Duke, however, did not intend to look at the residence of forgotten Kings. Instead he went to a small village, where his horses stopped outside the Convent of the *Sacré-Coeur.*

Anybody who knew the Duke would have thought it a strange

place for him to call. Yet, once again he was expected, and a smiling
Nun opened the iron-studded door and led him through cool,
cloister-like passages to a room overlooking the Convent garden,
through the windows of which the sun was shining in a golden haze.

"His Grace *le Duc,* Reverend Mother!" the Nun said as she
opened the door.

A woman in white, writing at a desk in the window, rose to her
feet with a little cry of gladness.

She held out her hands and the Duke took them in his and bent his
head to kiss her cheek.

"How are you, Marguerite?" he asked.

"It is delightful to see you, Raven dear," she replied, "but it is a
great surprise. I thought you would be far too busy in London to
visit Paris, unless it was on your honeymoon."

As she spoke, she saw that her brother's eyes darkened and a
scowl disfigured his handsome face.

Perceptive as she had always been, Lady Marguerite said quickly:

"What is wrong? What has happened?"

"That is what I have come to talk to you about," the Duke replied. "Shall we sit down?"

"Of course. I have ordered you some wine and some of the little
biscuits that you remember are a specialty of my Convent."

The Duke smiled, but there was no need for a reply, for as the
Reverend Mother spoke, a Nun came in through the door with the
wine and biscuits on a tray.

She set them down beside the sofa, made a respectful curtsey, then
left the room.

The Duke looked at his sister.

Although she was fifteen years older than he, he thought she still
looked a young woman and had not lost the beauty that had made
her so outstanding when she had made her début.

The late Duke of Ravenstock and his wife had been confident that
their only daughter, Marguerite, would make a brilliant Society marriage.

The Ball they had given at Ravenstock House had been attended
not only by every eligible young aristocrat in the whole of *Debrett,*
but also by a large number of younger sons of reigning Monarchs
and foreign Princes.

It was not quite what they had expected but at the same time it was acceptable when Lady Marguerite had fallen in love with the elder son of Lord Lansdown.

He was somewhat older than she was, had made a name for himself in the Army, and was a serious, rather unsociable character. His name had never been connected with any woman and he was in fact known to be dedicated to his Regiment.

The moment he saw Lady Marguerite he had known she was the one woman who had ever mattered to him and he had lost his heart irretrievably.

The Duke and Duchess had agreed to the marriage and it was arranged that it should take place in six months' time.

Marguerite, because she felt as if she were walking in the sunshine of Paradise, was prepared to do anything that was asked of her as long as eventually she could marry the man she loved.

They were together every moment that Arthur Lansdown could get away from his Regimental duties. Then, two months before they were due to be married, he was sent abroad on a special mission to the Sudan where there was a rumour of trouble amongst the tribes.

Since no hostilities had broken out, there was not the slightest expectation of his being in any danger. But he was assassinated by the knife of a tribesman who was intent on a revenge which existed only in his own distorted mind.

For Marguerite, her world came to an end. She would not listen to anything anybody said to her, nor would she accept any form of consolation from her family.

Because she could not bear to be in any place where she had been with Arthur, she left England despite every protest and entered a Convent in France.

She was accepted into the Catholic Church, and although her father and mother pleaded with her almost on their knees to give herself time to recover from her bereavement, she would not listen to them.

She eventually took the veil irrevocably when she had not yet reached her twenty-first birthday.

Because she was extremely intelligent and also very rich, as the years passed she rose from being an ordinary Nun to having what

was to all intents and purposes her own Convent on the outskirts of
Paris.

It housed a number of Nuns who came from families of equal importance to that of her father, and also Novices who the Church
thought should consider and think before they finally vowed away
their freedom to spend their lives in prayer and chastity.

Lady Marguerite won the approval not only of her Cardinal in
France but also of the Pope and officials of the Vatican in Rome.

The Duke could understand that in her own way she provided a
service that was unique within the Church, giving those who were as
intelligent and as well-born as herself a chance to serve God and at
the same time not to waste their talents.

Some of the Nuns under his sister had written books which had
been acclaimed in the outside world, while the embroidery and the
lace that came from the Convent of the *Sacré-Coeur* evoked the admiration of everybody who saw it.

Every time the Duke visited his sister he realised that despite the
fact that the Social World thought she had wasted her life, Marguerite was in fact a very happy woman and entirely self-sufficient.

What was more, her vocation had given her a sympathy and an
understanding which made him know that he could turn to her in any
emergency in his own life, and that was why he was here now.

Lady Marguerite poured out the wine for him, then seated herself
beside him to ask gently:

"What has happened, Raven?"

"I do not want to talk about it," her brother replied harshly. "But
I want you to find me a wife who is pure and untouched!"

If he had meant to startle his sister, he certainly succeeded.

But Lady Marguerite did not exclaim or in fact say anything. She
only looked at him with an expression of surprise in her blue eyes,
which then turned to one of compassion.

"Why have you come to me, Raven?" she enquired after a long
pause.

"Because I know that only here amongst your young women who
think they may have a vocation will I find a girl who has not been
contaminated by the world—or should I say by other men?"

There was no escaping the bitterness in his voice, which told Lady
Marguerite without explanation what had happened.

She clasped her hands in her lap and looked away from her brother before she said:

"If ever I doubted the efficacy of prayer; you have now convinced me that it is always answered."

The Duke did not speak. He merely waited for her to go on, and finally his sister continued:

"I have been praying about a certain problem for some time, and now, when I least expected it, when I felt the answer lay in a different direction altogether, you are here."

"You can give me what I have asked you for?" the Duke enquired.

His sister gave a sigh.

"I could do so. At the same time, I am afraid. I question whether it is something I should do."

The Duke's lips twisted as if he knew what she was thinking, and after a moment he said:

"Suppose you explain to me in so many words what you are thinking and the reason for your prayers?"

As if she was shaken out of her habitual serenity, Lady Marguerite rose and walked towards the window.

She stood looking out on the sunlit formal garden, and on the green lawns she could see some of her young Nuns wearing white habits that she had designed to seem less austere and certainly less ugly than those worn in most Convents.

The veils of the Novices were white and transparent, and instead of the heavy leather shoes that were habitual to other Nuns, those in the convent of the *Sacré-Coeur* wore light slippers so that they moved more gracefully.

The Duke waited, and after a little while, as if she had made up her mind to tell him what she was thinking, his sister turned from the window.

"Eight years ago," she began, sitting down again in the chair she had recently vacated, "a child was left outside the gates of the Convent. She arrived in a carriage, and after those who had conveyed her here had rung the bell, they immediately drove away. A Nun opened the door and brought her to me. She carried in her hand an envelope which contained the sum of five thousand pounds and a few words written on a piece of paper."

"Five thousand pounds!" the Duke exclaimed.

"It was a very large sum," his sister said, "and the letter, which I will show you, said:

"This is Anoushka. Her father is English and wishes you to bring her up. She is, however, not to take the veil until she is over twenty-one, and then only if it is her wish to do so. Money will be provided for her to have the best teachers available."

Lady Marguerite ceased speaking and the Duke asked:

"Was that all? There was no signature?"

"No, nothing. The writing was educated, and I think it was that of as Englishman."

The Duke raised his eye-brows and his sister gave a little laugh.

"I was guessing, just as I have guessed all through the years, but I have come to no conclusion."

"How many years?" the Duke asked.

"Anoushka is now nearly eighteen, and my problem is what I should do with her."

"You do not intend to keep her until she is twenty-one and let her become a Nun?"

"No."

"Why not?"

"For two reasons. First, because I do not think she is suited for the confined life. She is brilliantly intelligent, extremely talented in many ways, and has a strange character which I find hard to understand."

Lady Marguerite paused, and the Duke said:

"And the other reason?"

"Two years ago I received the sum of seventy thousand pounds. Since then there has been no more."

"There had been some previously?"

"Yes. Every two years after her arrival I received another five thousand pounds. Of course I have not spent it all, but with seventy thousand pounds Anoushka is a very wealthy young woman."

"So what do you intend to do with her?"

"That was my problem, and I was seriously considering whether to approach one of our relatives to ask her to introduce the girl to Society and let her see the world outside these Convent walls."

Lady Marguerite gave her brother an almost pleading glance as she said:

"I have prayed and prayed for what was best to do, and now you are here."

"It does indeed seem obvious that I am the answer to your problem and your prayers," the Duke said.

Lady Marguerite did not have to speak.

"But you are thinking of my reputation," the Duke went on, "and of course that I have recently announced my engagement to another woman. Let me make this clear—that engagement no longer exists."

Lady Marguerite was still silent, and the Duke continued:

"As for my reputation, the family, as you well know, have been pleading with me for years to have an heir. That is what I now intend to do, but my wife must be, as I have already said, pure and untouched. I will not tolerate the woman who shall bear my name being anything else."

Again there was a note in the Duke's voice which told his sister very clearly what had happened.

"I cannot imagine Anoushka being married to somebody like you!" she said after a moment. "I hoped that perhaps she would find a man who would love her and whom she would love, but I was well aware that one of the difficulties would be that she has no name."

The Duke gave a slight shrug of his shoulders.

"Is that important?"

"Socially, it would certainly raise a difficult problem."

"Whoever she might be," the Duke said, "there would be few people brave enough to question my wife's antecedents if I did not wish to speak of them."

Lady Marguerite knew this was true, and she said:

"We also have to think of the family, Raven. Although I am absolutely convinced that Anoushka is an aristocrat in every sense of the word and that her blood is as blue as ours, we have to face the fact that she may be a love-child."

"So have been many who have adorned history, especially in France," the Duke said.

Lady Marguerite gave a little sigh.

"I feel as if I am dealing with a problem which is too big for me," she said. "How could I have guessed, how could I have anticipated for a moment when I was praying about Anoushka's future that it could be linked with yours?"

She looked at her brother pleadingly as she said:

"Am I doing the right thing, Raven? Or have you talked me into it? Perhaps I am wrong in even considering a life for her outside these walls. At the same time, my experience here has taught me to know when an enclosed life is right for a young girl, or whether she should live in a very different way and above all know the happiness of having a husband and—children."

There was just a little tremor as Lady Marguerite said the last word, which told the Duke, if he had not known it already, that she still was faithful to the memory of the man to whom she had been engaged.

Having known what had seemed a perfect and complete love, she would never forget it.

"I think, Marguerite," the Duke said, "you have answered your own questions, and where this girl is concerned you can trust to your instinct, which often gives far better guidance than the logic offered us by our brains."

Lady Marguerite smiled.

"Thank you, Raven. That is very complimentary, and I like to think you are right. My instinct tells me that Anoushka belongs to a far broader world than I can offer her. At the same time, you must realise that she knows nothing of the life you lead and which you take as a matter of course."

Suddenly Lady Marguerite got up from her chair to say:

"Here we are talking as if something has been decided between us. I have been hypnotised by what you have asked and am no longer thinking straight. How can you possibly marry a girl you have never seen and who has never seen you?"

"Now you are listening to your mind and not your instinct," the Duke said. "You know as well as I do that in many Eastern countries the bride and bridegroom seldom see each other before the actual wedding-day, and even if we had met, I doubt if the girl in question or those concerned with her, which in this case is yourself, would turn down the chance of her becoming a Duchess."

"That is very cynical, Raven."

"But practical," the Duke replied.

"I still cannot think why, after you have walked in here with such a ridiculous proposition, we have sat down and talked it over as if it were quite a usual thing to happen."

"It may be unusual but it is not ridiculous," the Duke said, "and just as I have turned to you for help, so you are prepared to give me exactly what I have asked for."

"Wait!" Lady Marguerite said. "You are going too quickly. First you must meet Anoushka. Then you must decide how you can marry a young woman without a name and without the family being horrified because they have not been consulted."

"Let me make this absolutely clear. As regards my marriage I will consult no-one!" the Duke replied. "I am not concerned with the family or with anybody else. I intend to be married immediately. I have no wish to explain my reasons to you or to anybody else. Let me simply say that this is something I intend to do, and nobody shall prevent me!"

There was something so positive in the Duke's voice and another note in it that made Lady Marguerite look at him apprehensively.

For the first time in all the years she had known him, she thought that her brother looked not only grim but cruel.

There was an expression in his eyes which she had never seen before, and it made her say quickly:

"Whatever has hurt you, Raven, do not let it spoil you. You have done many things of which it is impossible not to disapprove, but you have always been kind and generous and because you have been happy you have given happiness to other people."

She put out her hand and laid it on her brother's arm.

"I know you are suffering," she said gently, "but those who are innocent of any crime towards you must not suffer too."

"I do not know what you are talking about," the Duke said defensively.

"I think you do," Lady Marguerite answered, "and remember, hatred is a boomerang which always eventually hurts oneself."

"I am not admitting I hate anybody," the Duke said. "I am only avenging an insult in a way which will be extremely effective."

"You will make somebody unhappy?"

"I sincerely hope so."

"That is very unlike you, and perhaps because you have been so lucky in your life, the moment has come when you have to pay, as everybody else does, for what you have received."

"You have forgotten your Bible," the Duke said mockingly. " 'An eye for an eye, and a tooth for a tooth.' That is justice!"

"If you read only a few more verses you will find that we should forgive our enemies."

"Perhaps I will do that, but only after they have been punished."

Lady Marguerite sighed.

"I have a feeling, Raven, that you are making yourself both judge and executioner, and that is a mistake."

"How can you be sure of that?" her brother asked. "And now I wish to see Anoushka."

He knew as he spoke that Lady Marguerite was regretting what she had told him, and perhaps regretting even the prayers she had expended in asking for a solution to her problem.

The Duke put out his hand to lay it on his sister's.

"Stop worrying, Marguerite," he said. "As you say, I have done many reprehensible things in my life, and I have gained a reputation which has undoubtedly shocked the elder members of the family. But I have never, as far as I can remember, done anything unsportsmanlike or behaved dishonourably to a woman who trusted me."

There was a note of sincerity in the Duke's voice, which made his sister look at him searchingly. Then she smiled.

"I know that is true, Raven, so I will trust you. But of course, whether you wish to marry Anoushka, whether she is the right person for you, is something you must decide for yourself."

"Exactly!" the Duke agreed.

His sister again rose to her feet.

"I will go now and find her. If she is not what you expect, or what you want, then you will have to look elsewhere."

The Duke did not reply, and only when his sister had left the room did he pour himself out another glass of wine and walk to the window.

He did not see the sunshine outside and the Nuns looking like flowers against the well-kept yew-hedges.

Instead he saw Cleodel's face in the moonlight as she smiled at Jimmy, then drew him from the balcony into her bedroom.

The Duke's fingers tightened on the stem of his glass until there was a faint sound and he realised he had cracked it.

It was then, as he prevented the wine from spilling to the floor, that he wished he could encircle Cleodel's white throat with his fingers and throttle her.

For the first time in his life he felt like murdering somebody, and he knew that what he wanted was undoubtedly an eye for an eye and compensation for the murder of his ideals.

That was what Cleodel had killed, the ideals that with her youth and beauty she had resuscitated within him after he had lost them in his philandering and raffish life.

Because she had stood for everything he ideally desired in a woman, he had set her in a shrine in his heart that before had always been empty.

Now she had despoiled and defiled it, and he hated her with a violence that surpassed every emotion he had ever felt before.

Yesterday in the train carrying him towards Paris he had imagined the satisfaction he would have felt if he had followed his first impulse and climbed up onto the balcony to enter Cleodel's bedroom.

He would have struck Jimmy and frightened Cleodel until they had pleaded with him on their knees for mercy.

Then he realised that that would have been a very primitive form of revenge which perhaps would have lowered him to their level.

What he was planning now was far more subtle, far more intelligent, and far more hurtful. Already he was quite certain that Cleodel would be wondering frantically what had happened and why he had not communicated with her.

Then this morning her father would have opened the pages of *The Times* or *The Morning Post* and seen the announcement that the marriage had been postponed.

His consternation would be farcical, the Duke thought, and he wished that he could only watch it.

He imagined the questions, the suppositions, the explanations the Earl and Cleodel would try to find. Then a letter would be sent to Ravenstock House, and the Earl would follow it and demand to see him and to be given an explanation.

The Duke was certain that Mr. Matthews would carry out his instructions to the letter.

Then there would be nothing the Sedgewicks could do but wait, and try to find answers to all the questions they wanted to ask while the wedding-presents continued to pour in.

The Duke gave a sharp laugh, and it was not a pleasant sound.

Yes, the revenge he had planned was far cleverer than anything that could be gained by physical violence, and when he took the next step in his plan, then there would really be consternation and speculation which would sweep through Mayfair like a tornado.

Cleodel, who would be at the centre of it, would eventually guess the reason for her fiancé's disappearance.

The smile on the Duke's lips deepened.

He heard the door open behind him and turned round.

Because he had been looking out into the sunlight, for the moment it was difficult for him to see at all clearly, but he heard his sister's voice say:

"Here is Anoushka!"

CHAPTER THREE

LADY MARGUERITE moved towards her brother and as she reached him with the girl beside her she said:

"Let me, Anoushka, present my brother the Duke of Ravenstock."

Anoushka curtseyed. With the sun on her face, the Duke could now see her clearly, and she was not the least what he had expected.

Because he had been so bemused by Cleodel he had supposed that any very young girl he decided to marry would look in some way a replica of her—a young face, fair hair, blue eyes, and an expression that had seemed to him completely innocent.

But Anoushka was completely different.

She was slender, taller than average, and her face framed by the transparent veil of a Novice was so unexpected that he could not remember ever having seen a woman who looked in the least like her.

She was lovely in a very different way, and although he knew she was young she did not look it.

Instead, she had a kind of ageless beauty that he thought might be found on a Greek statue or perhaps engraved on the tombs in Egypt.

Her face was dominated by her large eyes, which seemed somehow mysterious and not what he would have imagined those of a young girl to be.

As he went on looking at her he realised that her nose was straight and classical and her lips might have been chiselled by a sculptor in Ancient Rome.

But what he had not expected, and what was so astonishing, was that she seemed to vibrate as a personality in a way that he had known before only when he had met people of great distinction in their own particular field.

He had been aware that a force and power radiated out from them in a manner that was impossible to put into words and yet was indisputably there.

At his first glance at Anoushka he could understand his sister finding her a problem and feeling that she should not and could not be confined within the walls of a Convent.

The Duke had the strange and fanciful idea that she was like an exotic bird imprisoned in a cage that was too small for her.

Then he told himself that he was being foolishly fanciful.

All he had asked for was a girl who was pure and untouched, and this was what he was being offered.

Because he felt he must speak, he said to Anoushka:

"I understand from my sister that you have lived here for ten years?"

"That is true, *Monseigneur*."

He noticed that she gave him the title reserved for the Princes of the Church, and he knew it was a compliment, although whether it was paid to himself or simply to his sister's brother he was not sure.

"And you have been happy here?"

"Very happy, *Monseigneur*."

"Perhaps you found it strange after the life you led previously."

Anoushka did not reply, and he realised that she was not hesitating or choosing her words but was deliberately remaining silent.

The Duke looked at his sister and Lady Marguerite said:

"Anoushka told me when she first came here that she had been instructed never to speak of where she came from, and she has obeyed those instructions to the letter."

The Duke wanted to ask why she should be so mysterious, and he thought that was the right word to describe her anyway. She was mysterious: an enigma that was intriguing although it might prove to be extremely irritating.

After a moment he said:

"I wonder, Marguerite, if it would be possible for me to talk to Anoushka alone? I think you would want to explain to her why I am here, but it is something I would prefer to do myself."

His request was obviously unexpected, and Lady Marguerite looked at him appealingly before she said in a low voice:

"Do you think that is—wise so—soon?"

"I see no point in waiting, and I have not the time to do so."

His sister's eyes searched his face.

He knew she was worried, almost distressed. At the same time, because he was the head of the family and, despite everything, she respected him, she was finding it hard to refuse.

"You can trust me," the Duke said with a smile, "not to do anything to upset Anoushka—or you."

Lady Marguerite drew in her breath. Then she said: "It is, as you well know, very unconventional, but I will leave you for ten minutes."

She walked towards the door, but before the Duke could move, Anoushka opened it and dropped a curtsey as her Mother Superior walked through it.

Then she shut the door quietly and turned round to look at the Duke.

Her eyes, which he now realised were so dark as to be almost purple, were watching his face.

He had the feeling that she was not looking at him as a handsome man, and this surprised him because she could not have seen many of them, and certainly none like himself.

It was as if she was looking far deeper than the surface, almost as if she searched for his soul.

Then the Duke said:

"Shall we sit down?"

She walked towards him with a grace that reminded him of Eastern women whom he had seen balancing water-vessels on their heads and moving like Queens.

With his hand he indicated the sofa, and when Anoushka sat on the edge of it, her back very straight, her eyes looking directly at him, he took an arm-chair facing her.

He noticed that she had the same stillness and serenity that he had always admired in his sister, and after a moment he said:

"My sister has told me your strange story, and also that she has decided that as you are now eighteen you should leave the Convent and see something of the world outside."

"I would like that."

"You do not wish to take your vows and become a Nun?"

"It is something I have considered, but it is difficult to make a judgement until I have seen the outside world, of which, living here, I know very little."

"That is understandable," the Duke said, "and because my sister has been worrying and praying over what would be best for you, I have what I think is an answer to her prayers and your problem."

He waited for Anoushka to ask him what this was, but she remained perfectly still, her eyes still looking at him speculatively as if, he thought, she weighed up everything he was saying.

Because he wished to surprise and perhaps startle her, he said abruptly:

"What I have to suggest is that you should marry me!"

Now there was undoubtedly an incredulous expression in her strange eyes, and it was only after a long silence that she said:

"Are you asking me, *Monseigneur*, to be your wife?"

"I would hope I could make you happy," the Duke replied, "and in case you do not understand, your position as my Duchess will be one of the most important in England."

"And you think I am suitable for such a position?"

"You will naturally have a lot to learn," the Duke replied, "but I will be with you to teach you and protect you from making mistakes."

As he spoke, he thought he was making it sound a proposition that was too businesslike, too cut-and-dried to appeal to a young girl.

But he felt that Anoushka would rather hear the truth frankly and honestly than have it dolled up in pretty phrases, although he had no idea why he should have thought that.

As he waited for her answer, he thought cynically that most women would go into raptures if he had even hinted at making them his wife.

"I have never thought of being married," Anoushka said in a low voice.

"If you are not anxious to become a Nun," the Duke said, "then surely marriage is the obvious alternative once you have left these Convent walls."

"It is a subject that has not appeared on the curriculum in my studies."

"Well, I hope you will now consider it," the Duke said. "I wish to marry immediately, for reasons I will not explain, and as we are in Paris I can easily provide you with a fashionable trousseau which any young woman would find exciting after wearing the robes you have on now."

As he spoke, he thought that this was an inducement no woman of his acquaintance could possibly resist.

Paris was the El Dorado of fashion, and the gowns of Frederick Worth which the Duke had bought for many of his mistresses meant as much to them as the jewels with which he encircled their necks or clasped in their ears.

But there was not the excitement that he looked for in Anoushka's eyes.

"You said," she remarked in her soft clear voice, "that you will teach me how to be your wife. But suppose I fail and you are disappointed?"

The Duke realised she was thinking of him as one of the teachers who his sister had told him had been specially engaged for her studies because the money had been provided to pay for them.

"I have been told," the Duke replied, "how exceptionally intelligent you are. Therefore, I cannot imagine that you will find it hard to learn what you will find both interesting and enjoyable, and I assure you I am very experienced in the subjects we shall study together."

He smiled as he spoke because it seemed an almost ridiculous way to describe the union between a man and a woman.

Then as he did so he knew that to Anoushka what he was saying was serious and something she must contemplate with her brain.

It struck him then that because of her upbringing, her feelings had been subordinated entirely to her intellect, and he found himself wondering how long it would take before she would respond to him not as a teacher but as a man.

Anoushka was obviously turning over in her mind what had been said, and now she asked:

"Have I really a choice in what I do, or has the Reverend Mother decided I must leave the Convent with you, whether I wish it or not?"

The Duke was startled.

"I am sure that my sister would not force you to do anything you would not wish to do," he answered. "At the same time, may I say that what I am offering you is something which most women would be very eager to accept."

"I have a feeling that any other woman you would ask to be your wife, *Monseigneur,* would not be as ignorant or as inexperienced as I am. It would therefore be easier for them to adjust themselves to your requirements."

"I have already told you that I will prevent you from making mistakes," the Duke said, "and as we shall not return to England for some time after we are married, we will have a chance to get to know each other, which should make things simpler than they would otherwise be."

Again there was silence. Then at length Anoushka said:

"May I have a little time, *Monseigneur,* to think this over?"

"Certainly," the Duke replied, "but I think you really mean that you intend to pray about it."

Anoushka gave him a faint smile.

"Here in the Convent they are one and the same thing, and it is easier to think in the Chapel."

The Duke rose to his feet.

"Very well then. I suggest that you go to the Chapel and I will wait here until you are ready to give me your answer."

As he spoke, he felt that he was putting pressure on her. But he knew she was suitable for his requirements and he wished to get on quickly with his revenge on Cleodel.

"I will try not to be any longer than is necessary," Anoushka said in the same soft, quiet voice in which she had spoken before.

She looked at him straight between the eyes as she spoke, then curtseyed and moved towards the door.

The Duke did not open it for her, he only stood watching her leave, thinking he had never before had such a strange conversation with a woman.

Then he walked to the open window almost as if he needed air.

Once again he looked grim as he planned his next move, and it was one which Cleodel would find extremely unpleasant.

It was not more than five minutes before Lady Marguerite came back.

"I met Anoushka going to the Chapel," she said. "She told me she was considering the suggestion you made to her and she wishes to think about it."

The Duke gave his sister a rather wry smile.

"It is certainly unusual for any woman to wish to pray over any proposition I have made to her!"

"Anoushka is different, as I have already told you," Lady Marguerite said, "and I too have been thinking."

"And of course praying!" the Duke said almost mockingly.

His sister ignored the interruption and went on:

"If Anoushka decides to marry you, though there is always the possibility that she may refuse . . ."

"Really, Marguerite," the Duke interposed, "are you seriously suggesting that a girl of eighteen would refuse to be the Duchess of Ravenstock?"

"You and I know what it means and entails," Lady Marguerite replied, "but to Anoushka it is just a name. Do remember, Raven, that she knows nothing of the world except what she has read in books, and those which come to the Convent are very carefully chosen, I can assure you."

The Duke did not reply and she went on:

"To Anoushka it would be like coming from another planet where they had never heard of the ordinary, everyday things that make up your life—racing, cards, Balls, dinner-parties, the Theatre!"

She paused, then went on:

"You and I know what those mean, and when I speak of them they conjure up for us memories of what we have seen and done. But to Anoushka they are just words of one, two, or three syllables!"

Lady Marguerite paused to see if her brother was following her, then finished:

"She cannot, however imaginative she may be, have any idea what such activities are really like, or the people who take part in them."

The Duke did not reply, and after a moment his sister said:

"Now that I have had more time to think about it, the whole idea seems absurd and quite impracticable! Go away, Raven, and find some young woman who at least has been brought up in the same way as we were."

Her voice softened as she went on:

"I know something has upset and hurt you, but I do not feel that by marrying Anoushka you will feel any happier or give her the happiness she deserves."

"I intend to marry her," the Duke said.

There was an inflexible determination in the way he spoke, which told his sister that he was about to be difficult.

"I should not have mentioned her in the first place," she said as if she spoke to herself. "If she leaves here, I want her to find happiness."

"Which you are quite convinced I cannot give her."

"Let me put it another way," his sister replied. "I want her to find love, the love I knew with Arthur, the love that is so glorious and wonderful when a man and woman find it together that it is a gift from God."

The Duke moved restlessly across the room.

"And suppose she does not find this idealised love which happens, as you are aware, to very few people? Will you not feel you have deprived her of a position which most women would give their eyes to attain?"

"I understand what you are saying," Lady Marguerite replied, "of course I do. At the same time, Raven, I am frightened. For the first time in many years I feel indecisive and I do not know what is right or wrong. You are undermining my confidence in myself."

"Listen to me, Marguerite," the Duke said, "I came to you for help and you have given me what I asked for."

Lady Marguerite's eyes met her brother's defiantly, then as if she felt she could not go on fighting him she suddenly capitulated.

"Very well, Raven," she said, "I will allow you to marry Anoushka, as long as she agrees to do so, on one condition."

"What is that?"

"Because you are what you are—a very experienced, sophisticated man with a reputation," Lady Marguerite said, "I want you to give me your word of honour, which I know you will not break, that while you marry Anoushka in name, she remains as she is for three months—in your own words, pure and untouched—before you actually make her your wife."

The Duke looked at his sister reflectively.

"Do you think that is wise? I have always thought that any marriage should be normal if it is to have a chance of being successful."

"The marriage you are contemplating is not normal from the very beginning," Lady Marguerite replied. "It is not normal for you to come here demanding a girl who had been brought up as a Novice."

Her voice sharpened as she went on:

"It is not normal for people in our position to marry out of our class or, if you prefer it, our special environment, and certainly it is not normal for you to find waiting for you, as if by fate, somebody like Anoushka."

The Duke did not speak and Lady Marguerite said insistently:

"Promise me this, Raven, please promise me. You will set my own mind at rest, and I believe it will eventually help you and Anoushka to come to an understanding of each other."

There was a sob in her voice as she said:

"Because I love you I have always wanted your happiness in a very different way from how you have found it up to now."

"It is not wise to ask too much," the Duke replied lightly.

"Well, you and I at any rate could never tolerate second-best!" Lady Marguerite flashed.

"That is true," the Duke replied.

As he spoke, he thought that that was what he had been about to accept in Cleodel: second-best, skilfully disguised with an intent to deceive.

Thinking how near he had been to making her his wife and how later he would have realised he had been tricked and there would have been nothing he could do about it, he felt he should be grateful rather than angry.

"Do you need any money, Marguerite?" he asked unexpectedly. "I suppose I should express my gratitude to you in the usual manner."

Lady Marguerite shook her head.

"I am still a rich woman, Raven, which is why I am allowed to run the Convent very much my own way. But you can thank me by giving me your promise, which I have not yet received."

"Very well," the Duke conceded. "I promise!"

"And you may break it only if Anoushka asks you to do so."

"Thank you," the Duke said a trifle sarcastically.

He was thinking that he had never been with a woman who had not, with every word she spoke, every glance from her eyes, and every movement of her lips, invited his kisses and a great deal more.

He wondered how long it would be before Anoushka followed the example of all her predecessors, with of course the exception of Cleodel.

But she had Jimmy!

He had been making love to her when he was borrowing her father's horses. And perhaps every night when they were in London, Jimmy had sneaked up the ladder onto her balcony to share her bed.

Once again the Duke saw everything crimson before his eyes and felt his anger rising in his throat and almost choking him.

Then there was a knock at the door.

"Come in!" Lady Marguerite said.

It was Anoushka. She entered the room, closed the door behind her, and walked without hurry to where Lady Marguerite was standing.

She made a small curtsey, then stood straight and still, waiting for permission to speak.

Lady Marguerite looked at her. "You have found the answer you were seeking, Anoushka?" she enquired.

"Yes, Reverend Mother."

"Will you tell me what it is?"

"I have decided I would like to accept the proposal the *Monseigneur* had made to me, but only, Reverend Mother, if you consider I am capable of fulfilling the position of his wife."

"I am sure you will do that very adequately, my dear."

Lady Marguerite looked towards her brother as she spoke, and the Duke, feeling as if he were taking part in a strange drama in which he was not quite certain if he was the hero or the villain, walked forward.

He took Anoushka's hand in his and lifted it perfunctorily to his lips.

"I am very honoured that you should accept me as your husband," he said quietly, "and I will do my uttermost to make you happy."

*

The Duke, having returned to his house in the Champs Élysées, sent for his French Secretary, *Monsieur* Jacques Tellier, who managed his possessions in France, and told him his exact requirements.

When he heard of the Duke's intention to be married the following morning, Jacques Tellier was obviously surprised, but at the same time he was too tactful to say so.

"My congratulations, *Monsieur le Duc*," he said. "I will go at once to *La Mairie* to make arrangements for the Civil Ceremony."

"Afterwards a quiet Service will take place at the Chapel attached to the Convent of the *Sacré-Coeur*," the Duke said briefly.

As he spoke, he remembered that before he had left the Convent he had said to his sister:

"I presume Anoushka is a Catholic?"

"She came to our Services and was instructed by the Priests who are attached to the Convent."

"What do you mean by that?" the Duke had asked, knowing the answer was not clear-cut.

"I have always had the feeling that before she came here, Anoushka had been brought up in the Russian Orthodox Church."

"Her name is certainly Russian, so her mother may have been Russian. But surely she would have told you so."

Lady Marguerite sighed.

"I do not really have time to explain it to you, but it was quite obvious that although she was only eight years of age, Anoushka had been told that she must never speak of her life before she was left on our doorstep, and because she is so different from other girls she never has done so."

"Not about anything?"

"Not about her religion, where she lived, who her parents were—nothing!"

"I cannot believe it!" the Duke said.

"It is certainly incredible. At first, because I thought she was suffering from the shock of separation from those she loved, I did not press her to tell me anything, but I thought it would gradually emerge."

"But it did not?"

"She had never dropped a hint or shown, either by her familiarity with anything or by her knowledge of anything different from what she was doing here, that she had known any other life."

"I find it very hard to believe," the Duke said.

"So did I," his sister agreed, "but, as I have told you, she is different from any other child I have ever met. Perhaps the Buddhists would account for it by saying she is a very old soul."

"So you think the religion in which she was brought up was Russian Orthodox?"

"I am only guessing," Lady Marguerite replied.

"It certainly seems very strange," the Duke said, "but I presume she will not object to being married as a Catholic to a Protestant?"

"I will ask her, but I feel she will make no objections," Lady Marguerite replied. "In fact, she doubtless knows already that you are not of her faith, because they all know here that I changed my Church when I came to France."

She smiled before she added:

"As you will understand, the younger Novices here are always very interested in asking me what my life was like when I was their age."

"And you tell them?" the Duke enquired.

"I tell them what I think is good for them to know," Lady Marguerite replied, and he laughed.

When the Duke had left the Convent he sent a groom to one of the most exclusive dressmakers in Paris.

It was no use asking *Monsieur* Worth for a gown, because he designed individually for each of his clients.

That, the Duke decided, would come later, but he wished Anoushka when she left the Convent to set aside all the trappings of a Novice and become at least superficially a worldly young woman dressed traditionally as a bride.

"It would be the start of her new life," he thought, "and as I intend it to continue."

It was not compulsory at a Civil Marriage for the bride to be present in front of the Mayor. Therefore, the Duke had attended to all the formalities and his Secretary had stood proxy for Anoushka.

When the documents had been prepared and stamped, the Mayor had taken him warmly by the hand and wished him a long life and many children.

The Duke had bowed his gratitude and wondered what the Frenchman would think if he knew that he had sworn that for three months his bride would remain untouched and as pure as when she had left the Convent.

When he went to bed the night before, he told himself that in a way it was a good idea.

He had no wish to make love to anybody at the moment, and he thought that even to touch Anoushka's lips would make him remember Cleodel and the passion she had aroused in him.

"How can I forget her?" he asked himself, and felt she would haunt him for the rest of his life.

When he came down to breakfast he sent for *Monsieur* Tellier and instructed him that a notice should be sent to the French newspapers and then telegraphed to the newspapers in London.

This was the moment he was waiting for and was the rapier-point of his revenge.

The notice had been worded very carefully:

His Grace the Duke of Ravenstock was married quietly in Paris yesterday. The Duke and Duchess, after a few days in the French Capital, will proceed on their honeymoon to Nice in the South of France.

The Duke had written it down in his own hand, then read the announcement and reread it to be quite certain that it was exactly what he required.

He only wished he could witness the consternation which such an announcement would produce when it was published in the English newspapers.

At first, he thought, his friends would find it so incredible that they would not believe it.

Then it would be realised that there was something strange about it, coming so shortly after the previous announcement that his wedding to Cleodel had been postponed.

It would not take long to discover that the bride was not the Earl of Sedgewick's daughter.

It was then that the gossip and speculation would sweep through Mayfair like a whirlwind.

"What can have happened?"

"Who can she be?"

"Why had the Sedgewicks no explanation?"

"How could the Duke, unpredictable though he is, have treated Lady Cleodel in such a way?"

Not even his closest friends like Harry would know the real answer, and perhaps only Jimmy would have a suspicion of the reason for his disappearance from London and his speedy marriage to somebody else.

He was sure that the women who had been jealous of Cleodel for succeeding where they had failed, and who had disliked her because she was young as well as lovely, would then gradually begin to guess what had happened.

Why should he run away, which was very unlike him, unless he had a good reason for doing so? The answer could lie only with the woman he had left behind.

It was a revenge even crueler and more hurtful because there would be nothing Cleodel could say, nothing she could do.

It had all happened too quickly for her to pretend that it was she who had changed her mind at the last moment or even that the Duke and she had quarrelled.

At first she and her parents would be too bewildered to find any plausible excuse for the sudden disruption of all their plans, and the Duke was sure that the only possible action they could take would be to leave London and retire to the country.

This would mean that once again Cleodel would have to forego the Balls at which she had shone so brilliantly.

She would not be able to attend the Assemblies and the Receptions that were such an intrinsic part of the Season, nor would she appear in the Royal Enclosure at Ascot.

Of course, she would have Jimmy.

But the Duke guessed cynically that Jimmy would be conspicuous by his absence and would make no effort to comfort the girl whom he had instructed so skilfully.

It was a revenge, the Duke congratulated himself, that few men would have had the intelligence to think out and few the audacity to carry through.

To make certain that nothing went wrong, he also sent the Courier who had accompanied him to Paris back to England to make sure the newspapers had the announcement exactly as he had expressed it.

After two days at Ravenstock House, he was to return to give a comprehensive report on exactly what had occurred.

"If any of Your Grace's friends wish to visit you in Paris, what shall I say, Your Grace?" the Courier asked.

"Tell them I am on my honeymoon and have no need for company other than that of my wife," the Duke replied. "You are to answer no questions about her, however hard you may be pressed on the subject."

To make quite certain that the Courier knew nothing, the Duke had arranged for him to leave Paris before the actual wedding took place, and he wondered how the Earl would approach the man, veering, he was sure, between bribery and bullying in order to learn what he wanted to hear.

There was an expression on the Duke's face that his sister would have recognised as one of cruelty, as, looking resplendent in the evening-dress in which every Frenchman was married, he was driven by his coachman down the Champs Élysées.

Because he was determined to start his marriage with Anoushka on what he thought was the "right foot," he was wearing the Order of the Garter across his right shoulder.

The Garter also glittered below his knee, and he thought as he looked at himself in the mirror that it was a pity that Cleodel could not see him and be aware of what she had missed.

He realised now that under her soft, hesitating little act was an ambitious social-climber who was determined to get to the top of that prickly tree which so many had attempted to scale and failed.

But she had very nearly succeeded.

This was what infuriated the Duke more than anything else: the knowledge that he, who had always prided himself on his brains, his intuition, and his almost uncanny perception where pretence, hypocrisy, and insincerity were concerned, should have been caught by one of the oldest tricks in the world.

There was never a man born who did not feel protective and at the same time chivalrous towards a very young and innocent girl; there was never a man who did not like to think of himself as a Knight in shining armour, prepared to fight and kill the dragon that threatened the pure maiden.

The Duke could deride himself for being so gullible, but Cleodel had in fact played her part very cleverly, and of course Jimmy had been a good teacher.

"Damn them! Damn them!" the Duke wanted to cry out as he thought of how they must have plotted and planned every move of the game in which he had been as green as any yokel up from the country.

However, now he knew that he had the last laugh, and his revenge would brand Cleodel as clearly as if, like the Puritans in America, he had burnt an "A" for "Adultress" on her white skin—so very white, so soft to his touch.

Then he could see her again, the light in her eyes, the radiant smile on her lips as she looked at Jimmy on the balcony, and he knew that his revenge had so far not helped him to forget.

CHAPTER FOUR

THE DUKE waited in the magnificent Salon of his house for Anoushka to come down to dinner.

Once again he was wearing the elegant evening-clothes in which he had been married, but without his decorations and the Order of the Garter.

As he sipped a glass of champagne, he thought that he had certainly had an unusual wedding, and very unlike what he had always anticipated he would have.

The marriage he had planned with Cleodel would have been one of the events of the Season, with St. George's Church packed to overflowing with the elite of the country, and leading the distinguished guests present would have been the Prince and Princess of Wales.

The Queen would have sent a representative, and there would have been members of many European Royal families present to make it such a distinguished occasion that it would have been talked about long after it had taken place.

The Reception at Ravenstock House would have filled the Ball-Room to capacity, and if some of the guests preferred to walk in the garden, his gardeners had been working over the last month to make it a picture of perfection.

Instead, the only witnesses of his marriage to Anoushka had been his sister, Lady Marguerite, and an elderly Nun who played the organ with what the Duke recognised as outstanding skill.

He had expected that the other members of the Convent would be present, but then he had realised that it might have distracted them from their quiet life and perhaps put unsuitable ideas into the Novices' heads.

Therefore, on arrival at the Convent, the Nun who had opened the door had escorted him straight up to the Chapel where his sister was waiting for him.

"I thought you should know, Raven, that the Bishop of Paris, under whose aegis we are as a Convent, has come especially to marry you," she had said. "He will be supported by our usual Priest and two Servers. Otherwise there will be nobody in the Chapel but ourselves."

The Duke had smiled.

"A quiet marriage, Marguerite," he had said, "and the way I would wish it to be."

"If you will go in," his sister had replied, "I will bring Anoushka."

The Duke had walked into the small Chapel which he felt was redolent with the faith of those who worshipped there.

The Bishop and the other Priest were wearing spectacularly ornate white robes which he guessed had been embroidered in the Convent, and the altar was massed with flowers.

The organ played softly, and after he had waited a few minutes his sister came up the aisle with Anoushka walking beside her.

The Duke turned to watch their progress and realised that Anoushka, wearing the wedding-gown he had sent her, for the first time since she was eight was not dressed in the robes of a Novice.

The gown he had sent was softly draped at the front and swept to the back with frill upon frill of pleated gauze to make both a bustle and a train.

He had also ordered a fine lace veil which covered her face, and her head was encircled by a small wreath of orange-blossoms.

She did not carry the bouquet he had sent her, but instead she held in her hand a Prayer-Book with a mother-of-pearl cover, which the Duke suspected belonged to his sister.

He noted that Anoushka walked proudly with her head up, and her eyes were not on the ground as was usual when a bride approached the altar and her bridegroom.

Instead, through her veil he could see her looking at him and he wondered what she was thinking.

The Service began, and as it was a marriage of mixed religions it was very short.

The Bishop blessed them with a sincerity that made the Duke feel somewhat ashamed.

His marriage was taking place primarily—in fact entirely—as an act of revenge, and he could not help remembering his sister's words that she wanted Anoushka to find the love that she herself had found with Arthur Lansdown before he had died.

"I will be kind to her and give her everything she wants," the Duke vowed pensively to himself, and knew at the same time that what he was doing was intrinsically wrong.

When the marriage was over and the Duke walked out of the Chapel with Anoushka on his arm, he knew his sister expected them to leave immediately.

"The carriage is waiting, Raven," she said, "and I can only give you my good wishes and pray ceaselessly that you will both be very happy."

She looked at the Duke as she spoke, and he knew exactly what she was saying to him.

He kissed first her cheek, then her hand.

"Thank you, Marguerite," he said.

He helped Anoushka into the closed carriage that was waiting, and as they drove away he turned sideways to look at his bride, thinking that he had had no opportunity to do so until now.

Her veil was thrown back over her head so that he could see her hair for the first time.

He had thought it was dark, but now he saw that it was a strange, indeterminate colour to which he could not put a name.

Perhaps, he thought, it was the result of her parents having different nationalities. It seemed almost to have silver streaks against a colour that was neither dark nor fair, and made him think of the ashes of a burnt-out fire.

Once again he realised how different her beauty was from that of any other girl he had known.

Then as he went on looking at her, her eyes met his and she asked anxiously:

"Do . . . do I look . . . all right? I feel very . . . strange, and when I first saw this gown it made me . . . laugh."

"Laugh?" the Duke questioned.

She smiled, which he had never seen her do before, and her face seemed suddenly transformed as if by sunshine.

"I thought it seemed very amusing that a gown should have so much decoration at the back and so little at the front," she explained.

"That is the vogue set by Mr. Worth, who is the King of Fashion," the Duke replied.

He realised that Anoushka was looking at him to see if he was serious.

"Are you saying that a man made this gown?"

"He designed it," the Duke corrected, "but he has over a thousand people working for him."

Anoushka laughed, and he thought it was a very pretty sound, clear and spontaneous, and quite different from the rather affected laughter of other women he knew.

"I cannot imagine a man designing gowns for women," she said, "I thought sewing was an entirely feminine occupation."

When the Duke laughed, she said:

"I was thinking last night what a lot of things I have to learn, but if they are all going to be like my gowns, then I shall find them very funny."

That was true, the Duke thought now, and if Anoushka had been surprised at what she saw and heard, he was astonished at her reactions to the new world, which, as his sister had said, was to her like stepping onto another planet.

When they had first talked together she had been dressed as a Novice and she had been very serious as she considered whether she should or should not marry him.

He had therefore anticipated that he would find her seriously weighing up everything she discovered and approaching it in the same manner as that of a pupil attending a lesson with a teacher.

Yet, so many things seemed to amuse her that the Duke found himself laughing too, and the afternoon passed very differently from what he had expected.

He found that when she was animated, especially when she was laughing, her face had a new beauty that rather intrigued him, and she had a sparkle in her eyes which for the moment at any rate swept away the mystery in them.

Above all, he liked the sound of her laughter.

It struck him halfway through the afternoon that Cleodel had seldom laughed, but when she did so it was a hesitating little sound as if she forced it to her lips, in the same way as she had made her voice sound shy, young, and a little nervous.

As the Duke thought of her, there was a frown between his eyes and his lips tightened.

Anoushka, who had been inspecting the paintings in his house, turned from one of them which they had been discussing to ask him a question, then the words died on her lips.

"What have I . . . said which is . . . wrong?" she asked.

"I did not hear what you asked me," the Duke admitted.

"B-but you are . . . angry."

"Not with you," he replied quickly. "It was just something I thought of."

He tried to smooth away the frown and force a smile to his lips, but he realised that Anoushka was looking at him in the same way as she had done at the Convent when he had felt she was looking beneath the surface and seeking his soul.

Because he could not help being curious, he asked:

"What are you thinking?"

She did not reply but turned her head away to look at the painting.

"I asked you a question, Anoushka."

"I . . . I do not wish to . . . answer it," she replied, "because it might be . . . something you do not . . . wish to hear."

The Duke paused for a moment before he said:

"I think we should establish now, once and for all, that as we are married it would be a mistake for us not to be frank with each other. You have asked me to teach you, so I shall tell you honestly if you are doing or saying something wrong, and I shall not expect you to be offended."

"No, of course not," Anoushka said quickly.

"And the same applies to me," the Duke said. "I will not be offended or upset at anything you say to me, and let me beg of you to be frank and truthful. The one thing I will not tolerate is if you lie to me."

He spoke almost furiously as he remembered how Cleodel had lied to him.

"I will not lie," Anoushka said, "and the answer to your question is that what you were thinking was . . . ugly, and in some way it . . . spoilt you."

The Duke stared at her.

"What do you mean—spoilt me?" he enquired.

"You look so magnificent but it is not only how you look,"

Anoushka replied. "I think you are also noble, kind, and compassionate, which is why I agreed to . . . marry you."

She paused, and as the Duke could not find words in which to reply, she went on:

"Because just now you were . . . different from what you have appeared before, I . . . thought it was something you should control and forestall."

The Duke was speechless.

Anoushka had spoken to him in a quite impersonal manner, which he realised was the way he had been speaking to her.

There was nothing intimate about it, nothing of the soft allurement which might have been expected to pass between a man and a woman, even if they were not attracted to each other.

Instead it was an entirely logical, dispassionately thought-out appraisement, and he was intelligent enough to recognise it as such.

"I understand what you are saying," he said after a moment, "and thank you for being so honest with me."

"You are like your paintings," Anoushka said, "and I could not bear to think that any of them might be damaged."

Then, as if the subject was closed, she asked him questions about the very fine examples of pink Sèvres porcelain, which led the Duke to tell her the story of how *Madame* de Pompadour had started a China Factory.

She listened to him attentively. Then she said:

"I have read about *Madame* de Pompadour in one of the history-books, but when I asked my teacher about her she refused to answer, saying she was not a woman with whom I should concern myself. Why was that?"

The Duke thought this was a hurdle he would have to jump sooner or later, and he replied:

"She was the mistress of Louis XV."

"What does that mean?"

"You have no idea?"

"Not really," Anoushka replied. "In the history-books of France there seem to have been a lot of women who wielded great power though they were not aristocrats. How am I to understand if nobody will explain to me why they were so important?"

The Duke thought for a moment. Then he said:

"The Kings of France, like Kings everywhere, had their wives chosen for them for reasons of policy, so that the uniting of two Royal families might strengthen their throne or their country." He paused.

"But because he was also a man with ordinary desires, the King often chose a woman whom he found attractive to be his companion."

As the Duke spoke he watched Anoushka's face and knew by the expression in her eyes that she was trying to understand exactly what he was saying.

"Did the King love the woman who was his mistress?" she asked.

"Usually," the Duke replied, "and Louis XV not only loved *Madame* de Pompadour but was faithful to her, which was unusual."

"You mean that some Kings have had more than one mistress?"

"I see you will have to read about Charles II of England," the Duke said, "who had many mistresses, all of them very beautiful, one of the most important being a Frenchwoman. I have a portrait of Louise de Keroualle in my house in the country, which is one of the finest that was ever painted of her."

Anoushka did not speak for a few seconds. Then she asked:

"If Kings have mistresses, do ordinary men have them too?"

"Only when they can afford them."

"You mean . . . they are expensive? Why?"

"A mistress expects to be rewarded for her services . . ." the Duke began.

"What do those services entail?" Anoushka interrupted.

The Duke thought for a moment.

He felt it might be a mistake to pursue this conversation so soon after they were married. At the same time, it was inevitable sooner or later in the world in which Anoushka would live with him.

"A mistress reciprocates her protector's attention as best she can," he said, "and you will learn, Anoushka, that she expects to be paid, either with money or jewellery, for her kisses and any further show of affection a man requires of her."

Anoushka thought this over in silence until she said:

"It seems . . . very strange. I always thought that love would be given and was not something for which one would expect . . . payment of any sort."

The Duke appreciated the quickness of her mind, but he said:

"I suggest we leave this subject. It is certainly not something we should be discussing on our wedding-day."

Anoushka looked at him.

"I think because you say that it means that you have had mistresses you would not wish me to know about."

"If I have, it is not something I should be discussing with my wife," the Duke retorted.

He spoke sharply, then realised it was a mistake.

"I am . . . sorry if that was . . . wrong of me," Anoushka said humbly, "but you . . . did say we were to be . . . frank with each other."

The Duke felt as if he had walked into a maze and for the moment had lost his way.

"I meant what I said," he replied. "It is just that today, of all days, I want you to learn about things that are beautiful, like my paintings and a great many other things in this house."

"I understand," Anoushka said, "and everything you tell me is of interest to me."

The Duke knew this was true, and a little later, when he thought his explanations to Anoushka's questions had been very skilful, he said:

"Tomorrow I intend to take you to meet *Monsieur* Worth and get him to design some special gowns for you that will express your personality and your individuality. Only he can do that, which is the reason why he is hailed as a genius."

He thought Anoushka looked pleased, and he went on:

"Tonight when you go upstairs to dress for dinner you will find several gowns waiting for you that I have ordered to tide you over until Worth's creations are ready, and I hope that the bonnets and the other accessories that go with them will please you."

"I hope somebody will show me how to put them on."

"An experienced lady's-maid will do that," the Duke replied, "and as a *Coiffeur*, the most famous in Paris, is coming to style your hair, I think you will soon begin to feel you are a very different person from the one you have been in the past."

"A *Coiffeur?*" Anoushka questioned. "That means a hair-dresser."

The Duke smiled.

"Another man!" he said. "Henri is the most famous *Coiffeur* in

Paris. It is not only difficult to obtain his services, but he charges an astronomical sum to attend you."

"I can see it is very expensive to be a Lady of Fashion," Anoushka said. "I am only hoping you will think I am worth it."

Because her eyes were so expressive, the Duke knew he could read her thoughts: she was thinking that in accepting so much from him it was almost as if she were his mistress.

He wondered what she would say if he explained exactly what was expected of a mistress and also a wife.

Then he remembered his promise to his sister, and thought that as they had three months of chastity imposed upon them, it would be a mistake to talk too soon of things which might make his promise hard to keep.

*

The door of the Salon opened and Anoushka came in.

She was wearing another exquisitely beautiful gown which became her even though it did not have the special, unique touch that only Worth could impart.

It was made of very pale pink tulle with a bustle billowing out behind it and with tulle framing her shoulders, which the Duke realised for the first time were pearly white.

She looked so lovely as she advanced towards him that he felt as if he should applaud.

Henri had certainly created a masterpiece with her hair. It was coiled round her head in the way that the Princess of Wales had made fashionable in England, and it accentuated the Grecian look that the Duke had noticed the first time he had seen her.

At the same time, he thought that while she had none of Cleodel's pink-and-white, little-girl prettiness, she indeed looked young, pure, and untouched in a way that was more spiritual than physical.

She came towards him and as she reached him she laughed.

"You are right, *Monseigneur*," she said. "I feel very unlike myself. In fact when I looked in the mirror I saw a stranger staring at me. But there is one thing that worries me."

Her laughter died away and now she looked at him a little nervously.

"What is it?" the Duke asked.

"Is it really correct and not immodest to . . . wear so little on my . . . chest and arms?"

The Duke noted that she did not blush because he was a man looking at her, but her eyes were as uncertain as her voice.

"You will find," he replied, "that you would look very strange indeed if your evening-gowns were not exactly like the one you are wearing now, with perhaps an even lower décolletage."

"What is the idea?" Anoushka asked. "It is colder at night than it is in the day, and it seems more sensible to be covered up, especially in the winter."

"But not so attractive," the Duke said. "When you see a Ball-Room filled with women dressed as you are now, they look like beautiful swans gliding round the room, and the men who partner them appreciate the whiteness of their skin."

He did not wait for Anoushka's reply but went on:

"As I appreciate yours. I have a present for you."

He picked up a green leather box from the table beside him and held it out to her.

"This is . . . for me?" she asked.

"A wedding-present," the Duke replied. "And because we have been married in such haste, we have, I am glad to say, no letters of thanks to write, and no rose-bowls, entrée dishes, or candelabra we do not want."

"Is that what people generally send when one is married?"

"Dozens of them," the Duke answered, thinking of the presents laid out in the Ball-Room at Ravenstock House.

"Do the bridegroom and the bride give each other presents?" Anoushka enquired. "I have nothing for you."

"You can buy me a present later if you wish to do so," the Duke replied.

"But . . . I have no money."

"My sister did not explain to you that you are in fact a very rich young woman?"

"Is . . . that . . . true? Then . . . Pap. . . ."

The Duke realised she had been about to say the word "Papa," then had stopped herself.

"I would like you to finish that sentence, Anoushka."

She shook her head, and he said:

"I think you were going to speak of your father."

Anoushka was looking down at the green box he had put into her hands.

She opened the lid to see arranged on black velvet a diamond necklace, bracelet, ear-rings, and a ring.

They flashed and glittered as she stared at them, and the Duke realised that she had no intention of answering his question.

"I hope these will give you pleasure," he said. "They will belong to you personally, although there are also a great number of very fine jewels which are heirlooms worn by every Duchess of Raven-stock."

"They are . . . very beautiful," Anoushka said, "and I never thought I should own anything like this, although I have seen such jewels in pictures and drawings."

"These are yours," the Duke said, "and I will show you how to put them on."

As he spoke, he took the necklace from the box and put it round her neck, fastening it skilfully at the back.

He found himself thinking how many necklaces he had given in the past to women who had always been eager for jewels, but this was certainly the first time he had ever given them to a woman who had never owned any before.

Having fastened the necklace, he took the ear-rings and fixed them to the small lobes of her ears.

He had ordered them to be made specially for ears that had not been pierced, and he thought that as hers were so small she might find the ear-rings heavy and difficult to keep on.

Only as he fixed the second one did he realise that Anoushka could see her reflection in the mirror over the mantelpiece and was watching what he was doing.

Then she gave one of her spontaneous little laughs and said:

"I would feel like a Queen if I had a crown."

"Are you in an obscure way asking for a tiara?" the Duke en-quired.

She looked at him to see if he was serious before she answered:

"I would never ask for anything when you have been so generous to me already, and I know what a tiara is. Will I have to wear one now that I am your wife and we go to parties?"

"Invariably," the Duke replied. "In London every woman wears a tiara at the big Balls and Receptions, and especially when they dine at Marlborough House with the Prince and Princess of Wales."

For a moment he thought Anoushka looked nervous. Then she said, as if she was consoling or comforting herself:

"I suppose really it is only a jewelled bonnet."

The Duke laughed.

"A very good description, but there is no need to be nervous. I will tell you what you must wear and when you should wear it."

"That is what I would like you to do," Anoushka said, "but as you have already chosen my new gowns, I wonder how you know so much about how a woman should look, when I am sure most women have no idea what a man should wear?"

She spoke as if she was thinking out loud. Then she said quickly:

"Do not answer that quesion. I am sure I am talking nonsense. It only seems strange to me, since, having always been with women who know nothing about men, it never struck me that men would know about us."

"Not about Nuns," the Duke agreed, "but about ordinary women with whom I and most other men like to spend a lot of time."

"Why?" Anoushka enquired.

"Because I find women extremely attractive, I like to look at them, admire them, and . . ."

The Duke hesitated. Then he took the plunge:

". . . sometimes to make love to them."

"Even when you are not married?"

The Duke nodded.

"Then the ladies to whom you make love are your mistresses?" Anoushka said.

"Not always," the Duke replied. "As I said this afternoon, it is too soon to explain a somewhat complicated subject in detail."

As he spoke, he was thinking that it would be very difficult for him to put into words the difference between a mistress who was a Courtesan, or what the Bible termed a "harlot," and a Lady with whom one had an *affaire de coeur*.

However, he was saved from answering any more of Anoushka's questions because as he clasped the diamond bracelet round her wrist and put on her finger the ring which matched the whole suite, the Butler announced dinner.

After an excellent meal in the candlelit Dining-Room, the table decorated with white flowers, the Duke did not linger over his port but went with Anoushka to the Salon.

"As the night is so young," he said, "I thought it might amuse you to visit one of the places of amusement in Paris. There are quite a number of them, of which I suppose you are not aware, and tomorrow we might go to the Theatre."

Anoushka's eyes widened.

"Can we really do that?"

"There is nothing to stop us, unless you do not want to see a Play or listen to an Opera."

"But I would like to do both!"

"Then you will certainly have your wish," the Duke answered. "Tonight I will take you to a Restaurant where there is also dancing and we will have supper there."

"You realise I cannot dance?" Anoushka asked in a low voice.

"You shall have lessons as soon as I can arrange it," the Duke said. "In the meantime I will teach you a few steps myself."

"That would be very exciting, but I wonder what the Mother Superior would say."

"You are not at the Convent now," the Duke replied, "and the only person to whom you are responsible for your behaviour is your husband."

"I feel rather embarrassed at being so ignorant of all the things you do and also the things you talk about," Anoushka said.

"There is no reason to feel like that," the Duke replied. "I have promised to teach you, and let me say I find it an intriguing task, especially as you react to most of the new things you encounter in a different way from what I expected."

"What did you expect?" Anoushka asked.

The Duke considered for a moment.

"A frightened young woman who would be prudish and disapproving of most of the things I have suggested."

Anoushka smiled.

"I do not wish to disapprove of anything," she said. "It is only that everything is so strange, but at the same time so funny."

"What is funny now?" the Duke enquired.

"I was thinking how funny the servants look dressed up in that elaborate livery and the food on silver plates which must be very valuable. It is funny too that you have so many houses belonging to you when you are a man alone, without a wife to entertain for you and with no children."

"That is something that can be remedied in the future," the Duke said in a quiet voice.

"You mean that we can have children?" Anoushka enquired.

"I sincerely hope so."

"I would like that," she said, "but how can we do it? They always talked at the Convent about our being the 'children of God,' but they never explained how, as we had ordinary parents, we came into the world."

"As this is a subject which we must find time to talk about, shall we postpone it for the moment?" the Duke asked. "The carriage is waiting now to take us to see the bright lights of Paris."

Anoushka smiled and he saw the excitement in her eyes.

A servant produced a fur-trimmed wrap which matched her gown, and the Duke allowed his red-lined cape to be placed over his shoulders, and took his tall hat, gloves, and ivory-headed cane from one of the footmen.

As the Duke joined Anoushka in the carriage, she asked:

"Why are you carrying a stick? We are not walking."

"It is the correct thing to carry in the evening," he replied.

"Like a lady carrying a fan?"

"Exactly!"

"I think it is a funny thing to do."

"I have never thought about it," the Duke admitted, "but I suppose it is, in a way, just as it is unnecessary really to carry gloves which are seldom put on."

"I am putting mine on. Is that correct?"

"Of course," he answered. "A lady should always wear gloves when she is not at home."

"Always?"

"It would be thought strange if her hands were bare."

"But we can have a bare chest?"

"It may seem somewhat incongruous," the Duke said, "but I do not set the fashions, which have evolved ever since Eve was particular about what shaped fig-leaf she should wear!"

Anoushka's laughter rang out.

"Do you really think there was fashion in the Garden of Eden? Whenever our Priests told us the story of how Adam and Eve were expelled after they had realised they were naked, they always seemed to hurry over how they clothed themselves when they were outside in the wilderness."

"I am sure they found it embarrassing to talk to young girls about nakedness," the Duke said.

"It cannot really be wrong if we are all born naked," Anoushka argued.

"I have not said it is wrong," the Duke replied, "but it would be cold if you went about without clothes, and certainly you would be very disillusioned when you realised that someone whom you admired very much in a gown such as you are wearing now had very ugly legs, or a thick waist."

Anoushka laughed again.

"We were never allowed to talk about our legs at the Convent and some of the girls had very fat ones. I am glad mine are thin."

The Duke wondered if he dared say that he was looking forward to seeing them, then decided that was too intimate.

He realised that Anoushka was talking to him quite naturally, as she might have talked to another girl, and he thought that when he had asked for a wife who was pure and untouched he might also have added the word "unawakened."

That was what Anoushka was, he thought, completely unawakened to the fact that a man could be an attractive being, and that her feeling for one could be something very different from what she felt towards a Priest, who was the only type of man she had seen up to now.

Unless of course she could remember the men she had encountered before she had been left at the Convent.

He thought over how she had nearly spoken of her father when he had told her she was rich, and he was sure that she was about to say that if she had money it meant that her father was dead.

As they drove on he told himself that sooner or later he would get her to talk about her past and discover exactly who she was.

It would be intriguing to try to find out where she came from, who were her parents, and what was her name.

If there was one thing the Duke enjoyed, it was being challenged either to prove himself in the field of sport or to use his brain in some unexpected manner.

Now he found himself determined, however difficult it might be, to unravel the tangled chain of events which had brought Anoushka to the Convent, to discover who had paid for her education there and finally had left her what to any woman was a considerable fortune.

Because of what she had so very nearly said, he felt sure now it must have been her father, but if so, why had he never been to see her?

Why had he hidden her in that mysterious way?

It would have been more understandable if it was her mother who, having produced a "love-child" had placed her in the Convent for safety, and then had somehow been able to provide such large sums of money for her.

"I must get to the bottom of this," the Duke told himself.

He felt a sudden enthusiasm for the task he had been set, and it swept away for the moment at any rate the haunting memory of Cleodel.

*

The place to which the Duke took Anoushka was one of the most respectable Restaurants in Paris, but after the dinner was over the tables in the centre of the room were cleared and a Band played popular dance-tunes.

The Duke had been given one of the alcoves that surrounded half the room where they were a little raised above the tables on the floor and therefore had a better view of the dancers.

Having dined so well at home, the Duke ordered only champagne and some spoonfuls of caviar, which he was sure Anoushka would never have eaten before.

When it came, he thought, she looked at it in surprise, and he explained:

"This is caviar. It comes from Russia and is one of the great specialties that gourmets enjoy."

"Caviar!" Anoushka said almost beneath her breath, and there was a lilt in the tone which the Duke did not miss.

"You have heard of it?" he asked.

"I thought I should never eat it again!" she replied.

The Duke did not reply. He only knew this was another clue and a very helpful one.

He had been sure, from what his sister had said, that Anoushka's mother must have been Russian.

He remembered that when he had visited St. Petersburg five years ago, the women he had met at the Winter Palace were all extremely beautiful and that many of them had the large, mysterious eyes that he thought might almost be replicas of Anoushka's.

At the same time, she did not look completely Russian, and he knew that was because her father was English.

It was the combination of the two that made her look so unusual.

He waited until she had finished her portion of caviar, eating it quickly with a fork and refusing the hot toast she was offered to go with it.

"Will you have some more?" he enquired.

Anoushka looked at him doubtfully.

"Would it be greedy if I said 'yes'?"

"I want you to enjoy yourself," the Duke said, "and I am glad you like caviar. It is something I like too, and I am quite sure it is a delicacy they did not provide you with at the Convent."

"I am sure, with the exception of the Reverend Mother, none of the Nuns had ever even heard of it."

"I am surprised that you liked it when you were a child," the Duke said, thinking he was being rather subtle. "I feel most children would think it greasy."

Anoushka did not reply.

She merely looked at the dancers and after a moment said:

"I think the Reverend Mother would be shocked by the sight of a gentleman putting his arms round a lady's waist."

"But the Reverend Mother is not here," the Duke said, "but I am. And I think, as we agreed to be frank with each other, that you are evading my questions."

She looked at him before she said:

"Please . . . you must not be angry . . . but . . . it is something I cannot . . . answer."

"Why not?"

"Because I have . . . given my word."

"To whom?"

"That is another question to which I cannot . . . reply."

"I can understand your keeping your words of honour to everybody except one particular person," the Duke said.

"Who . . . is that?"

"Your husband. You must realise that the Marriage Service today made us one person, and therefore our loyalty is not to anybody else but only to each other."

Anoushka was silent for a moment before she asked:

"Are you . . . sure that is . . . right?"

"It is how I interpret the marriage-ceremony, and I am sure if you ask your Father Confessor he will tell you the same thing."

Anoushka sighed.

"I think you must explain to me what is expected when one is married, since the Nuns and Novices never had husbands and are not allowed to talk about them."

"But now you are married," the Duke said, "and I am here to explain to you what a husband means, and also what a wife should and should not do."

Anoushka was looking not at him but at the dancers, and yet he was aware that she was listening to him.

Then the Duke thought again that it would be a mistake to get involved in such a difficult conversation so soon after they were married.

And yet, because he was aware that, ignorant though she was, Anoushka had a quick and very intelligent brain, he told himself it was going to be difficult to keep to commonplace and banal subjects when there were such intriguing fundamental ones waiting for them, all of which he knew opened up new horizons which she did not even dream existed.

Then he realised that she was not only very lovely but unique.

He did not miss the glances she had received when they had come in and the way the men at the adjacent tables kept looking at her.

He knew she was supremely unaware of their admiration, intent only on looking at what was happening, with the eyes of a child.

"That is what she is in so many ways," the Duke thought to himself. "At the same time, she has a brain which when it is developed will make many men look foolish."

The dance-floor was now crowded, and as one couple who had obviously had too much to drink bumped into another couple, one of the women slipped and fell down on the floor.

Anoushka gave a little gurgle of laughter.

"Has that happened because the floor is so slippery?" she asked.

"No, it is because those people have been drinking too much and are unsteady on their feet," the Duke replied.

"I have heard of drunkenness," Anoushka said, "but I did not know it made it difficult to walk or to dance."

"In most cases it means that people are rather noisy and laugh too much."

He saw the look of apprehension on Anoushka's face as she pushed her glass of champagne to one side, as if she was afraid to drink any more.

"You need not worry that it will happen to you," he said. "I have told you I will look after you."

"Please do that," Anoushka said. "I would be horrified at myself if I behaved like the woman over there!"

The Duke watched the woman now giggling stupidly as two men tried to lift her to her feet.

Then as the other dancers passed they looked at her contemptuously, raising their eye-brows and shrugging their shoulders in a typically French fashion.

"I think it is . . . degrading," Anoushka said, "for a woman to . . . behave like that. I do not . . . like to see it. Please . . . can we . . . go?"

The Duke put a number of franc-notes on the table and rose to his feet.

"Of course," he said. "It was a mistake to bring you here in the first place."

They walked out of the Restaurant, the carriage was called, and when it arrived the Duke told his servants to open the hood.

As they drove off with the stars shining above them, Anoushka said in a nervous little voice:

"Perhaps it was . . . wrong of me to ask you to take me away . . . I am . . . sorry if I . . . spoilt your enjoyment."

"You did nothing of the sort," the Duke answered. "What you have just seen is something which I am sure rarely happens at that particular Restaurant. You were just unfortunate, and it is not the sort of behaviour you are likely to come in contact with elsewhere."

As he finished speaking he realised that Anoushka was not listening.

Instead, she was looking up at the stars with her head thrown back. The line of her long neck had an almost classical beauty as they passed the street-lights which revealed both her profile and the glitter of diamonds on her white skin.

She looked ethereal, and after a moment she said:

"The sky is so beautiful at night, and it seems strange that men and women do not look at the stars instead of dancing in a small stuffy room."

"They dance because they want to be close to each other," the Duke replied, "and the stars are far away."

Anoushka turned her head to look at him.

"Are you saying that the men and women we saw tonight dancing together want to be close to each other because they are . . . in love?"

"No, of course not," the Duke replied. "But most women who are unmarried are seeking a husband, and men like to dance with any woman they find attractive."

Anoushka thought this over. Then she said:

"I do not think I really want to dance, but if I did, it would be much more pleasant to dance alone."

CHAPTER FIVE

THE FOLLOWING day, the Duke thought, was filled with Anoushka's laughter.

There were so many things that amused her, to his surprise, since he had never thought of them as being in the slightest degree funny.

First, she had found the Champs Élysées as alluring as did the children who flocked there every morning.

Green and picturesque with the great private mansions scattered amongst the trees, it also provided numerous side-shows with Punch and Judy, roundabouts, miniature carriages drawn by goats, and stalls selling toys, gingerbread, and balloons.

As he watched Anoushka's eyes shining and listened to her exclamations of joy and the sound of her laughter, the Duke realised that this could not have been part of her childhood.

He longed to ask her questions, but he knew if he did so she would lapse into one of those repressive silences which he could not break.

Instead he drove her round Paris in an open Chaise to see the sights.

The half-finished Eiffel Tower made her laugh too.

"Who could have thought of such a monstrous monument?" she asked when he explained that it was to be the centre-point of an Exhibition.

"I agree it is not particularly beautiful," the Duke replied, "but at the same time there will be a magnificent view from the top of it when it is finished."

When they drove beside the Seine, Anoushka did not laugh, but she was fascinated by the animated scene on the great river, with its *bateaux-mouches* gaily decorated with pendants and streamers, and the *bateaux-lavoirs* for washer-women.

When they were driving along the wide boulevards, Anoushka was again laughing at the strange people sitting outside the *Cafés*, the Dandies, and the ladies of both the *Monde* and the *demi-monde* displaying the latest and most outrageous fashions.

She still found the bustle funny, although her own gown had one which was so skilfully made that on Anoushka it did not seem an exaggerated form of dress but added to her grace and the dignity with which she moved.

Finally the Duke took her to meet Frederick Worth in the Rue de la Paix.

He was used to women for whom he had bought clothes speaking of Worth almost as if he were a god.

They treated him with a reverence that made the Duke feel that they were quite prepared to kneel down and worship him if he would create for them the gowns they wanted. Therefore, he was not prepared for Anoushka's reaction.

Now as he looked through her eyes at the great man who came from Lincolnshire and who had slept under the counter as an apprentice, the Duke could understand the quiver at the corners of her mouth and the irrepressible twinkle that lit the purple of her irises.

In his fur-trimmed velvet coat, with the beret he always wore on his greying hair, and speaking in his bombastic manner, Worth, when thought of as an ordinary man, was indeed funny.

Because he knew the Duke was very rich, the famous designer studied Anoushka closely, then appreciatively.

There was silence as he walked round her, regarding her from every angle before he said, and his voice was entirely sincere:

"It will be a pleasure and a privilege to dress somebody whose beauty is so different from that of my other customers."

Anoushka looked at the Duke to see if what Frederick Worth was saying pleased him.

"That is what I thought myself," the Duke said quietly, "and my wife needs an entire trousseau as quickly as you can provide her with one."

It was then that Anoushka saw the great man in action.

His assistants hurried with silks, tulles, velvets, brocades, cloth of silver, lace, gauze, all of which he threw casually over Anoushka's shoulder, held them against her waist, or tried them in all the colours of the rainbow against her skin.

Then he was scribbling sketches on pieces of paper, calling for more and yet more satins, spangles, fringes, tassels, and feathers, until Anoushka felt she would be swamped by her clothing and left with no individuality of her own.

It was the Duke who inspected the sketches, listened to Mr. Worth, and decided what should be made.

Only when they drove away and Anoushka felt as if she must breathe deeply to resuscitate herself did she begin to laugh.

"How dare you laugh at the most acclaimed man in all Paris!" the Duke said with mock severity.

"He was so funny!" Anoushka said. "All those people running round him like busy little ants, and he giving orders as if he were creating the world rather than a gown."

"You are committing *lèse-majesté*," the Duke complained. "If he were aware of it, he might refuse to design for you, and then where would you be?"

"Perhaps like Eve, looking for fig-leaves, but in the Bois rather than the Garden of Eden," Anoushka replied, and the Duke joined in her laughter.

He took her to luncheon at the Pre Catelan in the Bois because he wanted to see what she would make of the beautiful *Amazones* who galloped between the Porte Dauphine and the Champs des Courses, and stopped there to refresh themselves and exchange gossip.

Until he arrived there he had forgotten that he knew so many people in Paris that it was inevitable that he should find himself surrounded by friends and that Anoushka would be the object of their intense curiosity.

He introduced a number of people to her, then he quickly moved her away to a secluded table under the shelter of one of the trees.

"We will have a very light luncheon," he said, "because tonight I intend to take you to a Restaurant where there is no dancing but where the food is superlative and those who dine there think of little else."

"I think that food must be very important to the French," Anoushka remarked.

"That is true," the Duke agreed. "They have in fact two national passions which absorb them to the exclusion of all else."

"What is the second one?" Anoushka asked.

"Love," the Duke replied.

She looked at him in surprise.

"Do you mean that they think about it almost as if it were a subject of study?"

"To the Frenchman it is an Art, as important as painting, music, sculpture, or food."

"There must be a great deal to learn about love."

"A Frenchman takes a lifetime to be proficient in it."

The Duke saw that Anoushka was puzzling over what he had said. Then three people came up to the table with exclamations of delight at seeing him.

Leading them was an Englishwoman with whom the Duke had had a fiery, tempestuous affair which had ended only when her husband, who was a Diplomat at the Court of St. James's, had been moved to another country.

La Comtesse de Portales, as she was now, was still exceedingly beautiful and was well aware of it.

Her red hair and slanting green eyes had held many men captive, and the two Frenchmen who accompanied her were both friends of the Duke and were delighted to see him.

"I intended to call on you this afternoon," the *Comtesse* said, "to offer you my congratulations and of course my good wishes for your happiness. You know, dear Raven, that I want you to be happy."

She looked up into the Duke's eyes in a manner which said without words that she thought it was very unlikely he would find that elusive goal except with her.

"You are even more beautiful than I remember, Madelaine," the Duke said courteously, raising her hand to his lips.

She smiled at him intimately before he said:

"Let me present you to my wife. Anoushka, *la Comtesse* de Portales, who was an irreparable loss to England when she left it."

Anoushka curtseyed, and as the two men were shaking hands with the Duke and congratulating him on his marriage, the *Comtesse* looked her up and down in a manner that was very different from the way she had looked at the Duke.

Then as if she decided to make something very clear she said:

"I was most surprised to hear of the Duke's marriage. He has been a very close and very dear friend of mine, and I thought he might have informed me of his intentions."

Anoushka looked at the woman with interest, and she thought she could understand why the Duke admired her.

She was certainly extremely beautiful, and yet instinctively Anoushka felt that beneath the surface she was not a good woman and that the attitude she had towards her was unpleasant.

"You must visit my house," the *Comtesse* continued, "and you must not mind, Duchess, if your husband and I have a great deal to say to each other. As I have already told you, he is a very, very dear friend."

There was an acid note in the *Comtesse*'s voice that Anoushka did not miss.

Then she realised that this lady was angry because the Duke had married her.

Quite suddenly she thought the reason was very obvious.

"Were you my husband's mistress, *Madame?*" she enquired.

The other woman was turned to stone and for a moment there was silence from sheer astonishment. Then she said furiously:

"How dare you ask me such a thing! I have never been so insulted in my whole life!"

Her voice rose as she spoke, and the Duke and the two men talking to him turned their heads to see what was occurring.

Then as the *Comtesse* stalked away, her bustle moving behind her like the tail-feathers of an angry turkey, the two men murmured their apologies and followed after her.

The Duke looked at Anoushka.

"What happened? What did you say to upset her?" he enquired.

"I . . . I am sorry if what I said was . . . wrong," Anoushka answered.

As if overcome by what had happened, she sat down again at the table and the Duke did the same.

"But what upset her?" he asked again.

Anoushka looked towards the Restaurant where she could see the *Comtesse* speaking angrily and waving her hands about and insisting on leaving while the gentlemen tried to persuade her to stay.

"I had no idea that what I said would . . . make her so . . . cross," she said, "or . . . that it was . . . rude."

"What did you say?" the Duke insisted.

"She told me how much you . . . meant to each other, and I . . .

asked her if she had been your . . . mistress," Anoushka said in a low voice.

As she spoke she looked at the Duke pleadingly, begging him to understand that she had not meant to be rude or insulting, but had merely thought it was the logical explanation of the way the *Comtesse* was speaking of him.

For the moment the Duke looked stern, then quite unexpectedly he laughed.

"You are . . . not angry?" Anoushka asked.

"It was my fault," he said. "I can understand how this all evolved from our conversation about *Madame* de Pompadour. I should have warned you never to call a woman a man's mistress to her face, as it is certainly not a compliment, especially when she is a lady who, if she has love-affairs, tries to do so very secretly and everybody pretends to know nothing about them!"

"But was she your mistress?" Anoushka asked.

"That is a question which you must understand I cannot answer, because it is dishonourable for a man to betray a woman's secrets or to mention her name in public."

"Or to his wife?"

The Duke felt that once again he had stepped into a maze.

Only last night he had been telling Anoushka there should be no secrets between them, and now he was saying that where he was concerned there must be one.

He found himself wondering how he had ever gone through life until now without becoming so involved in the inevitable laws of social behaviour and finding them so difficult to explain.

Then as he was silent Anoushka said:

"I am sorry . . . very sorry to have . . . done anything . . . wrong, but I did warn you that because I am so . . . ignorant I was not the . . . right sort of wife for you to marry."

"What you do or what you say at the moment does not concern our marriage," the Duke said. "You might just as well say your School is a bad one and you should not be there because you got one lesson wrong. What actually is wrong is the inadequacy of your teacher."

Anoushka smiled and it swept the worry from her eyes.

"I do not think even your worst enemy could call you inadequate," she said, "and you are, I know, a very clever man."

"And you think you are capable of judging me?" the Duke asked sarcastically.

"I can only compare you with the other people I have met, the teachers who came to the Convent specially and told me they were the best in Paris. And of course we were instructed by some of the most important Priests in France. Even the Cardinal called on us once or twice a year."

"So you felt you could appraise their talents and intelligence when you were gaining their commendation," the Duke remarked cynically.

He knew as he spoke that he had upset her, and as she looked away from him across the garden he said quickly:

"Believe me, Anoushka, I am pleased and honoured that you should admire my intellect. It is something I want you to do."

"I-it was . . . presumptuous of me to comment or to compare you with other people."

The Duke realised that she was far too perceptive not to have realised that it had flashed through his mind that it was an impertinence and that a young and supremely ignorant girl who had lived only in a Convent should criticise him even favourably.

Then he realised that from her point of view it was the greatest compliment she could pay him.

It was a fact that although she had been incarcerated between four walls, she had nevertheless studied under people who were high in their own professions and who, unlike the majority of his friends, used their brains.

He had no idea as he was thinking about her that Anoushka was reading his thoughts, and after a moment she said:

"Now that you are forgiving me, I am glad . . . so very glad. Please . . . do not let what I have done . . . spoil our luncheon . . . and I promise I will never say such a thing again."

She looked so lovely as she was pleading with him that the Duke thought he would have to have been made of granite not to respond wholeheartedly to what she said.

"Forget the whole episode," he said. "It is of no importance."

"But your friend . . . the *Comtesse*."

"I will send her some flowers and an apology," the Duke said, "and there is no need for me to see her again."

Anoushka looked at him quickly.

"But perhaps you want to . . . and if so, I could stay at home and you could go to her house . . . alone."

"I have no wish to do that," the Duke replied, and realised to his surprise that it was the truth.

After luncheon they drove round the Bois. Then as it was very hot the Duke took Anoushka back to the house and they sat on the terrace overlooking the garden and felt the faint cool breeze coming from the Seine.

"It is cooler here," Anoushka said as the servants brought them long drinks of fresh lime-juice.

"Personally, I find it unpleasantly hot," the Duke said. "Tomorrow we will leave for the South of France, where it will be hotter still, but there will be breezes from the sea and we will have nothing to do but enjoy the sunshine until my yacht arrives."

"Your yacht?" Anoushka questioned.

"I have sent for it to come to Nice," the Duke said, "and I think perhaps we will cruise down the Mediterranean, stopping at any country that interests you."

He watched her face as he went on:

"There is Italy, Sicily, Greece, and of course if we were very adventurous we could go on to Constantinople and into the Black Sea."

He thought Anoushka drew in her breath, but he was not sure.

Then quickly, before he could say any more, she said:

"Please, let us do that. It is something I would like above all things, and I am never sea-sick."

The Duke thought this was definitely an inadvertent clue about her secret past, but he made no comment except to say:

"The gowns from Worth will have to follow us, but I think you will find that one or two will be ready tomorrow, and I have already ordered some more from the dressmakers from whom I bought the one you have on."

"I am afraid I am costing you a lot of money."

"You have forgotten that you could pay for them yourself."

"Of course! I have forgotten, because at the Convent we never had any money! But there is something much more important I must do."

"What is that?" the Duke asked.

"You said that I could buy you a present which I could pay for myself, and I want it to be a very, very expensive one, because you have given me so much."

"Not as much as I intend to give you," the Duke replied. "I am finding it fascinating to dress a woman 'from scratch,' so to speak, and one who is content to let me have my own way."

He might have guessed, he thought after he had spoken, that Anoushka would not let such a remark pass.

"I think what you are saying, *Monseigneur,*" she said, "is that you have dressed other women in the past. Were they your . . ."

The word "mistresses" hovered on her lips, but she bit it back.

The Duke smiled to himself.

He wondered how many dozens of gowns he had been coaxed into paying for by the women who had granted him their favours.

There had also been furs—ermines and sables—and jewels, so many necklaces, ear-rings, bracelets, and brooches that he had lost count.

He was well aware that the women to whom he had made love, whether they were Ladies of Quality or *demi-mondaines,* thought that because he was so rich that it was only right that he should pay for the privilege to the utmost that they could extract from him.

Of course they gave him presents in return, but always things that were small and of no intrinsic value.

It was something new to have a woman wish to pay back what he was spending in the same generous way that he gave.

"What I wanted to do," Anoushka said, "was to give you something you do not have already. But this would be impossible if all your houses are as perfect as this one. But I have thought of something that I could give you, if you would help me choose it."

"What is that?" the Duke asked.

"A horse," Anoushka said. "The horses you have here in Paris are very fine, and from what you said when you were talking about your stables in England, I think those you have there must be finer still."

He looked at her in surprise as she went on:

"Could you please choose a really fantastic horse, one that is so good and so fine that it will win lots of races? Then if I could pay for it, I feel it would bear comparison with the diamonds and gowns which you have given to me."

The Duke was amused and rather touched.

"Thank you, Anoushka," he said. "Nobody else is likely to give me a horse for a wedding present, and I would like it above all things."

Anoushka clapped her hands together like a child.

"When can we choose it? And where?"

"As soon as we get back to England," the Duke said. "There is a Sales-Room in London called Tattersall's, where I buy quite a number of my horses. Or we can visit some of the Breeders and see what they have to offer."

Anoushka's eyes were shining as she said:

"I was not wrong! I thought that was what you would like. I am so glad!"

"We will choose it together," the Duke said. "And now there is another thing I want to ask you."

"What is that?"

"Can you ride?"

"Not well enough to ride with you," she said in a low voice. "I . . . used to think I rode well . . . but that was a long time . . . ago."

"You mean you rode before you went to the Convent?"

The Duke realised that he had caught her off her guard, and for a moment she did not know what to say.

Then, as if she felt there was no harm in admitting that it was the truth, she said:

"Yes . . . but I am sure riding is . . . something one does not . . . forget."

"We will soon find out," the Duke said, "but I would rather you started at home on my own horses than here in Paris."

"Yes . . . of course," Anoushka said quickly. "It would be very humiliating if I fell off in the Bois where there are so many people . . . and please . . . will you teach me yourself?"

"Of course," the Duke agreed. "And I am sure, from the way you move, that you will be a very fine rider."

"It is something I am sure all Englishmen do well."

The Duke was aware that she was thinking of her father, and he said:

"I hope you will always think so, and as an Englishwoman,

Anoushka, and as my wife, you must learn to hunt, for it is something I very much enjoy in the winter, and I have my own pack of fox-hounds."

"Explain to me, explain to me exactly what that means," Anoushka said. "I did know once, but I may have forgotten."

By the time they went back for dinner, the Duke thought he had never spent a more unusual and intriguing afternoon.

He was beginning to find it fascinating to learn the extreme contrasts in Anoushka's knowledge. In some subjects, the academic ones, she knew as much as he did, if not more, but in others there were voids of ignorance, and because she demanded it he tried to fill them.

He found himself understanding why parents liked to answer the questions their children asked them, to read to them, and to instruct them.

But Anoushka was not a child, and she had a rapier-like intelligence which made her never miss a point and a memory which he found so retentive that everything he said to her was remembered and catalogued for future use.

When she came into the Salon before dinner he thought it ridiculous, with her looks, for her to concentrate so insistently on her mind, or for him to do so.

Every time she changed her gown it seemed to him she took on a different beauty as the colours themselves were reflected differently in her eyes.

The *Coiffeur* was also trying out different styles on her hair, and the Duke found it difficult to say which he preferred.

Tonight she was wearing a gown of silver and white which he had bought because it seemed to him appropriately bridal.

The silver was echoed, he thought, in the strange silver streaks in her hair, and round her neck instead of diamonds she wore a necklace of large Oriental pearls he had sent to her room before dinner, which were glowingly translucent against the whiteness of her skin.

She looked very young, very ethereal, and almost like a sprite arising from the Seine rather than a Duchess of the Social World.

As she crossed the room towards him her eyes were watching the expression on his face. He knew she was wanting his approval and was nervous in case there was something wrong with her gown.

She stood waiting for him to speak, and after a moment he said:

"You look very lovely! Is that what you want me to tell you, or has your mirror done so already?"

She gave a little laugh before she said:

"How do you know I looked at my reflection hoping it would tell me the truth?"

"That is what every woman does when she wears a new gown, and if you had not liked what you saw, you would have changed into something else, and I would have had to wait for you."

"I would not have dared to be late," Anoushka replied, "but I would have been upset if you had not approved."

"When we have been married a little longer you will grow tired of my compliments," the Duke said lightly.

Anoushka shook her head.

"They are very, very exciting for me because I have never had any before."

"I suppose that is true," the Duke conceded. "That is why, if for no other reason, you will find it amusing to be with men rather than shut away with nothing but women!"

"Do all men pay women compliments?" she asked.

"I promise you will receive a great many before you are very much older," the Duke said.

His prophecy very soon proved to be true, because when they arrived at the Grand Vevour, a small but very exclusive Restaurant where he had taken Anoushka to dine, two of his French friends hurried to their table as soon as they were seated.

When the Duke presented them to Anoushka they kissed her hand and, speaking fluent English, paid her compliments which made her look at them wide-eyed.

"How can Raven, who has always beaten us in every race, have carried off yet another prize so alluring, so exquisite," one asked, "without our even being able to compete for it?"

"Are you saying that I am the prize?" Anoushka asked ingenuously.

"Of course, Duchess, although 'prize' is an inadequate word. You are a star glittering out of reach, the moon for which every man yearns, and the sun which Raven has now made exclusively his when you should really shine your radiance for the benefit of all mankind."

They said a great deal more before they went back to their own table, and when they were gone Anoushka said with laughter in her voice:

"You were quite right. I enjoy compliments, and I hope I have many, many more."

"The two gentlemen you have just met are unusually poetic," the Duke said drily. "An Englishman will simply tell you you are a 'good sport' and a 'fine figure of a woman'! And even then they will feel they are being over-effusive!"

Anoushka laughed. Then she asked:

"And what compliments do you pay to the ladies you admire and . . . love?"

"That is something I must not tell you," the Duke replied.

"It is a secret?"

"Not exactly a secret, but indiscreet, and something that would make the average wife jealous."

There was silence. Then Anoushka said:

"You mean . . . that if you . . . admire another woman . . . I should be jealous?"

"It is what most women would be."

"But . . . why?"

"Because I am your husband, and I am supposed to be interested only in my wife, and of course be faithful to her."

"And was the lady we met today not married when you were, as she said, 'very close friends'?"

The Duke thought that once again he had been "hoist with his own petard" and was relieved that for the moment, while they were served with one of the exotic courses he had ordered and the waiter hovered over them, it was impossible to speak intimately.

But he might have guessed that what he had said was being turned over in Anoushka's mind, and when the meal was finished and there was only the coffee left in front of them and a glass of brandy for the Duke, she said:

"Could I ask you a question?"

"Of course," he answered.

"Now that we are married, if you see a woman you think beautiful and attractive . . . and want to say loving things to her . . . am I to pretend that I do not . . . know what is happening?"

"Let us hope it is something that will not happen," the Duke replied, "but if it does, it should be something that is kept secret from you, and certainly it would be beneath your condescension to interfere."

"But you said that most wives would be jealous."

"I think all women are jealous of a rival," the Duke said evasively.

There was silence. Then Anoushka said:

"Then, supposing I listened to compliments from another man and found him interesting . . . would you pretend not to notice?"

"Certainly not!" the Duke said sharply. "That is something that must not happen, and as my wife you must behave decently and with propriety, which means there would be no other men in your life except me."

Once again he was thinking of Cleodel as he spoke, and he was sure that if he had married her she would have continued her affair with Jimmy.

The whole idea disgusted him, and without his meaning to his voice had sharpened and he answered Anoushka almost ferociously.

Then as he finished speaking he thought he might have frightened her and he should try to somehow soothe her feelings if she was upset. But before he could speak she said in a quiet voice:

"That does not seem fair!"

"Fair?" the Duke queried.

"For a man to be entitled to do something, but not a woman. Surely if it is right for the husband it must be right for his wife, and vice-versa."

The Duke realised she was arguing for the sake of it and not because she felt personally involved.

At the same time, he thought, seeing what he had suffered with Cleodel, he should make things clear from the very beginning.

He took a sip of his brandy before he said:

"There is something I want to tell you, Anoushka."

"What is that?"

"When I came to the Convent I was seeking a wife who would be different from all the other women I have ever known."

"In what way?"

"I asked my sister to find me a girl who, because she had been brought up as a Novice, would be pure and untouched. It was then that she suggested you."

There was a long silence. Then Anoushka said:

"I think . . . what you are saying is . . . that the women and girls you have met outside the Convent, in the world in which you . . . live, were neither of those things."

This, the Duke thought, was rather sweeping, and he prevaricated by answering:

"It is difficult to be sure, and although one must always believe that they have been brought up to keep themselves chaste until they marry, there is always the chance that they have been tempted into an indiscretion."

"You mean they might have met men about whom their parents knew nothing, and who would . . . kiss them?"

The Duke understood how this fitted in with the conversation he had had with Anoushka earlier, and he said:

"That is what I meant, for girls, even in the most aristocratic families, have for instance Riding-Masters and meet other men employed by their fathers. There are also men who are unscrupulous and find very young girls attractive."

Once again his voice sharpened as he thought that that was what Jimmy had felt about Cleodel.

"You said you did not want to tell me what had happened in the past," Anoushka said in a low voice, "but I think you have been hurt . . . wounded . . . and it is something you . . . have to forget if you are to be . . . happy again."

The Duke could find no words in which to answer her. He only knew that she had an extraordinary power of perception where he was concerned, and it would be impossible for him to refute anything she had said.

Instead he changed the subject, talking about the Palais Royal, in which the Grand Vevour was situated, describing what it had been like when it was the private house of the *Duc* d'Orleans, and how overnight he became a very rich man when he turned it into a place of amusement with Casinos and Restaurants.

Anoushka listened wide-eyed. Then she said:

"Did the men in those days come here with their wives?"

"Certainly not!" the Duke replied. "Ladies never go to such

places, and when we leave Paris for England, Anoushka, you will not be able to dine in a Restaurant."

"Why not?"

"Because it is something which a woman in your position, what we call a 'lady,' cannot do."

"But there are Restaurants in which you may dine?"

"Yes," the Duke admitted.

"With a woman who would be your mistress?"

"Speaking generally and not personally," he said, "the answer is 'yes.'"

"It seems to me that the women I am not supposed to talk about have a far more amusing time than I will."

"That has been said before," the Duke replied, "but it depends what you call amusement. You, Anoushka, being a Duchess, have a great social position. You will entertain all the most interesting and important people in the land. They will stay with us in the country and dine with us in London."

He saw that she was listening intently, and went on:

"People will look up to you and admire you, especially on my Estate where at Ravenstock alone I employ two thousand people. They will expect you to be interested in them and to look after them."

"How should I do that?"

"My mother would call at their cottages. She also wished to be told when anybody was ill. She gave a party for them at Christmas, and I think I am not exaggerating when I say that everybody loved her."

"And you think they will love me?"

"I am sure of it."

"And do they love you?"

"I hope so. I think perhaps they respect and admire me, and know that I will always be just and generous in anything I do which concerns them."

The Duke smiled as he continued:

"The women I do not wish you to talk about cannot have any of that, nor can they have children who can bear my name, and my eldest son will inherit my title."

There was just a touch of satisfaction in the Duke's voice.

For the first time he began to think, because he was describing it to Anoushka, that he would really enjoy having a son, or sons. He would teach them how to shoot, how to ride, and to enjoy his horses and Estates as he enjoyed them himself.

"If we had a child," Anoushka said in a very small voice, "we would never have to part with it?"

"Never!" the Duke said positively.

He knew she was thinking that she had been parted from her parents, and now he was concentrating on the mystery of why she had been brought to the Convent and abandoned there.

Because he felt it was better not to ask her any questions he said:

"Our children will be with us when they are small, but the boys will have to go away to School. They will of course always come home for the holidays, and we can visit them when they are at Eton and see that they are always well looked after and have everything they want."

He paused before he went on:

"I am thinking that what you said is right, Anoushka. It is funny, and perhaps wrong, for a man to have so many houses in which to live by himself when they should be filled with children who laugh as you laugh, play, and find life exciting."

"If you can give me children," Anoushka said, "why can you not give children to the ladies whose names I am not allowed to mention?"

The Duke thought this was one of the questions he had anticipated would arise sooner or later, but once again he evaded it.

"I think we should leave now," he said. "Would you like to go somewhere else, or would you prefer to drive home with the carriage open? I think we should go to bed soon, as we are leaving early tomorrow morning."

"Yes, of course," Anoushka agreed.

They drove back under the stars and as she looked up at them as she had done the previous night the Duke had the strange feeling that she had for the moment forgotten his very existence.

He knew that any other woman would have been nestling against him, holding his hand under the rug, and waiting for him to whisper words of love in a low passionate voice.

But Anoushka sat upright and her head was tilted back as they drove in silence until they reached the Champs Élysées.

Then, as if she suddenly remembered him, she turned to look at the Duke and say:

"Are you really going to bed now, or do you intend to look for your friends, perhaps in the places you will not take me?"

The Duke was startled not so much by what she said but because once again she was reading his thoughts.

He had in fact been deliberating whether he should drop into Maxim's, knowing that because it was the most fashionable Restaurant in Paris, he would doubtless know most of the men in the whole room.

The women, who would be the smartest, most fashionable *demi-mondaines* in the whole Capital, would welcome him eagerly.

Then because he felt that if he went to Maxim's his presence there when he was on his honeymoon would reflect on Anoushka, and also because, surprisingly, he really had no wish for the superficial gaiety of Maxim's, he replied quite truthfully:

"No, Anoushka, I am coming to bed, and like you I shall think of all the interesting things there will be to do when we reach the South. I am sure you have a thousand questions to ask me, for which I shall have to find the answers."

"You do not mind answering them?" Anoushka asked anxiously.

"I promise you it is something I shall enjoy, although I am quite nervous of displaying my ignorance."

Anoushka laughed.

"That you will never do, and you have to teach me very quickly so that I shall not make mistakes like the one I made today."

"I told you to forget it," the Duke said firmly.

"I am trying to," Anoushka replied, "but I know that even if you have forgiven me, the lady to whom I spoke will hate me, and that is wrong because I am your wife."

"And as your husband I can tell you quite truthfully that it does not worry me and is really of no importance," the Duke said.

They stepped out of the carriage, and because it was after midnight the Duke did not go into the Salon to have another drink, but walked up the stairs beside Anoushka.

Their bedrooms were side by side, with a communicating-door which had not been opened.

They stopped outside the first door, which was Anoushka's.

"Thank you very much for such a delicious dinner and for talking to me," she said.

"It is I who should be thanking you," the Duke replied. "I have found our conversations very interesting and certainly original."

"You mean it would have been different if you had been with anybody else?"

"Very different," the Duke said with a smile, "and that is what makes knowing you so unusual, and I think I might almost use the word 'intriguing.'"

"So you have not been . . . bored?"

"Of course not! And I can say this quite honestly: there has not been a moment since we have been together when I have felt in the least bored or had the slightest wish to be anywhere else except with you."

Her smile was dazzling. Then she gave a little laugh.

"Now you are talking like a Frenchman," she said. "I thought you told me that the English never pay compliments."

"I am the exception."

"Of course," she replied. "And . . . please . . . because I like hearing them, will you pay me lots and lots of them and forget you are English?"

"Only if they are truthful," he said.

"I shall know if they are," she replied. "But actually any compliment is better than none."

The Duke laughed, and taking her hand in his raised it to his lips.

"Let me tell you one more," he said. "I like the quickness of your brain and I enjoy your laughter."

He kissed her hand, his lips warm on the softness of her skin.

As he did so he wondered if he should kiss her lips. Then he thought it was far too soon, and he remembered that Anoushka had said she had no wish to be touched.

He raised his head and, still holding her hand, he said:

"Good-night, Anoushka. Sleep well. There are new excitements tomorrow which I shall look forward to."

"It will be very . . . very exciting for me too."

She spoke eagerly but lightly and took her hand from the Duke's. Then she smiled at him as she opened the door of her bedroom.

He waited until the last frill of her bustle disappeared before he walked towards his own room.

He had the feeling that he was losing or missing something that he should not let escape him.

Then he told himself he was just being fanciful.

At the same time, as his valet helped him undress, he was thinking of Anoushka.

CHAPTER SIX

As THE yacht steamed into the Black Sea, the Duke was watching Anoushka's face, feeling sure that she was showing a significantly different kind of excitement in her eyes.

Intent on finding clues to her past, he had found one of curious significance the moment they had arrived at Nice.

They had stepped out of the special carriage attached to the train to find that as usual the Courier who had gone ahead of them had arranged for the Duke's own carriage drawn by his own horses to be waiting outside the station.

The morning sunshine made it imperative to have the carriage open, but there was a fringed linen canopy to protect them from the sun.

As they drove away, Anoushka had glimpses of the blue sea. Then after they had passed through the town and started to climb the hills above Nice to where the private Villas were situated, the Duke heard her suddenly give a gasp.

"Cypress trees!" she exclaimed in a rapt voice.

The words were spoken under her breath, and yet he heard them and saw the expression of surprise in her eyes.

Silhouetted against the sky were a number of cypress trees pointing like fingers towards the heavens, and he knew as they drove on that her eyes were on them rather than on the Alps in the far distance.

The Duke had by now learnt not to ask searching questions which embarrassed Anoushka because she felt she could not reply to them.

Instead he merely watched her, and he found himself intrigued and interested in a manner which he began to think was different from anything he had ever experienced before.

When he was alone he found himself wondering why cypress trees should have such an importance for her.

They were very familiar in France and Italy. Then suddenly a thought came to him which he felt was very illuminating.

He remembered that when he had visited Russia he had read a great deal about the history of the country and its Tsars.

Now at the back of his memory he recalled that one book had told him that the tall, lofty, romantic cypress trees had first been planted by the Empress Catherine on her journey with Potemkin to her Southern possessions.

From these trees were grafted all the many cypress groves and avenues which over the years had come to be typical of the Crimean landscape.

More especially was Odessa connected with cypress trees.

The Duke had felt as elated as if he had won a hard race or defeated an opponent in the boxing-ring.

"We will go to Odessa!" he thought to himself, but he was too wise to say so to Anoushka. He would let it be a surprise.

After they had spent only two days in his Villa, the Duke was so impatient to put his theory to the proof that early the next day they sailed for Villefranche as their first port-of-call.

It was a brilliant morning which soon became very hot, but they found the sea breeze pleasantly refreshing.

Anoushka was as delighted with the yacht as she had been thrilled, almost like a child with a new doll's-house, by the Duke's private coach on the train.

From little things she said, the Duke knew that she had been in a ship before, but obviously not a private one.

There was no hurry and they sailed slowly down the coast of Italy, occasionally stopping in some small port to go ashore and look at the local sights.

The Duke had no wish at the moment to take Anoushka to Rome or Naples, and he thought even Pompeii could wait for another time.

It was only when they reached the Greek Islands that he recognised this as a desire to be alone with Anoushka and not share her with the crowds and sightseers.

Then he admitted to himself that he was falling in love.

At first he could not believe it possible. He had been so sure after leaving England, with his hatred of Cleodel distorting his whole outlook, that never again would he care for a woman or let one in any way encroach on his heart.

And yet, as he watched Anoushka, as he listened to her questions and strove to answer them, he knew that he found everything about her entrancing.

It was not only her beauty which attracted him but something else that was very different.

He thought now that he should have become aware of the change in his feelings when, the day before they had left Nice, the Courier he had sent to London arrived to report what had occurred after the announcement of his marriage had appeared in the newspapers.

The man had described the astonishment amongst the Duke's friends, the scenes which the Earl of Sedgewick had made at Ravenstock House, and the difficulty Mr. Matthews was having with him and a great number of other callers.

Although the Duke could visualise it all vividly, he found surprisingly that it did not give him any elation or the satisfaction that he had expected.

Quite suddenly it did not seem to matter very much what had been said or done, and England was far away.

Even then, he would not face them for this reason, and it was only when the yacht was steaming towards Constantinople that he admitted that he loved Anoushka in a way he had never loved before, though he was puzzlingly uncertain as to what he could do about it.

In all his considerable experience he had never been with a woman for so long who had not fallen in love with him.

Because he himself was now genuinely in love, he could not blind himself to the truth, nor could he pretend that Anoushka's feelings were anything but those of a pupil for a much-admired teacher.

She listened intently to everything he said, with her huge eyes on his face and with a serenity which he admired and which he had never found except in his sister, Marguerite.

When they discussed academic subjects, Anoushka showed remarkable powers of concentration, and when they argued together the Duke felt he must polish up his brain to keep his end up, let alone defeat her.

On other subjects she was so adorably childlike that he felt at times it would be a mistake to awaken her to a very different point of view.

And yet he could not disguise from himself that he desired her as a woman and that it was not a child who made the blood throb in his temples, his heart beat alarmingly, and a desire rise that seemed at times to be almost uncontrollable.

Then, because the Duke had long practised strict self-discipline, he acted his part with what he told himself was an admirable restraint.

Only at times he wondered frantically whether he would be able to last one month, let alone three, without taking Anoushka in his arms.

But he had given Marguerite his word of honour, and he could break it only if Anoushka asked him to make love to her.

As she had not the slightest idea what this meant, and did not think of him as a desirable man, he thought despairingly that it could never happen and it was a barrier between them that he saw no way of demolishing.

"What am I to do?" he asked himself helplessly at night after Anoushka had gone to her own cabin.

As he could not sleep, he would stand on deck looking at the stars overhead and thinking that he was more lonely than he had ever been in his whole life.

He thought of the women who had tried by every trick that was known to attract his attention, who had contrived in a thousand different ways to get him to themselves.

He would never have believed that he could be in a position where he could not attract one young girl or bring even an expression of affection to her eyes or to her lips.

"Now that you have seen something of the world, what do you think of it?" he asked Anoushka.

He was genuinely curious to hear her answer.

They had by now sailed past Constantinople without stopping there, gone up the Bosporus and into the Black Sea, and now were sitting comfortably side by side on deck-chairs, after an excellent luncheon cooked by one of the Duke's most experienced Chefs.

He thought that Anoushka in a white gown made of muslin looked like the wild-flowers they had seen growing on the Greek Islands and which she had said must have sprung from the footsteps of the gods.

"What do you expect me to feel when everything you have shown me is so beautiful?" Anoushka replied. "When I was at the Convent I used to try to make pictures for myself of the places I read about, and they became part of my dreams. Now I think I must be dreaming."

"Are there any people in your dreams?"

"Sometimes."

"Real people?"

The Duke thought she hesitated before she replied again:

"Sometimes."

"Do you think in the future I shall ever be in your dreams?"

He mocked at himself as he asked the question, knowing it was one he had never asked before, because all other women with whom he had talked would have already told him plainly that all their dreams included him.

"How do I know until I do dream of you?" Anoushka asked in a soft voice which the Duke had long recognised as entirely impersonal.

"I shall be extremely piqued if I am not in your dreams," he said lightly. "After all, I am the only man you know."

"Do most women dream of a man?" Anoushka asked.

"Invariably," the Duke replied. "Women do not feel complete when they are alone. They feel that they need a man with them, not only in real life but also when they are asleep."

He paused, and when she did not answer he added:

"The man in their dreams is the one they are always seeking in their hearts."

"Do they want to marry him?"

"Of course," the Duke replied.

"Then what happens when they are married?"

He smiled to himself as he thought this was a question he might have expected.

"Ideally," he replied after a minute's thought, "a married woman will dream of her husband, but I am afraid that does not always happen."

"But you said," Anoushka answered, "that a married woman, if she behaves correctly, can never be interested in any man except her husband."

"That is what a husband expects, and what I would expect of you."

"But you will not be able to control my dreams," Anoushka said, "and if I dream of somebody else I shall be the only person to know I have dreamt something wrong."

"I should be very upset and hurt if I thought you were dreaming of another man," the Duke said, choosing his words with care.

"Then I will certainly keep it a secret," she said, "and I suppose you are allowed to dream of any woman you like and I must not be upset or hurt!"

"Would you be?" the Duke asked.

It was a leading question, but he had to ask it.

Anoushka was looking out to sea, and he knew she was thinking seriously over what he had asked her. Then she gave one of her unexpected lilting laughs.

"This is a very funny conversation," she said. "How can we be so foolish as to worry about our dreams? Mine are sometimes very complicated. Last night I dreamt I was flying over the sea. . ."

"Alone?" the Duke enquired.

"I think so," she replied. "It was a lovely feeling, sweeping through the air like a bird, and I was disappointed when I woke up."

The Duke gave a sigh.

Once again the conversation had veered away from himself, and he knew Anoushka was not thinking of him in any way except as a companion who was a mine of information.

"You have not forgotten," she said, "that you promised that when we reached the Black Sea you would take me sailing? I have never sailed in a small boat, and I think perhaps it would be almost like flying."

"We will sail in an hour's time, when it is a little cooler," the Duke promised.

He had already given the Captain instructions that they were to anchor in one of the small bays along the coast.

He did not want to arrive at Odessa until early one morning when he intended there should be plenty of time for him to watch Anoushka's reaction when she first saw the cypress trees, the spires, and the towers of the city ahead of them.

He would take her ashore, and perhaps then he would find out the secret which she had kept hidden for so long and which she had still not made up her mind to confide to him.

Perhaps then, the Duke told himself optimistically, when that barrier between them fell, she would feel herself closer to him than she was at the moment, and the restrictions would fall one by one.

He was watching her while he thought it over, and she was looking exceedingly lovely.

He suddenly felt such a desire to touch her that only years of self-discipline prevented him from putting out his hands, pulling her to her feet, and taking her into his arms.

It had been an agony, and yet a joy, when a week ago in a small harbour in the South of Italy, where they had rested for the night, a Band consisting of two violins and a man who beat tambourines, a cymbal, or rang bells played on the side of the quay.

They had been in the Saloon with the port-holes open to let in the night breeze.

Anoushka had run to one of them exclaiming with delight not only at the music but at the strange way in which the musicians were dressed.

Then the Duke had said:

"I think this is an excellent opportunity for me to show you how to dance."

As he had expected, she learnt very quickly, and was so light on her feet that he felt he was dancing with some mythical being rather than with a woman.

He danced her round and round the Saloon, and when the music stopped she clapped her hands in delight and begged for more.

When she became quite proficient and could follow his steps without difficulty, the Duke drew her a little closer and was aware how much the nearness of her slim body affected him.

Then as another dreamy waltz came to an end and they were both still, he kept his arm round her and looked down into her eyes, up-turned to his.

"Now we can dance together," he said.

His voice was very deep and had a passionate note which any experienced woman would have recognised.

"It is very exciting," Anoushka answered.

"Is it something you want to do again?"

"Of course! Again and again!" she replied. "Sometimes the girls at the Convent used to say they would like to dance, and those who had done so would try to describe what happened, but I never knew it would be like this!"

"Like what?" the Duke asked.

"Like being part of the music, so that I am not only listening to it but it is playing in my feet and in my body."

The Duke wanted to say: "You will feel the same about love," but he knew Anoushka would not understand.

Quite unselfconsciously she slipped away from his encircling arm and ran to the port-hole.

"We must wave to our little Band," she said, "and tell them how much we enjoyed their playing."

She waved as she spoke, and the Duke heard the men below them on the quay saying:

"*Grazio, Signora, multo grazio!*"

She turned to smile at the Duke and found he was very near to her.

"I should be saying the same thing," he said. "*Multo grazio, Signora!*"

She swept him a deep curtsey.

"*Grazio, Signora,*" she replied.

Her eyes were laughing up at his but they did not hold the expression the Duke wished to see.

The sailors had now erected a mast on the lightest of the lifeboats with a bright red sail which was moving slightly in the wind.

Anoushka seated herself in the stern, the Duke took the tiller, and they began to move over the water.

"This is exciting!" she said. "How fast can we go?"

"That depends entirely on the wind," the Duke replied. "The Captain thought it would be a little stronger later."

"I hope he is right."

She looked up at the sky, which was clear, although the sun was not so hot as it had been earlier in the day.

"What you have to do," the Duke said, "is to whistle. Every sailor knows he must whistle down the wind."

Anoushka laughed and pursed her lips.

The way she did so made the Duke long to kiss her, but while he was thinking about it he was busy adjusting the sail, letting the boom swing outwards so that they began to run a little quicker with the wind behind them.

"It works! It works!" Anoushka cried. "My whistle has brought the wind!"

It certainly seemed to have been effective, and the small boat increased its speed as the sail billowed out crimson against the deep blue of the water.

"Faster! Faster!" Anoushka kept crying, and the Duke managed by extremely skilful sailing to achieve what he thought to himself was quite an unusual speed.

They had been sailing for nearly half-an-hour when he looked up apprehensively and realised that the sun had vanished and instead of the pale, clear, translucent sky which he expected, it looked grey and somewhat turbulent.

The Duke looked over his shoulder.

Intent on pleasing Anoushka, he realised they had gone very much farther than he had intended, the yacht was out of sight, and he knew it would take them a long time to sail back.

"Keep your head down," he said to Anoushka, and swung the boom over to begin what he knew would require all his expertise as a yachtsman.

The Duke had done a great deal of sailing and was in fact exceedingly proficient at the sport, which he enjoyed.

Last year he had won a considerable number of races at Cowes in the Isle of Wight, and he always sailed against yachtsmen as experienced as himself when he was in the South of France.

Now he thought somewhat apprehensively that the weather was worsening rapidly, and knew he had made a mistake to come so far when both the wind and the sea in these parts could be unpredictable and treacherous.

"Is everything all right?" Anoushka asked.

"I am concentrating on getting us back to the yacht," he replied, not wishing to frighten her.

"The sea is getting rough."

"I had noticed that," he replied drily. "But you told me you were a good sailor."

"At least I was," she said, "but it would be very humiliating if you proved me wrong."

"One should never trust the Black Sea," the Duke replied, "even though it is my colour."

As he spoke, he wondered what Anoushka would think when she

heard the crowds shouting: "Raven Black!" "Raven Black!" when his horses thundered towards the winning-post.

It always pleased him to find that he was popular with the racing-crowd, knowing they had an instinct that was seldom wrong as to whether a man was a good sportsman or not.

"Why is black your colour?" Anoushka asked.

"It seemed appropriate because my name is Raven."

"It does not suit you."

"Why should you think that?"

"Because if you resemble a bird at all, you are more like an eagle. I was watching two this morning when we went on deck after breakfast."

"I was watching them too," the Duke said, "but why do you think I resemble them?"

"They are not only magnificent, and they are called the King of the Birds, but they also seem imperious and disdainful of mere mortals, almost as if they belong to another world than ours."

"Do you think that is what I do?" the Duke asked.

"I think you are imperious, and I think too that while you take part in many different social spheres and activities, you could never belong to anything or anybody except yourself."

"Why should you think that?" he asked sharply.

Anoushka did not answer, and after he had adjusted a rope he said:

"I am waiting to hear your answer to my last question."

"It is difficult to explain to you, but I feel that you are sufficient in yourself and do not need, as most people do, others to inspire, guide, lead, or comfort you."

"I suppose what you are suggesting is flattering in a way," the Duke said. "At the same time, it would be very lonely if I took you literally."

"What I am really saying is that people are complementary to you, and not you to them. You do not need help as another man might."

The Duke wondered what Anoushka would say if he told her how much he needed her.

But he knew once again it was too soon—much too soon.

Then he realised that he had no time to think about Anoushka but must concentrate on sailing the boat in what was obviously going to be a dangerously rough sea.

The Duke remembered far too late that the storms in the Black Sea could blow up in a question of minutes, and this was what was happening now.

The wind increased so that he was forced to use all his strength to keep the boat on course, and the sea suddenly changed from rippling white-crested waves to large overpowering ones.

The Duke looked round and the nearest land appeared to consist of high cliffs, and to go near them would be to risk being dashed against the rocks.

Then just beyond them he saw what appeared to be a small bay and beyond it a much lower coastline with trees coming almost down to the water's edge.

"We will make for the shore," he decided, and realised he had to shout the words at Anoushka to make her hear them.

She was sitting on the floor of the boat. She did not answer but gave him a smile that seemed to illuminate her face.

The Duke had no time to look at her again.

He was trying to work the boat by skilful tacking towards the shore, knowing he must avoid the cliffs and the rocks beneath them and make for the bay, or, if he missed that, the low-lying ground beyond it.

It was a slow process and an unpleasant one.

The wind almost tore the main sheet out of his hands. The boat was buffeted and swept from side to side, or else it pitched and tossed in a most unpleasant manner.

The Duke was fighting for every inch but making little headway. Then the rain came.

It came down torrentially, soaking them to the skin and creating a veil through which the Duke could not see. He could only hope blindly that he was still continuing in the right direction.

It was impossible to speak to Anoushka, nor could he do anything but attempt to keep the boat afloat while the rain teemed down with such violence that even through his yachting-coat it hurt his shoulders.

Then as he strove to look ahead, finding it hard to keep his eyes open against the force of the rain, the boat suddenly gave a violent jerk.

There was a scraping sound and the Duke knew that they had either run aground or hit a rock.

As he wondered frantically what he should do and how he should save Anoushka, a gust of wind that seemed almost like a whirlwind swung the boom round with a swiftness that took him by surprise.

It struck him with a violence against which he had no defence, and he was thrown, unconscious, to the bottom of the boat.

Then there was only darkness . . .

*

The Duke came back to consciousness as if from the end of a long tunnel . . .

First he was aware that he could think. A long way away there was a glimmer of light . . .

He felt as if he was struggling to breathe, struggling to live, and yet he could not move . . .

Then he heard a voice speaking, a voice he recognised, and he knew it was Anoushka's, but he could not understand what she was saying.

It puzzled him, and he thought for a moment that he had gone mad. Then he realised she was speaking in a strange language and knew it was Russian.

Her voice was still soft and clear, but occasionally she hesitated, as if she was trying to remember a word. Then she went on talking, and a man was answering her in the same language.

He seemed to have quite a lot to say in a voice that was slow and deep, and the Duke thought vaguely that he sounded educated.

Then he drifted away into unconsciousness.

*

When the Duke became conscious again there was only silence and he was aware of a pain at the back of his head.

Then he felt a sudden frantic fear that he had lost Anoushka.

He tried to open his eyes, but even while he was trying to do so, the darkness seemed to come towards him from the end of the tunnel, and he could not prevent it from overpowering him . . .

*

The Duke opened his eyes.

There was a bright warm light near him, and after a moment he realised it was a fire, the flames leaping high from large logs.

He tried to speak, to call Anoushka, and then she was beside him.

He stared at her, trying to focus on her face, and as he did so he realised that he was lying on a bed beside the fire.

It was a bed that was low on the ground, and Anoushka seemed to tower above him until she knelt down at his side.

"Can you speak?" she asked.

"Where—am—I?"

"You are all right, but I was afraid . . . so afraid . . . But you can . . . speak."

"Yes—I can—speak," the Duke replied in a louder tone. "You are not hurt!"

She smiled at him, and he saw that her hair was loose, which puzzled him.

"What—happened?" he asked.

"We ran into a rock," she said, "but a kind and brave man saved us. He carried you from the boat. I was so . . . terrified you would . . . drown."

The Duke heard the pain in her voice and wanted to put out his hand towards her. As he tried to do so, he realised he was lying naked beneath some warm blankets.

As if she knew what he was thinking, Anoushka said:

"You were lucky, very, very lucky! The man who saved you is a Doctor. This is his holiday house, right on the edge of the sea."

"Where—is—he—now?" the Duke enquired.

"He has left to go to the nearest fishing-village to arrange, as soon as it is daylight and the sea has subsided, for somebody to row to the yacht and tell them to join me here. It is very kind of him to do this."

"Very—kind!" the Duke agreed. "But—you are all—right?"

"I was not hurt. Fortunately, we were very near the shore. I was only afraid for you."

"The boom hit my head."

"Yes, I know. It knocked you unconscious," Anoushka said, "but there is nothing broken. The Doctor felt you over very carefully and said that although your head will ache for a day or so, you are very strong."

The Duke tried to sit up but found that it hurt him.

"No, lie still," Anoushka instructed, putting out her hand to prevent him from moving.

As she did so, the Duke saw to his surprise that she was wearing a man's shirt with the sleeves rolled up.

She gave a little laugh.

"Please . . . do not look at me . . . but as we were both soaked to the skin, the Doctor insisted that while he undressed you, I should undress too. Our clothes are drying, and although they will look a mess, we will be able to put them on in the morning."

"You are quite certain you are not hurt?" the Duke asked.

He spoke automatically, thinking as he did so how beautiful she looked with her hair falling over her shoulders, and the cotton shirt she was wearing open almost to her waist.

As she was kneeling he could not see how long the shirt was, but he had the feeling that when she did rise he would see her legs.

Once again Anoushka read his thoughts.

"I have only just changed after the Doctor left," she said. "I tried to find a robe or something to make me more respectable. I have been wringing out my gown, for the moment it is nothing but a wet rag."

"I am not complaining," the Duke said with a smile. "But I gather your Doctor friend has not provided me with anything?"

"We were lucky he was there," Anoushka said. "I should never have been able to carry you from the water, and certainly not undress you."

She spoke without any shyness and there was only laughter in her voice as she added:

"My instructions are to keep the fire going all night and see that you rest. If you are hungry there is some food and of course tea. What Russian would be without his tea?"

"I should like some tea," the Duke said.

He realised that they were in a little wooden hut and he knew it was just the type of place in which a professional man would wish to spend his holidays, presuming he had no wife or children.

It consisted of one room with a large fireplace that burnt logs, and a **bed** which was little more than several mattresses which were pulled close to the fire.

It was quite a large bed, with room for two people, and the Duke thought that if the Doctor was unmarried he doubtless, like all Russians, often had a companion to share his bed.

There were two chairs and a deal-table against one wall, and a dresser hung with cooking-utensils as well as having shelves for plates and cups.

On one wall there was a gun, along with several fishing-rods and a telescope.

Everything was scrupulously clean and tidy.

Anoushka, who was watching the reaction in his eyes, gave a little laugh.

"It is not as grand as your house in the Champs Élysées or your Villa in Nice," she said, "but I do not think I have ever been so glad of a roof over our heads when the Doctor fished us out of the water."

"I am indeed grateful," the Duke said.

As he spoke, he thought that his luck had not betrayed him.

He had been in some very tight corners in his life and on two occasions he had nearly died, but always he had been saved in the nick of time. Always it appeared that Providence or Fate was on his side, or his proverbial good luck saw him through.

He could imagine what would have happened if their rescuer had not been there. Even if they had not drowned, they might have had to spend a night cold and wet, which might easily have resulted in their developing pneumonia.

"Thank God for my luck!" the Duke said to himself.

It was very nearly a prayer, because he was not thinking of himself but of Anoushka.

"I will make your tea," she said, "and now you will see for yourself that I have thin legs!"

The Duke laughed.

"It is something I have been looking forward to."

She got up without any self-consciousness and he saw that the shirt she was wearing, which obviously belonged to a tall man, reached below her knees.

She had it tied round her waist with what he thought was a man's tie, and with her hair hanging a long way down her back, and her very slim figure, the Duke thought she looked very beautiful, though not in the least like a Lady of Quality or even an alluring woman.

Instead she seemed like some sprite who might have come from the Russian woods or even from the sea.

Only as she busied herself with the samovar did he catch a glance of her large eyes, and once again he was aware that she was more like a goddess from mythology than anything else.

The bed was warm and comfortable, the top mattress and the pillows being filled with goose-feathers, and the Duke, realising that the bruise on his head was not now as painful as it had been, watched his wife brewing the tea.

He knew that it was something she must have done in the past, for the samovar presented no difficulties.

"Are you hungry?" she asked.

"Not at the moment," the Duke replied, "only thirsty, as I suspect you are."

"I am looking forward to drinking this tea."

"It is something you have not done since you were eight," he remarked.

She did not reply, but she flashed him a glance that was somehow mischievous, as if she deliberately wanted him to be curious.

Then she brought two cups from the dresser, filled them, and sat on the side of the bed.

"How long will our host be away?" the Duke asked.

"He said it was quite a long walk to the fishing-village," Anoushka replied, "and he will not attempt to return until tomorrow morning, when he will bring us some more food."

"That is very obliging of him," the Duke commented.

"He is such a kind man. He told me he comes from Odessa and has such a big practice that he finds it difficult to get away from his work."

"It was fortunate that you could converse with him."

Anoushka looked at the Duke sharply. Then she laughed.

"You heard me speaking Russian?"

"Yes."

"Were you surprised?"

"With a name like Anoushka, it is a language you should be able to speak."

"Yes . . . of course."

She turned away to look at the fire, and he did not press her. He was content just to lie there, feeling the warm tea seep down through him and watching the flames flicker on the silver of her hair and the contours of her face.

"I have seen you in many different guises," he said at length. "As a Novice, as a bride, as a Lady of Fashion in Paris, and now as a peasant in Russia."

"If I am poorly dressed, what about yourself, Your Grace?"

"What could I be but Adam in a Garden of Eden alone with Eve?" the Duke replied.

Anoushka's laughter rang out. Then she said:

"You always have an answer. You are so clever, which makes it fascinating to be with you, because I can never guess what you are going to say next."

"That is exactly what I find about you," the Duke said, "and, as you say, it is very fascinating."

As he spoke he gave a little yawn, knowing that while he wanted to talk to Anoushka, the tea and the warm fire made him feel very sleepy.

Anoushka took his empty cup from him.

"You must go to sleep," she said. "The Doctor said you must rest, and it is important that you do so."

"I am tired," the Duke admitted.

"Then sleep," Anoushka said.

She put down the cup, and as he shut his eyes he felt her fingers soothing his forehead, moving over it in a manner which seemed mesmeric.

As she did so, he thought it was the first time she had touched him, and while he tried to think how significant this was, and thrilled to her touch, the world seemed to slip away from him and he was conscious only of the softness of her fingers before he fell asleep . . .

*

The Duke awoke and was aware that everything was very silent.

He thought, although he was not sure, that before he went to sleep there had been a lighted candle on the table.

Now there was only the light of the fire. There was no fear that it might go out, for there were huge logs on it which had not yet even begun to burn through.

The Duke looked for Anoushka, but at first he could not see her. Then he realised that she was beside him in the bed, with her head on another pillow, and was sound asleep.

For the moment he was astonished. Then he realised that it was the obvious and sensible thing to do, and he was only surprised that she had accepted it as such.

There was nowhere else she could have slept, except on a hard upright wooden chair, and because the bed was large and he was on the side of it nearest to the fire, there was quite a gap between them.

The Duke turned over cautiously so that he could lie on his side and look at Anoushka.

She looked very young when she was asleep, her eye-lashes were dark against her cheeks, and her hair was tumbled over the pillow and over her shoulders.

She was still wearing the shirt which the Doctor had provided for her. Her arms were bare, and one of them with its long slim fingers lay outside the blankets.

The Duke looked at her for a long time, then because he could not help himself, because everything seemed far away in another world and of no consequence, he raised himself towards her.

Very gently, almost as if he were kissing a child, his lips touched Anoushka's.

CHAPTER SEVEN

HER LIPS were very soft, sweet, and innocent, and while the Duke meant to be very gentle he could not help increasing the pressure of his mouth until he felt Anoushka stir and she opened her eyes.

"I was . . . dreaming about . . . you," she murmured drowsily, and he knew she did not realise what was happening.

"I cannot help kissing you," he said, "because it is something I have wanted to do for a long time."

Then he was kissing her again, kissing her insistently, demandingly, and at the same time tenderly.

He realised that she was still half-asleep, but instinctively her body moved towards him, his arms went round her, and he was holding her close against him as he kept her mouth captive.

As he did so, he realised that never in his whole life had he felt such a strange, ecstatic joy in kissing a woman.

While physically he was aroused, he knew there was something spiritual in his love, which he had never known before.

He wanted Anoushka as a woman, but at the same time he felt a reverence for her. He wanted to protect her, fight for her, and prevent her from ever coming in contact with anything that was ugly or wicked, wrong or disturbing.

It was difficult to put his feelings into words, and yet he knew he held something in his arms so perfect, so unspoilt, that he would fight with every fibre of his being to prevent her from being changed or shocked by the world into which he had taken her.

Even as he kissed her he knew with some part of his mind that she had got into bed beside him quite naturally, since it was the only place to sleep.

It had never struck her because she had no idea what a man could feel for a woman, or indeed a woman for a man, that there was anything embarrassing in being next to him.

This was the real purity which he had sought—the purity not only of the body but of the mind.

Then as he raised his head to look down at her, he saw that Anoushka's eyes were wide open, and she said in a whisper:

"I . . . I did not . . . know that . . . being kissed was . . . like that."

"Like what?" the Duke asked, and his voice was deep and a little unsteady.

"Like the . . . feeling I have when I am . . . praying."

"I love you, Anoushka!" the Duke said. "I have tried to prevent myself from telling you so until you loved me, but now that you are beside me I cannot help kissing you."

There was a note of anxiety in his voice as he added:

"You told me you do not like being touched, but, my darling, you have made it impossible for me not to do so."

She smiled and he felt as if a ray of sunshine filled the small hut.

"I like your touching me," she said simply, "and I would like you to kiss me again."

The Duke's arms tightened. Then when his lips were very near to hers he said:

"Tell me, my precious, what you feel about me. I have been patiently waiting—and it has been more difficult than I can ever tell you—for you to love me as a man."

"I do not . . . know what people feel when they are in . . . love," Anoushka replied, "but every day being with you has been like being taken up to Heaven, and every night . . . although I did not tell you so . . . you were in my dreams."

"Why did you not tell me?" the Duke asked.

"Because I did not know you loved me, and I thought because you had been hurt and wounded by some woman it had made it difficult for you to love anybody again."

"I love you!" the Duke said. "I love you as I have never loved before, but I was stupid enough not to guess you were somewhere in the world if only I could find you."

"Do you really . . . mean I am . . . different?"

"Very, very different," the Duke said, "so different, my lovely one, that it is going to take me a lifetime to make you realise how happy we shall be and how different you are in every way from any other woman I have ever known."

He smiled as he added:

"Up until now I have been your teacher. Now I am ready to become your pupil, and you can teach me about the love you feel for me, which you say is part of Heaven."

He did not wait for her answer, but his lips came down on hers and he kissed her until he felt her body quiver against his and knew that the fire that burnt in him had ignited a little flame in her.

But while his heart was beating frantically and his whole body throbbed with desire, the Duke remembered his promise to his sister, and he knew that because he had given her his word he could not break it.

He raised his head and as he did so one of the logs fell lower in the fire.

The flames leapt higher and by the light of them he could see Anoushka's face very clearly.

He stared at her, and he saw in the expression in her eyes the look he had longed to see, and knew that at last, after a wait of what seemed to him a century of time, she was awakening to love.

He realised too that her lips were parted and her breath was coming fitfully through them, and her breasts were moving beneath the thin cotton shirt.

Very gently, so as not to frighten her, he drew it away from one shoulder, then he was kissing her neck, the white skin of her chest, and the softness of her breast.

He knew as he did so that she was experiencing sensations she had never known existed, and when he looked down at her again she said:

"Love is . . . very exciting . . . why did nobody . . . tell me it was . . . like this?"

"What do you feel?" the Duke asked.

"As if the stars are all glittering in my heart," she said, "and little waves are running through my body, which makes me feel restless and at the same time very . . . very excited."

"And what do you want when you are excited?" the Duke asked.

"I want you to kiss me, and I want to be very . . . very close to you . . . closer and closer so that . . . as the Bishop said when we were married . . . we are really . . . one person."

The Duke knew she did not really understand what she was asking, but was only expressing desire in the most beautiful words he had ever heard said, which made him feel that he too had the stars glittering in his heart.

"I love you! I worship you!" he said. "At the same time, my darling, I cannot make you mine until you ask me to do so."

Anoushka looked puzzled.

"What have I to ask you?"

"When I took you from the Convent," the Duke replied, "because my sister wanted us to find the love she had known before she took her vows, she made me promise that while I made you my wife in name, I would not make love to you completely for three months or until you asked me to do so."

"I do not understand," she answered. "Do you mean that I can be nearer to you . . . than I am now . . . and there is more to . . . making love than just kissing?"

"Much, much more," the Duke said in a deep voice.

"And I can . . . ask you to do . . . that?"

"If you want me to."

She gave a little laugh and he thought that only she could have laughed at this particular moment.

"Of course I want you to love me," she said. "Please . . . please . . . teach me about love . . . the love that will make me your real . . . wife, and we shall be really . . . one person."

There was a touch of passion in Anoushka's voice that had never been there before.

As the Duke kissed away the last words, he felt as if the stars fell from the sky to envelop them, and the love that they felt for each other carried them into a Garden of Eden where they were alone and there was nothing else in the whole Universe but themselves and their love.

*

The Duke woke and realised it was dawn.

The light was coming between the wooden shutters which covered the small windows of the hut.

The fire had burnt down to smouldering ashes, but it was warm and he knew now that the storm had passed and it would undoubtedly be a very hot day.

Then he was aware that Anoushka was cuddled up against him, her head on his shoulder, her hair falling over his arm.

He looked down at her and knew it was impossible for any man to be happier than he was.

Last night when he had made her his, he was aware that they had both touched the peaks of ecstasy, which, with all his experience, he had not known existed.

He had tried to be very gentle with her, but they had been transported out of themselves into a rapture in which there was neither time nor space and they were blinded by the wonder of it.

Only very much later, when he was able to think coherently, did the Duke ask:

"My precious, my darling, I have not hurt you?"

"I love . . . you," Anoushka said. "I love you . . . I love you . . . and I want to go on saying so over and over again because it is . . . so glorious and even to speak the words is like hearing music."

"That is what I thought too," the Duke said, "and, my precious, I am very grateful to be alive and even more grateful to be here alone with you."

He kissed her hair before he said:

"But I never imagined that I would make love to you for the first time in a wooden hut and with only blankets on the bed."

"Does it matter?" Anoushka asked. "To me it is the most glorious place in the world! Perhaps it is a little Planet all by itself, to which we have managed to—fly, and which therefore belongs only to us."

The Duke smiled.

He was thinking of how his sister had said that to step outside the Convent would be for Anoushka to find herself on another Planet.

"All I know is," he said aloud, "that because we are here I not prevent myself from telling you of my love, although it was something which was bound to happen sooner or later."

"I am glad it was sooner," Anoushka said, moving a little nearer to him, "otherwise there might have been more days and weeks when you did not kiss me, and I should never have known how wonderful your kisses could be."

"And when I made love to you?" the Duke asked.

"I have no way to explain that," she replied. "I only know that I became one with you and you were not a man but a god from

Olympus, or perhaps an Archangel. Now I really belong to you and nobody can . . . take me from . . . you?"

The last words were a question and the Duke's arms suddenly tightened round her as he said fiercely:

"I would kill anybody who tried to! You are mine, Anoushka! Mine, now and for eternity, and I will never lose you!"

"That is what I want you to . . . say."

She looked up at him, and while there was a smile on her lips, there was a touch of anxiety in her strange eyes as she said:

"You told me I should feel jealous of you . . . but I did not . . . understand . . . Now I do. If you loved . . . anybody else but me . . . I think I should want to die!"

"You need not be afraid of that," the Duke said. "I have never really loved anybody but you. Like you, I had no idea what real love was like, until last night. Now I know that in the past I was accepting second-best, my beautiful darling, and it is something I shall never do again."

Anoushka put her small hand on his chest.

"How can you be so wonderful?" she asked. "How can there be a man in the world like you, who loves me?"

"You have not met many men, my darling," the Duke said, "but even if you had, I should still want you to think I am unique."

"But you are," she said, "because I think when God made us He intended us for each other . . . or is that . . . presumptuous of me?"

"It is what you should think," the Duke said firmly, "and what I think too. We were made for each other, Anoushka, and I can only be very, very grateful that I have found you."

Anoushka gave a little cry.

"Supposing you had not come to the Convent? Supposing you had married somebody else?"

The Duke had a fleeting thought of Cleodel and realised that now she was no more than a ghost in his life and he could hardly remember what she looked like.

"We should have trusted Fate," he said, "knowing that there is a Power that shapes our lives."

He spoke sincerely and thought it was something he would never have said a little while ago.

He had thought himself so self-sufficient, so much the Captain of his own destiny.

Now he knew that the Power of which he had spoken had saved him from the destruction of a marriage which was based on deception and trickery, and had taken him, in his thirst for revenge, to the Convent where he had found Anoushka.

He turned round so that he could hold her closer to him.

"We are neither of us going to look back on the past," he said. "I have done many things, my darling, which I have no wish to discuss with you, and which I do not wish you to know about. All I want to think of is the future—our future together."

"That is what I want, too," Anoushka answered, "and I will try every second, every minute, and every hour of every day to make you happy."

She lifted her lips to his as she spoke and as the Duke kissed her he felt once again the fires of love burning within them, and at the same time they were sanctified by a belief in the power of God that had never been there before.

Anoushka was his, with her body, her heart, and her mind. He knew as he made love to her that their souls were, in a way he could not explain, part of the Divine which had brought them together.

*

The sun was shining brilliantly when the Duke finally opened the shutters and the door of the hut.

Wearing a shirt that belonged to the Doctor and a pair of trousers that were too long for him, he thought the world seemed to glow with a light that came both from himself and from Anoushka.

She was wearing the same shirt that she had worn during the night and her hair fell silkily over it.

As she set the plates and cups on the table and found the food which the Doctor had told her they could eat, she looked very alluring.

Their own clothes were nearly dry, but the Duke said they should lay them out in the sun before they put them on.

"When we have had breakfast," he said, "I am going to swim in the sea."

"You are quite certain the exercise will not make your head ache?" Anoushka enquired.

"I have forgotten about my head," the Duke said. "I think loving you, my darling, is more efficacious than any cure the Doctor could prescribe!"

Anoushka laughed before she said:

"You can always suggest he try it on his other patients!"

The Duke turned from the open door to walk towards Anoushka and take her in his arms.

"Every time I look at you," he said, "you are lovelier than you were a moment before. I think it would be a mistake to waste time and money going back to civilisation. Let us live here for the rest of our lives, and you can wear what you have on now, although actually I prefer you with nothing!"

She laughed up at him completely unselfconsciously.

"It might be rather cold in the winter," she said. "The Russian winters, even in Odessa, can be very, very cold."

The Duke looked at her.

"Now you are going to tell me your secret?" he asked.

"Not at this moment," she replied. "I think you had a reason for bringing me to Odessa, and that is where I will tell you what I have never told anyone else."

"You shall have it your way, my darling one," the Duke said, and kissed her, at first gently, then with a fierce, demanding passion which seemed part of the sun.

*

It was the following morning before the yacht steamed into Odessa Harbour.

The Doctor had kept his word and sent fishermen to tell the yacht where they were, and it had actually arrived in the little bay near the hut at four o'clock in the afternoon.

The Doctor himself had reached them about midday, and after they had thanked him he had gone fishing and once again they were alone in the hut.

"I am so happy . . . I do not want to be . . . rescued," Anoushka said.

"Nor do I," the Duke replied.

He shut the door and bolted it, then carried her back to bed, and it was several hours later when they looked out to sea and saw the yacht steaming down the coast towards them.

The Duke had never seen Odessa before, but it was just as he had expected it to be.

Beyond the harbour, which was beautiful, he could see a great number of turrets and towers of the buildings which he knew from his study of Russia had been built by Prince Voronzov when he had become Governor-General of New Russia and Bessarabia.

Under his guidance, the land round Odessa had flourished.

The Duke was interested in seeing what he had read about the city. At the same time, it was difficult to think of anything but Anoushka.

He knew by the way her eyes shone that she was excited, and yet when she slipped her hand into his he knew she was also apprehensive.

He had already found that she had endearing little gestures that he had never expected before, after growing used to her serenity and her innocently impersonal ways.

As his fingers closed tightly over hers he felt everything she did, and everything she said brought him a new happiness, and he had never known that he could feel so different or so complete as a man.

He knew that he still had a great deal to teach her about love and that she was like the bud of a flower, its petals just opening to the sunshine.

The fact that he was the sun to Anoushka made him feel proud and yet at the same time humble as he had never humbled himself in the past.

"I love you!" he said to her a hundred times.

Yet he knew that words were inadequate to express the breadth and depth of his love, which grew every minute that he was with her.

The gang-plank was let down and the Duke saw one of the stewards hurry onto the quay.

He had been told to procure for them a *troika* to carry them to where Anoushka wished to go, and a few minutes later they saw one coming towards the ship.

It was drawn by three horses and was painted and carved in a very attractive manner.

The coachman, with long hair and a moustache and beard, swept his strangely shaped cap from his head with a courteous gesture as Anoushka explained to him in Russian where they wished to go.

She did not tell the Duke where she was taking him, but as the horses started off at what seemed a tremendous pace, she put her arm into his and said:

"This is something I never dreamt would happen."

"That you would come back here?" he asked.

"That I should be able to do so without being afraid."

"Afraid?" he questioned.

"No-one can hurt me now that I am your wife, can they?"

"No-one!" the Duke said firmly.

He laid his hand on hers and said:

"I knew last night, when we loved each other, that I would protect and fight for you and not allow anything or anybody ever to frighten you."

"I knew you felt like that," she said simply, "and it makes me feel different from the way I have felt all these years."

The Duke did not ask for an explanation. They were now climbing away from the lower part of the town where the harbour was situated, to where high on the cliffs which rose sheer above the sea there were the beautiful buildings which had been erected by Prince Voronzov.

They passed the Palace, then came to another very fine building, and the expression on Anoushka's face told the Duke that it meant something personal to her.

The *troika* stopped and they both got out. He thought she would go to the front of the building, but instead she led the way to one side of it, and the Duke realised it was a Chapel.

It was very ornately built and, in Russian-fashion, was painted in brilliant colours with a gold dome shining brilliantly in the sun.

The Duke opened the door and there was the scent of incense, and he saw that while the Chapel was not very large it was very beautiful.

There were Ikons on the walls, silver lamps hanging from the ceiling, and there were flowers, candles, and an inescapable atmosphere of sanctity.

Anoushka walked up the aisle and as the Duke followed her he saw that kneeling ahead at the Sanctuary was a Priest.

He was obviously deep in prayer, and as Anoushka stood still as if waiting for him, the Duke also waited, watching her.

Then, as if Anoushka's presence communicated itself to the Priest, he rose to his feet and turned round.

For one moment Anoushka was still, then she ran forward to kneel in front of him.

The Priest spoke and the Duke fancied it was a question, as if he asked what she needed.

Then she looked up at him from her knees and said in Russian:

"You do not recognise me, *Mon Père,* which is not surprising."

The Priest looked around and the Duke saw that he was a very old man and his hair was white, and he thought perhaps he had difficulty in seeing clearly.

Then he exclaimed, also speaking first in Russian and then in French:

"It cannot be—but it is! Anoushka! *Ma petite!* You are really here?"

"I am really here, *Mon Père,* and I have brought my husband to meet you."

"Your husband!" the Priest exclaimed.

Anoushka rose, and as the Duke came forward she said:

"This is Father Alexis, who baptised me when I was born, instructed me in my faith, and taught me my lessons before I went to the Convent."

The Duke held out his hand and the Priest bowed over it.

"I am the Duke of Ravenstock, Father," he said, "and, as Anoushka has told you, we are married."

"I pray you will both be very happy," the Priest answered, "and you must tell me all about it, my children. Come with me."

He led the way out by another door and they found themselves in a cloister.

The Priest took them through a door which led into what the Duke was sure was his own private house.

It was small, austere, but at the same time beautiful, and he led them into a room where while the furniture was sparse the walls were decorated with very fine Ikons.

Anoushka gave a cry of delight.

"This is where I came for my lessons, and only when I reached the Convent did I realise how well you had taught me."

The Priest smiled.

"I am glad about that, but let me look at you, Anoushka. You were a pretty child, but you have grown into a very beautiful woman."

Anoushka did not reply. She merely looked at the Priest as if she wanted him to say more, and, as if he understood, he added:

"You are very like your mother."

"That is what I wanted you to say!" Anoushka exclaimed. "But I think I have also a resemblance to Papa."

"How, when you were loved so much, could you be anything but like them both?" the Priest asked. "But you must sit down."

With his hand he indicated two chairs near each other, and when they had seated themselves he said:

"I am not surprised that you have married. I always felt somehow that you would not take the veil, and if it was God's will He would provide you with a very different life from that of a Nun."

"God has been very, very kind to me," Anoushka said. "And now, please, as I have kept the secret of Papa and Mama all these years, will you tell my husband what happened, because, as you can imagine, he is very curious."

The Priest smiled.

"That is not surprising, and although you were very young, Anoushka, you were wise beyond your years, and I knew you would never betray your father or do anything which might constitute a danger to him."

"It was not difficult to keep it a secret until I was married," Anoushka said.

She gave the Duke an understanding little smile as she spoke, and he said:

"I am very anxious to hear what this momentous secret is."

"Let me start at the beginning," the Priest said. "Anoushka's mother was born in 1830 and she was a niece of Tsar Nicholas."

"His niece?" the Duke murmured, realising the importance of her position.

"Her Serene Highness Princess Natasha," the Priest went on, "was born into a position of luxury and importance that I am sure I need not describe to Your Grace."

The Duke inclined his head to show that he understood, and the Priest went on:

"As she grew up, Her Serene Highness was very different from the other pleasure-loving Royalty at the Court of St. Petersburg. When she was twenty it was decided that she should marry, and a husband was chosen for her without her being consulted, which I am sure Your Grace will understand is traditional."

"Of course," the Duke agreed.

"The Princess, however, was appalled by the suffering of the Serfs and the poorer citizens of St. Petersburg, and, disliking the man who had been chosen as her husband, she decided to withdraw from the world and enter a Convent."

The Duke was listening intently but he did not interrupt, and the Priest continued:

"Because she thought nobody would listen to her while she remained at Court, Her Serene Highness ran away before anybody could stop her and travelled to Odessa, where her father had a Palace he never used and which had over the years fallen into disrepair.

"When the Princess arrived, she was so beautiful, so young, and so full of life that I told her I thought it was a mistake for her to withdraw from the world and she should think over seriously what she was about to do, before she finally committed herself."

The Priest smiled at Anoushka before he said:

"As perhaps you will remember, my child, your mother was a very determined person, and she told me she had made up her mind. I think she was also afraid that if she did not do something quickly, the Tsar would have her brought back to St. Petersburg."

"It was the Tsar Nicholas at that time," the Duke interposed.

"It was indeed, Your Grace, a cruel, wicked tyrant whose crimes have left an indelible mark on the history of our country."

As the Priest spoke he crossed himself, then continued:

"The Tsar sent members of the Secret Police to Odessa, but by that time the Princess had taken her vows in the small community of working Nuns, and I was able to send them away, saying that Her Serene Highness now belonged to God, and even the Tsar had no jurisdiction over her."

The Priest paused before he said:

"This, God forgive me, was not quite true. When I had accepted Her Serene Highness into the Church, I had made her submission to her vows revocable so that if at any time she wished to do so she could return to the world."

"But the Tsar was not aware of it?"

"No one was aware except myself," the Priest answered, "and of course the Princess."

There was silence for a moment as he thought back into the past. Then he said:

"After a few years the small community of Nuns moved from the very inadequate and uncomfortable house which was their Convent into the Palace. This was after Her Serene Highness's father had died, and he had left her the Palace in his Will."

"So the Palace became a Convent," the Duke said.

"Exactly," the Priest agreed, "and it was more convenient for me and for them. We also had room for a Hospital, which we arranged in one wing of the Palace."

"They were Nursing Nuns?"

"All of them," the Priest said, "and they are the only Nurses to be found in the whole of Southern Russia. Our Doctors are very grateful to have them, I can assure you."

The Duke knew it was very rare for women to be Nurses either in peace or in war, and he knew, having served as a soldier, how inadequate the military Doctors and orderlies were and that the troops more often died from lack of attention than at the hands of their enemies.

"Everything was peaceful and uneventful," the Priest went on, "until 1865, when Sir Reginald Sheridan came to Odessa."

"Papa!" Anoushka exclaimed.

"Your father," the Priest agreed. "He had been a great traveller, having been round the world several times, but the strain of the journeys had proved too much for his health, and he bought a house on the outskirts of the city, intending to write a book on his journeys and also to spend the rest of his life in a climate that suited him."

"I seem to remember an author by that name," the Duke said.

"I have copies of the three books he wrote," the Priest replied, "and I will give them to Your Grace."

"Thank you."

"Sir Reginald was not only a very distinguished man but also an extremely interesting one, and we became, I am honoured to admit, friends," the Priest said. "Then the second winter he was here he became seriously ill."

The Duke felt he already knew the end of the story.

"He was so ill," the Priest continued, "that, thinking he was dying, Her Serene Highness had him moved into the Convent, or Palace, whichever you like to call it, where he had a quiet room overlooking the garden and the sea, where we expected him to breathe his last."

"But he lived!" Anoushka cried in a rapt voice.

"He lived entirely owing to your mother's ministrations," the Priest answered, "and while she nursed him they fell in love."

The old man spoke quite simply. Then he went on:

"They had found a happiness together that could only have come from God, and they asked me what they should do about it."

"And what did you reply?" the Duke enquired.

"I married them," the Priest said simply. "It had of course to be a very secret marriage, because if the Tsar had learnt what had happened—even though he was not now the cruel Nicholas but Tsar Alexander II—Her Serene Highness's alliance, even with someone so highly distinguished as Sir Reginald, would not have been permitted."

"I can understand that," the Duke said.

The Priest sighed.

"I do not think I have ever known two people so happy, and it was easy for them to keep their secret when everyone thought Sir Reginald was still too ill to go back to his own house, and your mother was now the Mother Superior. They could therefore be alone without anybody else being aware of it."

"I can understand now," Anoushka said in a very low voice, "as I have never been able to do before, why they were so happy."

She looked at the Duke as she spoke, and he knew she was thinking of the rapture and ecstasy they had found together in the little hut.

He smiled at her, then forced himself to listen again to the Priest.

"Your father and mother were rapturously happy," the old man

was saying, "until several years later when Her Serene Highness discovered she was with child."

"How old was she?" the Duke asked.

"She was within a month of her fortieth birthday, so it was something neither she nor Sir Reginald had any idea might happen."

"What did she do?"

"Because of the white robes Her Serene Highness wore, it was
quite easy to conceal her condition until it was nearing the time for
her baby to be born."

The Priest was silent for a moment, as if he was remembering the
long discussions there must have been between the three of them.

"What did you do?" the Duke asked, as if he could hardly bear
the suspense of not knowing.

"We announced that the Doctor who was attending Sir Reginald
wished him to go to Constantinople for a second medical opinion on
his condition. Of course, he was too ill to travel alone and was therefore accompanied by the Reverend Mother, and her maid, who was
an elderly woman utterly devoted to her and who she would have
trusted with her life."

"So Anoushka was born in Constantinople," the Duke said.

"I wish I could remember it," Anoushka said with a sigh.

"You were born," the Priest replied, "and three weeks later Sir
Reginald with Her Serene Highness returned with you to Odessa."

"How did you explain the new addition to the Convent?" the
Duke asked.

"I am afraid that to make the story of Anoushka's appearance
convincing, we had to tell a number of lies," the Priest answered, "for
which I did many long penances."

"What was your explanation?" the Duke enquired.

"Sir Reginald announced that when he was in Constantinople he
had found a distant relative who had just given birth to a child. She
had been recently widowed and she had not enough money to return
home before the baby was born. Unfortunately, while the baby survived, she died."

"Very ingenious."

"To make it sound more convincing," the Priest went on, "Sir
Reginald announced that he had adopted the child as his own, and,
when she could speak, Anoushka called him 'Papa'."

"I loved Papa," Anoushka said, "and although nobody told me he had died, I knew it before my husband informed me that he had left me all his money."

"How did you know?" the Duke asked.

"It is difficult to explain," Anoushka replied. "I felt a sudden sense of loss, and when I was praying in the Chapel I suddenly felt him near me, so near me that I knew that it was true and he was no longer in Odessa, but in another world from which he could reach me."

"You were blessed, my child, by his presence," the Priest said, "and I know that because his thoughts were always with you, if he was able to do so he would come to you and be as near as he was permitted to be."

"What I cannot understand," the Duke said, "is why Sir Reginald sent her away."

"I am just coming to that, Your Grace. Her Serene Highness died unexpectedly when Anoushka was only eight years old. I think perhaps because she was older than the average when Anoushka was born, and the Doctor who attended her in Constantinople was not very skilful, she often suffered pains which she would not admit. She grew very thin and found it difficult to eat."

"I did not know this!" Anoushka cried.

"Nor did your father," the Priest said. "She was so happy with you both that she would never have allowed there to be a cloud in your sky. But I had known for a long time that she was not as well as she should be. Nevertheless, when she died it was a great shock."

"I can remember it!" Anoushka said in a whisper.

Because she sounded so unhappy, the Duke took her hand in his, and as if the touch of him comforted her she moved her chair a little nearer to his and held on to him almost as if she felt he was a lifeline, and she would not let go.

"It was then that I realised the full impact of Her Serene Highness's death," the Priest said, "and I knew it would be dangerous for Anoushka to stay here."

"Dangerous?" the Duke asked.

"I had to inform the Tsar in St. Petersburg that a member of his family had died, and I knew that the moment the news reached him, not only Court Officials but the Secret Police would descend on us to make enquiries as to the cause of Her Serene Highness's death. We had thought that living here, at what seemed like the end of the world, we were safe from gossip and the tongues of those who are always ready to make trouble."

"What did you do?"

"The important thing of which both Sir Reginald and I were aware was that, whoever her father might be, Anoushka was in fact Royal, the grandchild of an Arch-Duke, a cousin of the reigning Tsar."

"You mean they might have taken her away?"

"Most certainly they would have done so," the Priest replied. "She would have been taken to St. Petersburg and brought up in the life from which her mother had fled."

"Now I understand," the Duke said.

"I thought you would," the Priest answered. "That was why, even though it was a great wrench, Sir Reginald, thinking only of Anoushka, took her to France."

"You knew about the Convent of the *Sacré-Coeur* where my sister is the Mother Superior?" the Duke asked.

"I had heard of it through a Catholic Priest with whom I had a lifelong correspondence, and Sir Reginald knew Your Grace's family and had met some members of it."

"But it was your idea that Anoushka should go to France?"

"It was my idea, and Sir Reginald agreed that it would be the best and safest place for her."

"It was very hard to say good-bye to Papa," Anoushka said.

"I can understand that," the Duke agreed, "but he was saving you from a very much worse life. I do not think you would have been happy in St. Petersburg."

"Mama always spoke of it with horror," Anoushka answered, "and I knew she was frightened of the Secret Police."

"There is no-one in Russia who is not frightened of them even now," the Priest said, "and although things are better, it would be a mistake, Your Grace, for anybody here to know of Anoushka's real identity."

"I agree with you," the Duke said, "and I promise you that as far as I am concerned nobody will ever be aware of Anoushka's Russian origins, although I imagine there would be no reason, now that her father is dead, for not saying she was his child."

"Not in England, at any rate," the Priest said, "but I would rather you did not speak of it in Odessa."

"I will not do so," the Duke promised. "And now that we have come here and you have told me what I wished to know, I shall take Anoushka away."

He paused before he said quietly:

"Before we leave, I would like to ask you, Father, if you will bless us, because although we were married in a Catholic Church, I think it would make my wife happy to have a special blessing from you in the Church where she really belongs."

"There is nothing which would make me happier, Your Grace," the Priest replied simply.

As the Duke rose to his feet, Anoushka laid her cheek for a moment against his shoulder and he heard her whisper so that only he could hear:

"You understand! Oh, my darling, wonderful, precious husband, you understand!"

*

After dinner that night, the Duke and Anoushka went out on deck to look at the lights of Odessa.

The yacht was no longer tied to the quay but was anchored at the entrance to the harbour, from where they had a panoramic view of the town, the tall cypress trees, and the undulating country beyond it.

It had been beautiful in the day-time, but now at night it had a mystic glory that was accentuated by the moonlight on the golden domes and the glittering lights in the houses which looked like stars that had fallen down.

The real stars filled the great arc of the Heavens above them, and the moon sent shafts of light glimmering over the waters of the sea, making a picture that the Duke thought he would never forget.

When he realised that Anoushka, standing by his side, was very silent, he turned to look at her, feeling that no beauty, however sensational, could hold him when she was there.

As if she had need of him, because the sight of where she had lived with her father and mother and what she had heard today made her emotional, she moved closer to him and he knew she wanted the comfort and strength of his arms, and he held her close.

"What are you thinking?" he asked in his deep voice.

"That no woman could have a more intriguing and exciting background, but, my darling, although this must be a secret between ourselves, we must never forget."

"I knew you would you feel like that," the Duke said.

"What is so wonderful is that as Papa and Mama loved each other so tremendously . . . I was born of love."

The Duke did not speak, but his lips were on her hair as she went on:

"That is what I want our children to be born of, a love as great as theirs and ours, so that they in their turn will be able to give love as I can give it to you."

"And I to you, my precious, adorable little wife."

The Duke looked at the sky for a moment. Then he said, and his voice was very moving:

"I asked for a woman pure and untouched, and that is what I found, but I was also given someone so perfect that I want to fall down on my knees in gratitude."

Anoushka looked up at him, her eyes no longer mysterious but deep and dark with another emotion.

"I am talking about you, my darling, and love," the Duke went on. "To me they are one and the same. I love you until there are no words to express the depth, the breadth, and the width of it, so I can only live my life trying to make you understand what you mean to me."

Anoushka gave a little cry of sheer happiness.

Then she lifted her arms to pull his head down to hers.

"I love you, I love you!" she said. "If you are blessed by God, so am I! No other man could understand as you do. No other man could be so wonderful."

Her lips found the Duke's and for a moment as he kissed her he was so moved by what she had said that their kiss was as spiritual and ethereal as the moonlight.

Then as he felt her body pressed against his, the fire that was never far from the surface rise within them both, and it was not the light of the moon which enveloped them, but the golden warmth of the sun.

The Duke kissed her until their hearts were beating frantically and the flames were leaping higher and higher within them and there was only one way they could express the glory and wonder of their love.

"I love . . . you . . ." Anoushka murmured against his lips. "Show me how to make you . . . love me."

"I think it is impossible to love you more than I do already," the Duke replied. "But the night will prove me wrong."

He took one last look at the moon, the stars, the lights of the city, and he felt as he drew Anoushka below that their beauty went with them.

It was all part, as they were, of the love of God, which is purity itself.

Love at the Helm

AUTHOR'S NOTE

The Earl Mountbatten of Burma helped me with the historical background of many of my novels, especially those which concerned the Navy. The proceeds of *The Dream and the Glory* for which he supplied the details of English and French ships at the time of the surrender of Malta, were given to the St. John Ambulance Brigade.

Lord Mountbatten wrote the preface and supplied some pieces of information for *Barbara Cartland's Book of Useless Information,* sold in aid of the United World Colleges.

Just before he went to Ireland for a holiday, where he was brutally assassinated, we had planned a novel with a Naval background which was to be sold for another of the many charities which were so dear to his heart.

After his death the Prince of Wales set up the Mountbatten Memorial Trust and the proceeds of this novel will be in support of this fund. I discussed the plot with Lord Mountbatten and he gave me information relating to the American Privateers, the sea battles, the duties and discipline at the time, on a British two-decker.

I am also extremely grateful to Mr. John Barratt, Comptroller and friend of Lord Mountbatten for many years, who was himself in the Royal Navy, for correcting the final proofs.

When I was in Antigua a few years ago, I visited Clarence House, the Admiral's House, and Nelson's Dockyard. They were fascinating, as was the beautiful island with its perfect climate, lovely beaches and waving palms.

When in 1814 the war between Britain and the United States came to an end, it had brought nothing but loss to both sides. British Naval supremacy had inflicted great damage in the States and also brought American overseas trade almost to a halt. On the other hand, American Privateers of which 515 had been commissioned, had played havoc with British ocean trade, capturing at least 1,345 craft of all kinds.

Privateering continued on a small scale until the war with France ended a year later, then ceased for over fifty years.

CHAPTER ONE

1815

THE POST-CHAISE set Captain Conrad Horn down in Whitehall outside the Admiralty.

As he walked through the arched entrance he looked up at the anchor on the pediment over the four Corinthian columns and thought as he had before, that it was appropriately impressive.

He gave his name to the servant inside the entrance and saw a glint of admiration in his eyes, which Conrad Horn had grown used to, since his ship had docked.

It seemed to him as if the cheers which had greeted him were still ringing in his ears.

"Tiger!" "Tiger Horn!" "Tiger!" they had yelled as they lined the quayside and manned the yards and there had been applause and congratulations all the way to London.

It still seemed incredible that he had survived what, as a professional sailor, he knew was a voyage in which the odds had been stacked heavily against him.

And yet he had succeeded beyond his wildest dreams and the wreckage of French ships that he had left behind him would, he knew, be yet another nail in Napoleon Bonaparte's coffin.

He saw the servant returning, but before he could reach him, a man in uniform came out of a door in the passage and gave a cry of recognition.

"Conrad! I was hoping to see you."

He limped towards him and held out his hand which Captain Horn clasped fervently.

"John! How are you? I have worried about you, but did not expect to find you here."

"I have been lucky in that they have found a shore job for me, for there is not much chance of my going to sea again."

"You will hate that," Conrad Horn said sympathetically. "At the same time, you are still in uniform."

"I was afraid that I should be rusticated for the rest of my life, but the Surgeons pulled me through—or rather it was my wife, who is a better doctor than any of them."

"That would not be difficult," Conrad Horn said, with a twist of his lips.

There was silence as both men were thinking of the inadequate Surgeons on the ships who, shockingly unskilled, were little better than butchers and often caused the death of more men than the enemy.

"We are talking about me when we should be talking about you," Commander Huskinson said. "You know that you have all my congratulations, Conrad. Your reports have been the most exciting adventure stories I have ever read."

"I wish you had been with me."

"I wish I had too," his friend admitted. "Only you could have inflicted the terror of those night-attacks along the coast, and only you could have evaded the enemy when you were out-numbered in quite such a clever way."

They both laughed, for it had been almost a boy's prank by which Captain Conrad Horn had evaded two large enemy frigates in the Bay of Biscay.

His own small frigate the *Tiger* had already created so much damage to Napoleon's Fleet which had been so seriously depleted at Trafalgar that the *Tiger* was a marked vessel hunted by every Frenchman and all the powers in Europe they had subjected.

The incident to which John Huskinson was referring had occurred at dusk.

Realising he was not only out-numbered but out-gunned, Conrad Horn had strained his sails all through the night in an attempt to avoid his pursuers.

However, they were there the next day to continue the chase and when day-light died again, were perilously near the *Tiger*.

When it was quite dark, as a last resort Conrad Horn had played one of his tricks on the enemy.

He had a tub put overboard containing a lantern leaving the frigates to pursue it all through the night while he abruptly altered course.

When dawn broke the next day the two French frigates surveyed an empty horizon.

"I wish I could have seen the 'Froggies' faces!" Commander Huskinson laughed now, and Conrad Horn laughed with him.

The *Tiger* had not had to run away another time and the ships they brought home as prizes, besides those which had been sunk, had made Conrad Horn the hero of a country heartily sick of war and wishing only to learn of victories.

The liveried servant was waiting by his side to catch his attention.

"His Lordship will see you now, Sir," he said respectfully.

John Huskinson put his hand on his friend's shoulder as he said:

"Go and receive your congratulations. You are His Lordship's blue-eyed boy at the moment and I will not spoil the surprise by telling you what sweets he has in store for you."

"I am glad to have seen you, John," Conrad Horn said. "Take care of yourself."

As he walked away he was thinking not of himself but of the difference he had seen in his friend.

The wounds which had been inflicted on John Huskinson in battle had left him pale, emaciated, and very unlike the tall, up-standing man he had been before the battle of Trafalgar.

Conrad Horn sighed.

It always hurt him to think of how many men were not only killed in the battles at sea but crippled and incapacitated for the rest of their lives.

The servant opened an impressive-looking door and announced:

"Captain Conrad Horn, M'Lord!"

Conrad Horn entered a large, comfortable office overlooking Horse Guards Parade and as he did so, the First Lord of the Admiralty, Viscount Melville, rose to greet him.

"Welcome home, Horn!" he said, "and my congratulations and those of everyone in the Admiralty on your brilliant exploits. We are very grateful to you."

"Thank you, My Lord."

Viscount Melville resumed his seat at his desk and indicated a chair in front of it.

"Sit down, Captain Horn!" he invited.

Conrad Horn did as he was told, then waited a little apprehensively for what the First Lord had to tell him.

He knew what he had achieved should result in his being appointed to a larger ship than the small frigate he was commanding at the moment. Besides, it would take at least two to three months to refit the *Tiger* and make her seaworthy after the last battle in which she had been engaged which had resulted in extensive damage to her bows.

Every ship's Captain dreamed of the sort of ship he would like to command, but very few realised their ambitions, and at this particular time of the struggle with France every possible ship that could put to sea was being utilised by the Royal Navy.

Viscount Melville's opening sentence told Conrad Horn what he already knew.

"There are at the moment, Captain Horn," he said, "over six hundred ships in commission manned by 130,127 men."

He paused as if to make his announcement more impressive, then went on:

"And until this war is finished, every one of those ships are of vital importance in one part of the world or another."

Again he paused, but seeing there was no reason to reply Conrad Horn merely remained silent.

"We therefore cannot afford to lose any ship from the smallest brig to the largest three-decker," the Viscount continued, "and naturally our most precious ships of all, are those which are new and therefore, most effective."

There was a hint of excitement in Conrad Horn's eyes as the First Lord continued:

"You will remember," he said, "that the *Caesar* was the first of the new English two-decker eighties to be launched in 1793. Another ship, built at the same time, on very much the same lines but with additional improvements which we had learned from the French, became Admiral Nelson's flagship after the Battle of the Nile."

"I remember that, My Lord."

"It was on this occasion," the Viscount continued somewhat pompously, "that the *Franklin,* a new French eighty was captured, with their Vice-Admiral, and turned out to be so notable a performer under sail, that it was decided to build eight ships to her lines."

Again he paused and with his eyes on Conrad Horn's face, said slowly and distinctly:

"One of these is ready to go to sea within the next two weeks."

"Do you mean, Sir. . ." Conrad Horn began only to be interrupted as the First Lord continued:

"I mean, Captain, that your magnificent performance entitles you to take command of this ship which has been named by His Majesty: the *Invincible!*"

Captain Horn stared at the First Lord.

A new ship—a two-decker with forty-two and twenty-four pounders was very much more than he had ever expected.

"How can I tell you how grateful I am, My Lord?" he asked and knew there was an irrepressible note of excitement in his voice.

"Perhaps you should ask me first what are your orders," the Viscount said with a faint smile.

"I suspect the Mediterranean, My Lord."

"Then you are mistaken," the Viscount replied. "You are to sail first, Captain Horn, to Antigua."

He saw the surprise in the younger man's face and said:

"We have two reasons for sending you there. The second, which I will explain first, is that you should put a stop to the damage that is still being done to our shipping by the American Privateers."

As Captain Horn had been away for three years this was news to him and as the First Lord realised it, he explained:

"I expect you heard that during our war with the United States of America, they suffered heavily as a result of the blockades imposed on both sides."

"I must admit, My Lord, I had not thought of that sort of penalty affecting America," Captain Horn replied.

"I believe the British blockade brought commercial ruin to many American merchants, and if we are honest, Captain, the Americans had grounds for complaint about the high-handed conduct of Royal Naval Captains encountering their vessels on the high seas!"

Conrad Horn frowned.

"In what way, My Lord?"

"The discipline and our conditions of service in the Royal Navy have, not unnaturally, kept our ships permanently short of seamen who have sought better conditions and safety from the Press Gangs on American mess-decks."

Conrad Horn pressed his lips together.

He had always loathed the cruelty inflicted by the Press Gangs in forcing men into service with the Navy, usually without even giving them time to say good-bye to their wives and families.

He was also aware that on many ships, although not on his own, the conditions were appalling and the punishments brutal.

"I think the ill feeling between our nation and that of the United States," the First Lord continued, "has steadily increased during the war with France, and because at first we thought derisively that America with a Fleet comprising only seven frigates and a dozen or so sloops would never resort to war, we ignored the danger of their doing so."

"I heard of course, My Lord, that President Madison had signed a declaration of war in 1812," Conrad Horn admitted, "but it was all over last year and I did not realise it would do us any permanent harm."

"What we did not expect," the First Lord went on, "was large numbers of fast privateers which sailed out of American ports to prey upon British merchant traffic to and from Canada and the West Indies."

His voice sharpened as he said:

"They have even sailed across the Atlantic, to operate off the English and Irish coasts and as far afield as the North Cape, to harass the traffic to Archangel."

"They must have had very good ships, My Lord."

"They did and still have!" the Viscount agreed. "Their super frigates, faster and better built than ours, are manned by more thoroughly trained crews."

"I had no idea of this, My Lord!" Conrad Horn exclaimed.

"The depredations of American Privateers off the coast of Scotland and Ireland, for the past three years," the Viscount said, "produced such apprehension at Lloyds that it is difficult to get insurance policies underwritten except at enormous rates of premium."

"I can hardly believe it!"

"You will soon find when you are in those waters," the Viscount said dryly, "that the American ship-builders and designers have produced ships with such fine sailing qualities that they can out-sail all the frigates and sloops of the Royal Navy, besides the fast West Indian mail packets."

He paused, then he said:

"Food is essential to this island and that is why the *Invincible,* Captain Horn, must protect our trading routes and rid ourselves of the menace of these independent Privateers who have paid no attention to the peace which now exists between us and the United States."

"I can only say, My Lord, that I will do my best," Captain Horn said quietly.

At the same time his heart was singing with joy at the thought of commanding a new ship, a two-decker!

He was wondering if this was the end of the interview when the First Lord said:

"I told you, Captain, there were two reasons for your voyage to Antigua. I have not yet told you the first."

"No, My Lord."

"You will sail straight to Antigua because you will be carrying on board the prospective wife of the Governor."

There was a startled silence. Then Conrad Horn said in a tone that was obviously incredulous:

"A woman? Are you telling me, My Lord, that I shall have as a passenger a woman?"

"She is, in fact, I think, Captain Horn, a relative of yours. Her name is Lady Delora Horn, and her marriage to Lord Grammell has been arranged by her brother, the Earl of Scawthorn, who is, at this moment, in Antigua."

If the First Lord had fired a broadside at Conrad Horn, he could not have been the more astonished.

First because he had a rooted objection, as had all good Captains in wartime, to allow a woman so much as to set foot on his ship; and secondly, because she bore the same name as himself, and was one of his relatives, for whom he had not only a contempt but what amounted almost to hatred.

Conrad Horn's grandfather had been the younger brother of the third Earl of Scawthorn.

The two brothers had fallen out and started a family vendetta which had divided the Horns into two factions.

The fourth Earl had carried on his father's battle with Conrad Horn's father, who had been his first cousin, and there had been no communication between their various families, while they were always acutely aware of what the other was doing.

Conrad himself had always been far too busy at sea, since he was a midshipman, to be concerned with family feuds or what he thought was unnecessary bickering between grown-up people who should know better.

But he had, in fact, once met the present and fifth Earl of Scawthorn when he was in London, and decided he was the type of young man he most disliked.

His cousin Denzil had managed at a very early age to become one of the riotous Bucks who were despised and decried by all respectable citizens.

Having inherited the title when he was only twenty-two and with it a very large fortune, he had neglected the huge family estate in Kent except when he wished to give wild parties there and spent his time drinking, gaming and whoring in London.

His name was a by-word for noise and unnecessary violence in the Clubs he frequented, and the Cartoonists had a field-day depicting the scandals he caused and the miseries he managed to inflict on almost every woman with whom he came in contact.

Because he was heartily ashamed of the family connection Conrad Horn was brave enough to say now:

"I suppose, My Lord, it is not possible for Lady Delora to travel to Antigua in another ship?"

"As I cannot spare another two-decker to make the voyage, and the only three-deckers we have at the moment are under sail in the Mediterranean, I cannot think of any other way in which she can be conveyed in safety to her destination."

The Viscount's voice was sarcastic.

"You said, My Lord, that she is to marry the Governor, Lord Grammell?"

"Yes, that is correct."

"It can hardly be the Lord Grammell I remember being on a Board of Enquiry at the beginning of this century?"

"Your memory is not at fault, Captain. Lord Grammell must be well over sixty!"

Conrad Horn was frowning.

If his cousin Denzil had a bad reputation, so had Lord Grammell, as he had heard from various sources, since the enquiry in 1801 when he had thought him one of the most unpleasant, aggressive and foul-mouthed men it had ever been his misfortune to meet.

It seemed incredible that he should be marrying again at his age and to somebody who must be very much younger than he was.

At the same time, he asked himself, what did it matter what happened to any of his Horn cousins?

If Lady Delora was anything like her brother, which she probably was, she and Grammell would make a good pair.

Aloud he said:

"I understand my orders, My Lord, and may I thank Your Lordship and the Board of the Admiralty most sincerely and from my heart for entrusting me with this special mission? I shall pray that I will not fail you."

"I am sure you will not do that, Captain Horn," the Viscount said, "and good luck!"

The two men shook hands and Conrad Horn left the room feeling as if he was walking on air.

*

Later that night, after he had received his orders and detailed instructions from various departments of the Admiralty and had made arrangements to leave London first thing the following morning for Portsmouth, Conrad Horn pulled Nadine Blake into his arms.

He knew as her red lips were lifted to his that this was what he had been wanting for a very long time.

"Oh, darling Conrad, I thought I would never see you again!" she murmured.

Only after he had kissed her until they were both dizzy with passion did she manage to gasp:

"I love you! There has never been anyone like you and I have

missed you dreadfully. I swear I have missed you every moment of
the time you have been away!"

Conrad Horn smiled a little mockingly.

At the same time he wasted no words but lifting her in his arms
carried her from her Boudoir into the large luxurious bedroom that
opened out of it.

*

It was nearly two hours later before they were able to talk, and
lying back against the softness of Nadine's lace-trimmed pillows with
her dark hair against his shoulder Conrad asked:

"I suppose you have been misbehaving yourself as usual?"

"If I have it was your fault for leaving me for so long," she
replied, "and, darling, wonderful Conrad, there has never been a
lover as good as you. If you had stayed with me I would never have
looked at another man."

"That is one of your illusions which at the moment we both want
to believe," Conrad said, "and it is therefore perhaps a good thing
that I am leaving tomorrow morning."

Nadine started and exclaimed:

"Tomorrow! But it cannot be true! After two years the Admiralty
must give you some proper leave."

"Instead they have given me a new ship—a two-decker—the *Invincible!*"

Nadine gave a little cry.

"Oh, Conrad, I am glad! I know there is nothing that would please
you more. But what about me?"

"What about you?" Conrad enquired. "I am told that you have an
army of admirers."

"Who told you that?" Nadine asked defensively.

Conrad Horn laughed.

"My dear, you are far too beautiful and too notable not to be
talked about."

"Are you jealous?"

"Would it matter if I were?"

"I want you! I want you more than I have ever wanted any other
man! Does that mean nothing to you?"

"It means everything you want it to mean," Conrad answered,

"and if I were here I concede that I might be aggressive to anyone else on whom you bestowed your favours. So I must commend the Admiralty on their wisdom in sending me away so quickly."

"When do you sail?"

"In fourteen days."

"Very well," Nadine said, "in that case I am coming with you for at least half of that time. After that you will be too busy to think of anything except your ship."

"I think it would be a mistake. . ." Conrad began.

But Nadine's arms were round his neck, pulling his head down to hers, and what he had been about to say was silenced by her lips.

He knew she was right and that after two years at sea he deserved a holiday and the sort of holiday which only Nadine could give him.

He remembered how, when her husband had been killed in action, on the orders of the Captain of the ship in which he was serving, he had been sent to console several of the women widowed in the battle, by telling them of the bravery with which their husbands had died.

As soon as he saw Nadine Blake, Conrad Horn had thought her the most attractive woman he had ever seen in his life.

Her hair was dark and her eyes were green with gold lights in them and they slanted upwards in a manner that was both exotic and alluring.

She had a white skin, a perfect figure, and the sort of seductive manner of speaking which he found fascinating.

He was well aware before he called on her, that the marriage from her husband's point of view, had not been a perfect one.

George Blake had been one of the officers who was always over-eager to go ashore in search of feminine companionship in every port at which they called.

He would come back to the ship elated by some new conquest, wanting to talk of his amatory successes, and it was in fact, a long time before Conrad Horn was even aware that he was married.

He had known by the manner in which Nadine spoke of her husband's death that she was not in the least brokenhearted or even upset.

He gathered that unlike most officers' wives she was not in need of money, and he also learned during that first short visit that her family were of some social importance, and there was a comfortable house in the country waiting for her should she wish to leave London.

That she did not do so, he learnt a year later when Nadine was talked about as being the most attractive woman in a city filled with them.

At first he had not understood the knowing glances, the secretive smiles, the nods and winks that accompanied any conversation about her.

When the truth dawned on him he had made it his business to see her during his next leave.

He had been promoted to serve on a larger frigate and was accorded three weeks leave before he was required to report for duty.

On an impulse, thinking perhaps he might be snubbed for doing so, Conrad Horn had called on Nadine.

She had greeted him literally with open arms and for three weeks she was not at home to her other admirers, nor did Conrad have time to see any of his friends.

Their desire for each other was fiery, demanding and irresistible and it was only when he was forced to join his ship that Conrad realised wisely that fire could not burn so fiercely for long.

"Why must you leave me? Why must you go when we are so happy together?" Nadine had wailed.

He knew even as she protested when he had left her, that she would return immediately to being the social success she had been before his arrival.

There were a dozen men waiting to walk in through the door as soon as he had walked out of it.

Nevertheless it had been a comfort in the long, gruelling and at times, desperately trying years that lay ahead to know that when he returned, if he was fortunate enough to do so, Nadine would be there.

There was something between them, he felt, that was not love but a magnetism which drew them towards each other and ignited a blaze that it was impossible to resist, and equally impossible to quench.

He had seen her once again for a brief three days before he had taken over the command of the *Tiger* and now when he came to her tonight he had known that the attraction they had for each other was still as violent as it had been five years ago.

"I think you are even more beautiful than you were when I first saw you," he said now reflectively.

"Do you really think so?" Nadine asked. "Sometimes I feel I am getting old."

"At twenty-five?"

"Perhaps I have a few more years," she conceded.

"You could stop burning the candles at both ends and last very much longer."

"How could either of us ever be cautious, calculating?" she enquired. "We are both adventurous, impulsive, expensive, and I will never regret it."

What she had said was true, Conrad thought, and he enjoyed feeling that life was a wild adventure and that if he was killed tomorrow no-one could say that he had missed any of the opportunities that had been open to him.

"Perhaps you would be wise," he said quietly, "to marry while there are plenty of men to place their hearts and their coronets at your feet."

Nadine gave a little laugh.

"They may place their hearts there," she said, "but a great number are very stingy when it comes to offering me their names, and I have long ago decided that marriage is not for me."

"It should be," Conrad insisted. "A woman needs a husband to look after her."

"And a man a wife?"

She felt the shudder Conrad gave against her bare body and laughed.

"I know you would hate quiet domesticity," she said, "and being tied to one woman."

"As it happens, I have been tied to you for the last five years."

"Is that really true?"

"It is true, although I know I can hardly take much credit for such constancy since the opportunity of meeting women who attract me have been few and far between."

Nadine knew this was what she expected.

Conrad was too fastidious to entertain for one moment having anything to do with the type of woman whose favours could be bought in any foreign port.

"You are so attractive, my dearest, most adorable lover," she said.
"But one day you will want a son—What man does not?—to carry on
your name. Then you will marry some nice, smug, respectable young
woman, while I. . ."

She made a little gesture with her hands.

". . . will burn out both ends of my little candle and when they
meet that will be the end."

"Not until I come back from the West Indies," Conrad said.

"I might wait as long as that," Nadine answered.

Then as she laughed up at him he was kissing her again.

Kissing her violently, demandingly, passionately, as if he must
make up for what he knew would be long restless nights at sea when
the moon and the stars overhead would make him long for the
softness of a woman and the fire that Nadine could ignite so easily.

*

During the long journey to Portsmouth the following morning in a
post-chaise which despite good horses, was badly sprung, Conrad
Horn was half-asleep.

But while he was physically exhausted, his brain was active and
not in the least fatigued.

In fact, stimulated by what lay ahead he was thinking excitedly of
the *Invincible* and what he must do on arrival.

What annoyed Conrad was the knowledge that he must give up his
accommodation on the quarter-deck to his passenger.

It was infuriating that some unpleasant hard-faced relative, to
whom he would not give elbow-room if he had his way, would be occupying the extremely comfortable, if not luxurious, quarters in the
stern that were the Captain's prerogative.

On the quarter-deck of the two-deckers Conrad knew there was
the Captain's quarters which would obviously have to be allotted to
Lady Delora, and two small cabins, one of which was the Clerk's
office, the other belonging to the Captain's steward.

He supposed, as Lady Delora would undoubtedly bring some kind
of chaperon with her and a lady's-maid, these two cabins would be
given over to her attendants.

This meant that he must move down to the upper deck to take
over the cabin belonging to the First Lieutenant.

He, in his turn, would move out and displace the second Lieutenant, and so on.

There were only six cabins on the upper deck which meant that the most junior officer would have to move to the orlop-deck, again displacing some wretched minor officer, who would have to double up with somebody else, rather than move into the already over-crowded gun-room or sleep on the gun-deck with the men who slung their hammocks between their guns.

No-one knew better than Conrad Horn the strict etiquette that was observed among the men to whom the ship became their home, school-room, work-room and perhaps prison for sometimes years on end.

And because a ship to be a happy ship, must be worked not only with discipline but with justice, Conrad Horn cursed the woman who was disrupting by her mere appearance, the whole pattern of the ship's organisation.

But it was hard to feel like cursing any of them, even the sister of his cousin Denzil, when he saw the *Invincible* lying in the harbour and thought her the most beautiful sight he had ever seen in his whole life.

She was decorated simply because there had been a tremendous scandal some years ago when the decorations of a Royal Sovereign had cost such an astronomical amount of money that the Admiralty had sworn never to allow such extravagance again.

With the adoption of sash-windows the ship's stern had become designed to let in so much light and air that it was jokingly said it resembled a conservatory.

In fact, as Conrad knew, since Trafalgar Admiral Collingwood was an enthusiastic cultivator of pot-plants in his cabin.

Conrad had no intention of having any decorations that distracted either his or the seamen's attention from war, but he would not have been human if he had not realised that his ship, new from bow to stern, was not only seaworthy, but beautiful as only a sea-going man understands the full meaning of the term.

His officers had not yet come aboard with the exception of a few who were busy taking on crew that had already volunteered to sail in the new ship, or had been sent from ships which were being repaired in other dock-yards.

It was only after he had inspected the *Invincible* in every particular and found everything about her to his liking, that Conrad remembered that Nadine would be arriving at the best hotel in Portsmouth as she had promised to do.

Because he was so obsessed with his ship, he almost regretted that he had allowed her to persuade him to let her join him for at least a week.

However, if he was honest he knew there was very little for him to do except fuss over the few last details to be completed before they sailed, which were actually not his job but that of the officers serving under him.

Accordingly he went to the hotel and found as he had expected, that Nadine had already made herself very much at home.

She had not been a sailor's wife without realising that small extra comforts and luxuries could make a home out of the most unlikely rooms and in the most unexpected places.

As Conrad entered the Sitting-Room which she had forced the Proprietor of the Inn to arrange leading out of her bedroom, he was conscious of the exotic fragrance which hung on the air and which came from the perfume she used, and also from the flowers that seemed to decorate every dark corner.

Before he had time to look around, before he could even realise Nadine's background, she was in his arms.

Because he could not help himself, he was kissing her like a thirsty man who suddenly finds water in the middle of a desert.

CHAPTER TWO

CONRAD HORN began to dress himself with what was undoubtedly a thrill of excitement.

He eyed himself in the mirror and knew that his new clothes for his new command were worthy of the occasion.

His coat was of the finest blue broad-cloth, the heavy epaullettes which hung on the shoulders were of real bullion and so was the broad gold lace round the edges and the buttonholes.

His eyes lingered on the heavy gold stripes on his cuffs that marked him as a Captain with more than three years seniority.

He had tied his cravat of thick China silk with a precision which was typical and now he approved the cut of his white kerseymere breeches and his thick white silk stockings, which were the best he could buy.

Then he picked up his cocked hat, the button and lace of which were real gold, and his gloves which gleamed white against the sunburnt skin of his hands.

He looked around the bedroom to see he had forgotten nothing, then for the first time he thought of Nadine.

It seemed to him that she had left him a long time ago, but he had kept the rooms they had occupied at the hotel because he had not been expected to sleep on board until he took over officially, and it was therefore convenient not to move.

He did not realise until last night when he had told the Proprietor that he was leaving the following day, that Nadine had paid the bill up to the end of his stay.

For one moment he had felt angry, really considering it an insult, then he knew she had been thinking of him as she had done when she had left sooner than he had expected.

He had been awake very early one morning because inevitably he woke at dawn. He felt happy and relaxed after a night of love-making, and it was pleasant to feel the softness and fragrance of Nadine still close against him.

Then as his mind slipped away to his ship, the voyage that lay ahead of him and the Privateers whom he intended to capture, he realised that she too was awake and automatically his arm went round her.

"I did not want to wake you," he said, wondering how he had managed to do so.

"I want to be awake," she replied, "because I cannot bear to miss even a moment of you and I am leaving today."

"Leaving?" he exclaimed in surprise. "Why? You have only been with me for four days."

"Four very wonderful days and nights," Nadine said softly, "but, darling Conrad, I am growing jealous and that is something I never allow myself to be."

"Jealous?" he questioned in surprise.

Nadine gave a little laugh.

"I can stand up to any woman and defeat her, but you are obsessed by someone so adorable, so captivating that I have no chance."

There was no need to explain what she meant, but when Conrad would have protested she put her fingers against his lips to silence him.

"Do not trouble to lie, my wonderful man," she said. "Invincible by name, Invincible by nature, she already possesses you!"

Feeling for the moment embarrassed Conrad merely kissed the softness of Nadine's forehead, but she went on ruminatingly:

"When we are in London I possessed three-quarters of your mind and the whole of your body. Now I still possess your body, but although I find it irresistible, it is not enough."

"So you are determined to leave me?" Conrad said and tried as he spoke not to feel it was almost a relief.

"Prince Ivan has sent his carriage for me drawn by four superb horses. You really must see them!" Nadine replied. "I am also to have four out-riders, and so that I shall not be cold, he has included a cape of the finest sables I have ever seen!"

"So I should be jealous."

Conrad put his fingers under her chin and turned her face up to his.

She was very alluring, even in the pale light of the dawn, and when he looked at her slanting eyes, her provocative lips and the heavy

waves of her dark hair, he could understand why there would always
be men and more men ready to give her anything she desired.

The look in her eyes was very soft as she said:

"You know there is no need for jealousy, and when you come
back with more triumphs, more glory than you have already, I shall
always be there."

"You spoil me," Conrad said, "and you know how much you
mean to me."

He spoke ardently but Nadine laughed.

"Not as much as another much larger woman whose name I am
always expecting to hear on your lips even when you are making love
to me."

"If I called you by any other name than your own," Conrad said,
"it would not be *Invincible* but 'Incomparable'! There is no-one like
you, Nadine, and no-one who has ever given me so much happiness
as I have had these past four days."

"Thank you," Nadine said simply, "and there is always the future
of which I shall be thinking as the Prince's horses carry me back to
London."

She gave a little sigh, then in a different voice she murmured:

"But why should we waste the present?"

As she spoke she lifted her lips and as Conrad took possession of
her he knew that for the next few moments at any rate he would not
be thinking of the *Invincible*.

But when Nadine had gone it had been impossible to think of anything else.

There were still many things to do and every day he found more
important details that had to be seen to until sometimes he was
afraid they would not be ready to leave on the day appointed.

But yesterday everything seemed to swing into place at the last
moment.

The food and water came aboard, the last hammock was slung on
the gun-deck, and with a feeling of deep satisfaction Conrad Horn
realised that he had his full complement of seamen without one of
them being forced to serve by a Press Gang.

Almost the entire crew of the *Tiger* had signed on, and there were
men who had served with him on other ships and others who were
determined, because of his reputation, to be under his command.

There were also a few, mostly more experienced, who thought that the war would not last much longer and when inevitably the majority of ships would be laid-up, the newest built would be kept in commission.

Whatever the reasons, the ship's complement was formed and waiting for their Captain to take them to sea.

The only thing that spoilt the prospect, in fact the only "fly in the ointment," was the idea of starting his ship's maiden voyage with a woman aboard and a woman he already loathed because she was one of his relatives.

He wondered when he had the time to think about it, how old she was likely to be, and decided that as his cousin Denzil was two years younger than himself, that would make him thirty-one, his sister was therefore likely to be in her late twenties.

It seemed strange that she had not married, except that if she was as unprepossessing and unpleasant as her brother, it was obvious that no man had been fool enough to take her on.

Conrad had inspected his own quarters and decided that they were too good for any woman, and especially Lady Delora.

They were sparsely furnished, as any luxurious items were expected to be provided by the Captain himself, but the table that occupied a large amount of room in one cabin could easily seat twelve.

It made Conrad almost grind his teeth to think that he would not be able to entertain more than six officers in the First Lieutenant's Cabin which he had had to commandeer for his own use.

Then he told himself that the restrictions imposed upon him by his female guest could not last for more than twenty-five to thirty days.

Once he had set her down in Antigua to marry the Governor, he would be able to arrange the cabin to his liking.

In fact, while he complained, the Commander's Cabin was bigger and far more comfortable than any cabin he had occupied in the past.

A frigate was always unpleasantly cramped for anyone as large as he was and it was a delight in itself to be able to walk about the *Invincible* without having to bow his head or, if he was not cautious, to bash his brains on an oak beam.

Conrad, with a last look round the room, proceeded downstairs to where rather touchingly he found almost the whole staff of the hotel waiting to say good-bye and to wish him luck.

"It's been a great privilege to have you stay with us, Captain," the Proprietor said so sincerely that it was impossible to doubt that he spoke the truth.

The maids in their mob-caps curtsied and the waiters and pot-boys shook his hand.

There was a hired carriage waiting for him outside and instinctively he felt as if he was leaving his old life behind and starting a new one.

It was a cold day with a blustery wind coming from the sea.

As it had rained all night and the streets were thick with mud, the horses were forced to proceed slowly towards the harbour.

Conrad was thinking that in a few seconds he would have his first glimpse of the masts of the *Invincible* and hoping that "this damned woman," as he called her in his mind, would not be late in arriving because he wanted to leave on the dawn tide.

That meant it would be best to be anchored further out in the harbour.

He was surprised to see, despite the fact that it was still early in the morning and very cold, there was quite a crowd waiting to see him embark.

He found it difficult to remember his new fame after being for so many years, an ordinary Naval Officer whose comings and goings were of little interest to anybody outside the Service.

As his carriage drew up at the quay a cheer went up from the men and women waiting, many of the latter having husbands or sweethearts among the crew of the *Invincible*.

Despite the fact that the ship was as conveniently near to the quay as possible, there was nevertheless a stretch of water to be covered and a boat painted blue was waiting to convey Conrad to his ship.

When he came aboard they piped the side for him as Admiralty regulations laid down.

There was the Marine Guard at the present, the side-boys in white gloves to hand him up, the pipes of the boatswains mates all a-twittering, the Ships' officers waiting on the quarter-deck to shake hands with him in spite of the fact that they had seen him only the day before.

This was a formal occasion and the correct procedure was something the Navy laid down.

It was expected the Captain formally and with due ceremony, should take possession of the *Invincible* by making a tour of inspection just as if he was seeing it for the first time.

Conrad had already learnt the names of a number of the men under his command and was determined before they reached the end of the Channel, to know the names of the rest.

He had a retentive memory and he knew that by the time they were in the Atlantic he would know how many children each of his seamen had, who was expecting another addition to the family, and which man had already proved himself proficient as a yardsman.

When his tour of inspection was over, he invited his First Lieutenant Deakin who had been with him on the *Tiger* to come to his cabin.

There his private steward, Barnet, had a flat bottomed ship's decanter ready to serve them with a glass of madeira, and Conrad taking off his cocked gold-lace hat, sat down in one of the comfortable leather arm-chairs while Deakin took another.

"I can hardly believe it, Sir," Deakin said, as he had said a hundred times before in the last two weeks.

He paused and as Conrad did not speak, he went on:

"I expected you would get a decent ship but I never imagined you would pull out the biggest plum in the whole pudding with a new two-decker!"

"We have been very fortunate," Conrad agreed. "But we still have to prove ourselves, although that unfortunately will have to wait until we have deposited our guest at Antigua."

He thought that Deakin looked surprised and explained:

"We can hardly go charging about looking for a battle with a woman aboard!"

"No, of course not, Sir," Deakin replied. "But I understand there are still some French ships left in that part of the world and if we came upon one unexpectedly like, we could hardly run away."

There was a glint of amusement and also of anticipation in Conrad's eyes as he replied:

"That would be unthinkable! Let us hope that Her Ladyship is not too squeamish when it comes to the noise of gunfire!"

Deakin laughed, and knowing that he and his Captain were both hoping the same thing, raised his glass.

"To 'Tiger Horn'!" he said, "and may you, Sir, and this ship prove themselves to be invincible!"

*

It was dark and the lights of the *Invincible* were reflected in an uneasy sea splashing against her sides when the look-out of the quarter-deck announced:

"Here they come, Sir!"

Conrad, who had been pacing up and down like a caged lion for the last hour, looked towards the end of the quay.

He was just able to discern the carriage-lamps of a large and luxurious travelling chariot drawn by four horses proceeding cautiously to where a boat, manned by six shivering seamen from the *Invincible* had been waiting hour after hour.

"Damn the woman! It is about time!" Conrad Horn said under his breath.

While he was relieved that his guest had arrived, he could not prevent a surge of indignation sweeping over him because she was so late.

He had to force himself not to show his annoyance when Lady Delora was preceded on board by an official of the Foreign Office who, as Conrad had expected, had escorted her from London.

He was a middle-aged man and as he held out his hand he said:

"I can only express my regrets, Captain Horn, that we are tardy in reaching you. We had a series of mishaps on the journey, but I hope we have not delayed you over long."

"I am only relieved that you have arrived safely, Sir," Conrad managed to reply, hoping his voice did not sound too cold or even sarcastic.

He suspected that the delay was due to the woman who was just coming aboard, and he expected that she had either been late in starting, which would have been typical of her sex, or else had indulged in some temperamental scene which had wasted the time they should have been on the road.

"My name is Julius Frobisher," the gentleman from the Foreign Office was saying, "and the Viscount Castlereagh asked me to convey his congratulations on your promotion, Captain Horn, and also to thank you most sincerely for transporting Lady Delora to Antigua in a manner which he is certain will not only be safe, but comfortable."

"Thank you, Sir," Conrad replied. "I am deeply appreciative of the Foreign Secretary's kind words."

A figure wrapped in a heavy cloak now appeared beside Mr. Julius Frobisher.

"May I, Your Ladyship, present Captain Conrad Horn?" Mr. Frobisher asked.

The wind seemed to whip away the words from his lips and as he spoke, Mr. Frobisher had to hold tightly onto his high top-hat.

It was obvious that the woman beside him was having to clutch her travelling-cloak around her.

"I think, Sir, it would be best if we repaired immediately to Her Ladyship's quarters," Conrad said.

"But of course! That is most sensible!" Mr. Frobisher agreed.

Conrad Horn walked ahead to lead the way and the small procession followed him, first Lady Delora and Mr. Frobisher, then another woman to whom he had not been presented, but whom he suspected to be her chaperon, and lastly a lady's-maid, an elderly woman who moved slowly clutching a leather case which was obviously of some value.

Conrad led the way across the quarter-deck to the shelter of what should have been his cabin.

He had only just reached it and stood aside for Lady Delora to precede him into it, when he found beside him a young midshipman.

"Excuse me, Sir," the midshipman said in a low voice, "but the Captain of the Marines desires to speak with you, Sir. It's urgent!"

Conrad knew that the message would not have come at this particular moment had it not been important.

He turned to Deakin who was at his side.

"Take over, First Lieutenant."

"Aye, aye, Sir!"

Deakin, who was never at a loss, followed the ladies into the cabin and Conrad hurried to the lower deck to find out what was amiss.

It was, in fact, only a careless misplacing of the bullets for the marines' muskets which had been taken below but not deposited, as had been expected, in the magazine.

The Captain of the Marines had been afraid that they might sail without them, and it was over an hour before his anxiety was allayed and the missing ammunition had been found.

By that time, Conrad decided it was too late for him to pay his respects to Lady Delora and Deakin told him that everything was in order.

Her Ladyship, he said, had, in fact, been so tired after the journey that she had retired to bed immediately, not even wishing to partake of the meal which had been waiting for her.

Conrad also learnt that Mr. Frobisher had gone ashore.

"To tell you the truth, Sir," Deakin said with a smile, "I think he had no stomach for the sea and wanted only to get back to the hotel where he has booked a room for the night."

"I will have to apologise for my absence," Conrad said.

The First Lieutenant's eyes twinkled.

"I think, Sir, he was so glad to be rid of his charges and for his journey to be at an end, that he had no wish to prolong his farewells."

"Well, that, at least, clears the decks," Conrad remarked.

He had already given instructions to raise the anchor and move nearer the mouth of the harbour.

He thought as he did so, that if the wind held and they moved out on the early tide they would be well on their way towards the Atlantic before another night had passed.

He had a few hours sleep, but he was up again before dawn and as the wind brought them comfortably out of harbour into the open sea, he thought he had never been so happy in his whole life.

He knew that the first days at sea were going to be very busy ones.

There was the crew to be co-ordinated and made to feel they were part of a team, there was the gun-practice which was always of tremendous importance to men who had never worked together before.

And most of all, there was the handling of the sails and making the crew aloft realise that the ship's life and their own, depended on the speed with which they set them.

This was when he thanked God that Deakin was with him. Deakin had a passion for that kind of seamanship.

He had inspired the crew of the *Tiger* to achieve a record of eleven minutes and fifty-one seconds for sending up the topmasts and they managed to set all sail starting with the topmasts housed in twenty-four minutes seven seconds.

This was the kind of ambition that had to be instilled into a new crew, with far bigger and more complicated sails and with rigging that was likely to be sticky until it had been in use a number of times.

There were so many things to do that the morning seemed to pass like a flash, and it was only when he heard the ship's bell ringing that he realised it was noon and he had not even enquired after his passenger.

He excused himself on the grounds that a Lady of Quality was not likely to rise early, but because his conscience pricked him, he sent his personal steward, Barnet, who had been with him for years, to ask Lady Delora if she would receive him.

The answer came back that she would be delighted to do so, and feeling an uncomfortable moment was ahead of him, Conrad left the fo'c'sle and moved towards the stern.

The elderly maid he had noticed when she came aboard last night was waiting outside the cabin door to usher him in.

Conrad thought with a slight smile that she looked exactly as a lady's-maid should, having a gaunt, slightly grim face, greying hair under a neat cap, and wearing a small, white, starched apron over her black dress.

As a concession to the fact that it was extremely cold, her shoulders were covered in a black wool shawl.

She dropped him a perfunctory curtsy which told him she was not particularly impressed by ships' Captains, but she did not speak and merely opened the door to announce:

"Captain Conrad Horn, M'Lady!"

Removing his hat Conrad walked into the cabin, and looking across to where its occupant was standing by one of the port-holes, thought he must have made a mistake.

There was just a faint glimmer of sunlight coming through the dark clouds which illuminated the fair hair of a woman who turned at his entrance and he saw to his astonishment, that she was not the spinster he had been expecting, nor did she bear any resemblance to her brother.

Denzil Horn had a long nose, eyes that were too close together, and a face, young though he was, already lined with debauchery.

The eyes looking enquiringly at Conrad were the deep blue of the sea, set wide apart and had a questioning expression in them.

What was so astonishing was that the small oval face and the slim, softly curved body was that of someone very young, almost he thought, immature.

He saw, too, that Lady Delora was very lovely and at the same time, there was an unsophisticated and unspoilt innocence about her that he had never found in any woman and expected least of all to discover in the sister of the 5th Earl of Scawthorn.

They stood for a moment looking at each other and as if she suddenly remembered her manners, Lady Delora curtsied.

"I think we are related, Captain Horn," she said in a soft, little voice which was not only musical, but which told him she was shy.

"We are, I believe, second cousins, My Lady."

"Then may I say that, although it has been a long time delayed, I am glad to meet you."

She held out her hand as she spoke and Conrad took it in his, finding it was small and soft, and yet at the same time, there was a vitality about her touch that was unmistakable.

He flattered himself that he could always tell a man by his handshake and he elaborated on this point that some hands were very heavy and dull, while others vibrated with the personality of their owner.

It was a contention which had never failed him and he thought, now, that although she was so young, he was certain that Lady Delora had character.

"I understand," she was saying, "that this really is your cabin, and I want to apologise for being a nuisance. I am well aware how annoying it must be to have to give it up on your very first voyage in the ship."

Conrad was surprised that she should be aware of the inconvenience she had caused, and conventionally he replied:

"It is of course, a pleasure, My Lady."

There was a pause. Then she said:

"I have been hoping all the morning, that you would come to see me and I could ask you if I could see over the ship."

"Yes, of course," Conrad replied, "but I think it would be more convenient if I took you round a little later."

"Any time that would suit you," Lady Delora said, "and please. . ."

She was about to say something, then as if she thought she was being indiscreet, she stopped and looked away from him as if embarrassed.

"You were about to say, My Lady?" Conrad prompted.

"Perhaps it is something I should not say . . at any rate . . not so quickly."

"No, I am inquisitive as to what it might be."

She gave a little laugh.

"I was going to suggest that as we are actually cousins we should not be so formal, but Mr. Frobisher was telling me that as Captain of this ship, you are very important and even unapproachable . . or perhaps I am saying the wrong thing?"

"No, of course not," Conrad replied.

As he spoke, the ship gave a lurch and as she put out her hand to steady herself, he added:

"Perhaps we should sit down. You may find it takes you a little time to get your 'sea legs'."

She smiled and walked carefully towards a small sofa which was against one wall at the far end of the cabin.

"My 'sea legs', Cousin Conrad," she said, "are, as I have proved on previous occasions, extremely good, but I cannot say the same for poor Mrs. Melhuish who I am convinced, was sea-sick before we even left harbour."

"I am sorry to hear that," Conrad said gravely.

"She should never have come with me," Lady Delora confided, "but she is terrified of my brother, because it is only through his generosity that she is allowed to stay with me as a chaperon."

Conrad said nothing.

He had no wish to discuss his cousin Denzil with his sister and yet it was so surprising that she was so completely unlike anything he had expected that, as if he could not help himself, he said aloud:

"I must tell you that I was expecting someone very much older, but as our families have had no communication with each other for nearly two generations, I am somewhat out of touch not only with the age of my relatives, but even the number of them."

Lady Delora smiled.

"I remember my father telling me how his father and your grandfather quarrelled with each other. I have a feeling he had even forgotten the reason why the war between them first started."

"It certainly seems ridiculous," Conrad agreed. "But now we have met, Cousin Delora, in somewhat strange circumstances."

He was thinking as he spoke, that he was taking her out to marry one of the most repulsive men he had ever known.

As if she knew what he was thinking, he saw the colour rise in her face and a look come into her blue eyes which he had not thought it possible he would see, but which was unmistakably one of horror.

There was a moment's silence. Then she said:

"Please . . I would rather not . . speak of it."

"Of course not!" Conrad agreed. "I apologise. I have no wish to intrude on anything that is personal."

He spoke coldly, feeling his dislike of her brother sweep over him and suspecting that he was somehow being deceived by her appearance into thinking she was different from the rest of the Horns he had always avoided as his father and his grandfather had done before him.

As if he felt that she had snubbed him, he would in fact, have risen to his feet, if she had not put out her hand to say quickly:

"No . . please stay. I want to . . talk to you. In fact, I am glad . . very glad that you are here . . and you are a . . relative."

Conrad would have replied, but she went on quickly:

"I have heard of your brilliant exploits in the Mediterranean. The newspapers said such wonderful things about you, and I felt as I read them that I would like to meet you anyway. Then I knew it was lucky . . very lucky for me that you should be the Captain of this ship that is . . carrying me to . . Antigua."

There were a million things Conrad was longing to ask.

He could not think why she should have agreed to such a monstrous marriage with a man old enough to be her grandfather, and why when she had every excuse to stay in England because they were at war, she was intent on taking what must obviously be a difficult journey without considering the dangers that lay at the end of it.

Then he told himself that she had warned him once not to be inquisitive and she would certainly not need to do so again.

Because he was keeping a tight control on himself he looked somewhat grim and unapproachable, and this was brought home to him when Lady Delora said with a pleading note in her voice:

"Please . . please . . I did not mean what you . . thought I meant just now."

"I think perhaps it would be wise for us to forget that there is any blood connection between us," Conrad said slowly, "and to behave as if we were just strangers, as indeed we are. Let me assure you that my only wish is to see to your comfort and your well-being until we reach Antigua."

As he stopped speaking he saw Lady Delora clasp her hands together, and there was an expression in her eyes which made him know that she was pleading with him, almost supplicating him to understand before she said:

"I . . I had hoped that as we are . . cousins we could be . . friends."

"I hope indeed we shall be," Conrad replied, "for the short time that this voyage must last."

He felt somewhat cynically that there was no chance of their being friends once she had reached Antigua and he had handed her over to her brother and the bridegroom who was waiting for her.

"And . . friends help each other . . do they not?" Lady Delora asked.

"They should do, if it is possible."

There was a little pause before Lady Delora replied, almost as if the words burst from her lips:

"Then . . please . . if you are my friend, Cousin Conrad, will you tell me how I can be as . . brave as you . . are?"

For a moment Conrad felt he could not have heard her aright. Then as if he could not help himself, he asked:

"Of what are you afraid?"

Her eyes met his and he knew the answer before she could say it.

"Of being . . married," she said, little above a whisper, "to a man I have never . . met!"

Conrad stiffened.

"A man you have never met?" he repeated. "Then, why? Why in God's name are you going all this way to Antigua?"

"Because . . I have to," she answered. "Because I have no . . alternative . . but I am . . frightened . . desperately frightened!"

CHAPTER THREE

For a moment Conrad stared at Lady Delora as if he could hardly believe she was telling the truth. Then he said in a warmer and more friendly voice than he had used before:

"Suppose you tell me from the very beginning what has happened? To start with—why are you so much younger than your brother?"

As he spoke he realised that she was fighting for self-control and with an effort she answered in a quiet voice:

"Denzil is only my half-brother."

She saw the surprise in Conrad's face and went on:

"But after I was born Mama was never very strong and therefore it was rather like being an only child as I had no one to play with."

"Who was your mother?"

"She was American and I think Papa married her because she was so rich."

Again the surprise in Conrad's face was very obvious and Lady Delora went on quickly:

"I have never met my American relations, but I am sure they were delighted that Mama should marry a man of such importance, and as she was very young, she had no say in the matter."

"Like you," Conrad commented.

"Exactly like me!" Delora answered, "and that is why. . ."

She stopped as if afraid that what she was about to say would be indiscreet and after a second's pause Conrad said:

"Shall we agree it would be best in the circumstances for us to speak frankly to each other? I want to know exactly the position you are in, and as I am a relative it would not be disloyal to tell me what you are thinking and feeling."

"I want to do . . that," Delora answered. "I felt when I read in the newspapers how you refused to use such cruel discipline on your ship as other Captains do, that you would understand people's . . sufferings."

"I try to," Conrad said, "and if you confide in me, Cousin Delora,

I shall try to understand your problems and do what I can to help you."

He saw a little light come into her worried blue eyes and after a moment she began to speak, telling him in simple words a story which he could easily augment from his own knowledge of the Horn family.

Apparently after Denzil's mother died, the 4th Earl was desperate to have more children.

His first wife had been a weak woman and the treatment she had received from him had reduced her to a condition of nerves and misery which made her practically mental.

When she had finally died the Earl had considered it a merciful release and looked round for a young woman who would give him the children for which he craved, and above all more sons.

He was well aware, although he would not admit it, that his son Denzil already had a wild streak in him and might well grow up into a wild young man.

The death toll among young men who were always taking part in duels, drinking themselves insensible or riding in crazy steeple-chases where there was every chance of their breaking their necks, made it imperative for him to have a younger son to inherit if anything should happen to Denzil.

Although the Earl was immensely rich, no-one ever believes they have enough money, and when he heard that the daughter of one of America's richest millionaires was coming to London he decided that she would suit him admirably as a wife.

As Delora grew older, she realised how unhappy her mother was and how much her husband who seemed to her extremely old, terrified her.

Like the Earl's first wife, his second found it difficult not to grow weaker and ineffective from fear and unhappiness.

Although she fought to keep her health, her vitality gradually ebbed away until she found it easier to become more or less an invalid, agreeing to everything that was asked of her and making no effort to assert her own personality.

"Mama was very intelligent," Delora said, "she had been well educated and read a great deal. But every time she expressed an opinion she was either ignored or told she was a fool, so that gradually she hardly spoke to anybody except me."

There was a little sob in her voice as she said:

"I think I made her happy, in fact I know I did, and we used to laugh and talk together from the time I was old enough to understand what she was saying. But if ever Papa came into the room, Mama would lie back against the cushions and close her eyes as if she could not bear the sight of him."

Because she was much younger and stronger than her predecessor the second Countess took a long time to die. When she did, Delora had already lost her father, and her half-brother Denzil had become the 5th Earl.

"He had been away from home for so long enjoying himself in London," Delora said, "that I did not realise what he was . . like until soon after Papa's death he came back with a . . party of his . . friends."

Conrad saw her shiver as she remembered them with horror, and as he was well aware of the type of riotous Bucks and the fast, immoral women with whom his cousin Denzil associated, there was no need for Delora to elaborate on what had happened.

It was fortunate that she was still in the School-Room, but she had been aware of a great deal that went on in the house and knew that the older servants and her Governess heaved a sigh of relief when the Earl and his guests returned to London.

Soon he had come back alone and Delora found he was angry with her and learned the reason for it.

Delora's mother had a huge income during her lifetime, which legally was entirely at the disposal of her husband, and she had no say in the spending of it.

Her capital however, was administered in America by the Trustees of her father's estate and when she died they had made it clear that while they were prepared to give Delora an allowance which was more than sufficient for her needs there was no question of any large sum of money being released except to her husband when she had one.

"Now you understand," Lady Delora said in a low voice, "that as soon as Denzil knew this he was determined that I should be married."

There was a moment's hesitation before she added:

"He told me quite frankly that he intended I should marry a man who would share my fortune with him."

Conrad's lips tightened.

He had always loathed his cousin Denzil and everything he had heard about him, but it really seemed inconceivable that, scoundrel though he might be, he would choose a man of Lord Grammell's reputation for anyone so young and so obviously sensitive and inexperienced as Delora.

"When Denzil wrote to me saying I was to come to Antigua immediately to marry Lord Grammell," Delora went on, "I did not think I had to obey him."

"What did you do?"

"I wrote to him saying I had no wish to marry anyone I had not seen, and that I thought the idea of my marriage could wait until the war was over and he returned to England."

"That was sensible," Conrad approved. "What did he reply to that?"

Delora drew in her breath.

"He sent a gentleman from the Foreign Office to tell me that as Lord Grammell was Governor of Antigua and my half-brother was my Guardian I had no choice but to agree to the plans that had been made for me. He also brought me a letter from Denzil."

"What did that say?" Conrad asked.

He knew from the way Delora spoke that what the letter contained had been significant.

For a moment she found it hard to answer him. Then she said in a low voice:

"Denzil said that if I did not do as I was told he would shut the house and . . 'turn me out into the street'. Those were the actual words he . . used. He said he had the authority to stop me from having any money from the Trustees in America and that all the servants who had looked after me, like my Governess, my maid and my teachers, would go with me and he would not pay them a penny!"

"I can hardly believe it! I can hardly think any man would stoop to anything so despicable!" Conrad muttered.

"How could I let poor Mrs. Melhuish and Abigail starve?" Delora asked. "And the servants who looked after me were nearly all old and would have found it impossible to find other employment."

She made a helpless little gesture with her hands.

"That is why I had to . . agree to come on this . . voyage. You do understand?"

"Of course I do!" Conrad answered. "But I have no idea how I can help you to escape from the fate that awaits you at the other end."

His cousin was looking at him with the expression, he thought, of a small child who believes someone grown up will solve every problem and he told himself despairingly that he had no ready solution, nor was he likely to find one to save her from the situation in which she found herself.

"I am glad you have told me this, Cousin Delora," he said quietly, "and I promise you I will do everything in my power to think what I can do to help you."

He gave her a brief smile as he added:

"We have at least twenty-four days, which was the time Lord Nelson took to reach the West Indies, in which to think, and surely one of us can find an answer during that time?"

"You may . . and I shall . . pray that you will," Delora replied, "but I have thought and thought, and prayed and prayed, and all I can remember is how frightening Denzil's friends have always been and that the gentleman from the Foreign Office told me that Lord Grammell is . . sixty-six!"

"I thought he must be about that age," Conrad said and his voice was hard.

"What have you heard about him?" Delora asked.

"There is no point in my repeating what I have heard at this moment," Conrad replied.

Delora did not say anything. She was looking down at her hands and he felt in the silence that she was keeping something back from him.

"Suppose you tell me what you have learnt about this man your brother wishes you to marry?" he suggested gently.

"It was when Denzil first wrote to me . . before I replied refusing to go to Antigua as he had . . ordered me to do," Delora said in a hesitating little voice, "and I rode over to see the Lord Lieutenant of Kent."

"And you asked him about Lord Grammell?"

"Yes, although I did not say why I wanted to know. I . . I just asked Lord Rowell what he knew . . about him."

"And what did he tell you?" Conrad asked.

"Lord Rowell has always been very kind to me, and Mama liked him, so I knew I could trust him to tell me the truth."

"What did he say?" Conrad persisted.

There was a little pause, then Delora said in a low voice:

"He replied: 'Good Lord, child! Why should you want to know anything about that abominable man? A debauched creature I would not allow to set foot inside my house, and I certainly would not permit him to meet my wife or children!' "

"Did you tell Lord Rowell the reason why you asked the question?"

Delora shook her head.

"I thought of asking him to help me . . but I knew there was . . nothing he could do. He disliked Denzil, and Denzil . . disliked him. I was afraid that if he said anything to my brother then I would no longer be permitted to visit His Lordship and I had . . very few friends."

Conrad was certain that was true, and Denzil's behaviour, if published, would have caused him to be ostracised by every decent person in Kent.

His sins would obviously then repercuss on his sister's head so she would not be invited as she should have been, to take her place in local society.

"I suppose you have been presented at Court. When was this and how was it arranged?"

"Only after I had been told I was to marry the Governor of Antigua."

"Who arranged it then?"

"The Foreign Office. The gentleman who came to see me said it was imperative that I should be presented to the Queen before I took my place as the Governor's wife."

"And who presented you?"

"The Viscountess Castlereagh. I only saw her the night I arrived

in London, then we went straight to a Drawing Room at Buckingham
Palace and I was sent back to the country the next day."

"It seems incredible!" Conrad exclaimed.

"I think," Delora said, "that the Viscountess, and for that matter
the Viscount, disapproved of Denzil and that I was to marry Lord
Grammell."

Conrad could see all too clearly that while the Foreign Secretary
and his wife disapproved there was nothing they could do to interfere
with the private arrangements of the man who had been appointed as
Governor.

How Lord Grammell got the position he had no idea, but unpleasant though he was he obviously had influential friends in the House
of Lords, and it was certainly not the Foreign Secretary's business to
say whom he should or should not marry.

Conrad could understand all too clearly how Delora, small and
helpless as any little animal, was caught in a trap from which he
could see no escape for her.

The position she was in appalled him and revolted every instinct
of decency in him.

But that was a very different matter from knowing how Delora
could defy first her half-brother, who was her natural Guardian and
bore a distinguished title, and a nobleman who, whatever his reputation, was still the representative of the King with, in consequence,
considerable powers in the Island over which he ruled.

Yet there was no point in saying so to Delora, and Conrad merely
said:

"Listen, Cousin Delora, to what I am going to suggest to you."

She raised her eyes to his and he knew there was both hope and
faith in them, as if she felt he held a magic wand that could save her
when everything ordinary and commonplace must fail to do.

"What I am going to suggest," he went on, "is that for the moment,
while I am thinking how to save you from your plight, you try to
enjoy the voyage which at least is a new experience."

"It is indeed!" Delora answered. "At any other time I should be
so excited and thrilled to be in such a wonderful ship."

"Then look at it as a respite between the past and the future,"
Conrad said. "For the moment you have left the troubles you had at
home and have not yet reached those that lie ahead."

Delora gave a little laugh.

"What you are really saying is: 'Enjoy today and let tomorrow take care of itself!'"

"Exactly!" Conrad agreed. "And I promise you that everybody in the ship will try to make it as pleasant a journey for you as it is possible in the circumstances."

"Suppose we get involved in a battle?" Delora asked.

"If we do, which I doubt," Conrad replied, "you must trust the *Invincible* to prove her name, and try not to be frightened by the noise."

"I am not as chicken-hearted as that!" Delora retorted. "I think it would be rather exciting to see a battle, as long as you win!"

"If one occurs I will certainly make every effort to see that happens," Conrad said with a smile.

"After all they have said about 'Tiger Horn'," Delora laughed, "I think any ship which sees your flag coming over the horizon will run away in the opposite direction."

"You are very complimentary and I hope that is an accurate prophecy," Conrad said. "Now, Cousin Delora, I must go back to work."

He rose to his feet. Then he said:

"I am afraid as there is no sign of Mrs. Melhuish you will have luncheon alone but, if you wish, I could invite some of my officers to meet you at dinner this evening."

He saw Delora's blue eyes light up with delight.

"Would you really do that? I would love to meet them, and I could wear one of my new gowns."

Conrad laughed.

"There speaks the eternal woman and of course, we would be very flattered to see you in all your finery."

"Then that is a promise. What time should I be ready?"

"I will tell you that when I collect you after luncheon to take you on a tour of the ship."

"I was afraid you had forgotten that is what you promised me."

"You would have thought me very remiss if I had done so," Conrad replied. "Besides, it would be better for you to make your tour while we are still in the English Channel. Later it may be rough."

"I am not afraid of the sea," Delora said.

There was a shadow across her face as she added almost beneath her breath:

". . only of people."

*

Watching Delora making the young Lieutenants laugh and knowing that the eyes of every man at the dinner-table were turned in her direction, Conrad told himself that she was an entrancing child whose unaffected self-confidence would make her a success wherever she went.

He liked the way when he had come to her cabin to escort her down to the First Lieutenant's cabin on the Upper Deck, which he was now occupying, that she had been waiting ready for him, and when he appeared a smile seemed to light up her whole face.

"I am ready!" she had announced, "and as you look so magnificent I feel I should be wearing a tiara, only I do not possess one."

"I think it would look somewhat over-dressed on a battle-ship," Conrad answered.

He thought as he spoke that the little bunches of artificial flowers that Delora had arranged on each side of her head and which matched those on the hem of her gown were more becoming than any jewels could be.

She looked very young and the excitement of being taken to a dinner party made her eyes shine in the light of the lanterns hanging from the ship's beams.

Her gown was white, but as the new fashion decreed both the bodice and the hem of the slightly wider skirt were more elaborate than they had been for some years.

Because he wanted to pay her compliments but thought at the same time it was a mistake, Conrad said almost abruptly:

"It is cold tonight, and I suggest you wear something warm before we move out of this cabin."

"I have a scarf trimmed with fur," Delora replied and as she picked it up from a chair on which it had been lying Conrad took it from her and put it round her shoulders.

It framed her face and her long neck, and he knew with a faint smile as they walked down the companionway which led to the upper deck that his other guests would be bowled over by her appearance.

He had thought when he first saw the First Lieutenant's cabin in which he had ensconced himself that it would only dine six people comfortably and he therefore invited Deakin whose cabin it was and three other guests who were all under twenty-four years of age.

His Lieutenants whom he had chosen himself were a very good-looking lot, and because it had been a privilege to serve with him on the *Tiger* two of them belonged to distinguished families whose fathers had almost beseeched Conrad to take their sons into his ship.

The third Lieutenant, by the name of Birch, was a clever young man who came from a family of ship-owners and Conrad confidently expected him to prove himself an outstanding Naval Officer.

They were all, after their first startled look at Delora when they had seen her going round the ship that afternoon, ready to entertain her and to spend as much time in her company as it was possible.

In fact, Conrad thought with an inward smile, that if he was not careful Delora would prove a distraction which would not augur well either for the discipline of the men or the amount of hard work that was expected from those who manned a ship when she first put to sea.

At the same time, because he was desperately sorry and in a way apprehensive about his cousin, he was determined to make her next few weeks happy ones.

When he was dressing for dinner, Conrad had remembered what his feelings had been about his guest during the last fortnight and laughed to himself.

He had cursed the woman who had taken over his cabin and disliked more than anything else having to meet one of his own relatives.

Delora was different, so very different from what he had expected, that now he told himself he was already in the position of wishing to protect a girl who was being exploited in an outrageous manner by two unscrupulous villains.

"But what the devil can I do about it?" he asked aloud making Barnet jump as he helped him dress.

He asked himself the same question when dinner drew to an end and he found himself laughing with the other officers at the table at something ingenuous that Delora had said.

She was not trying to be funny, witty or clever, she was just her natural self and because quite unselfconsciously she said what came into her head, the young Lieutenants found it amusing and her entrancing.

"I was reading in one of the newspapers, Cousin Conrad," she said now, "how on your ship you encourage your seamen to play musical instruments, to sing and even to dance. That is something I very much want to see."

"I am afraid you will have to wait," Conrad replied, "until we find out what talent we have aboard. I have in fact always thought it is a good idea for men to play and sing, especially when things are going badly."

"Or when they are hungry!" one of the Lieutenants remarked who had been with him on the *Tiger*.

Conrad smiled.

He was remembering how on one voyage they had been so long without picking up fresh supplies that the food had become almost uneatable, and only by thinking hard of something else had he and those in the ship managed to swallow even a mouthful of the biscuits full of fat weevils and the salted meat that was so hard that no amount of cooking seemed to make it any softer.

One of every Captain's incessant problems was how to feed his men with even a passably edible meal when they were so long at sea before they could replenish their stores.

Beer turned sour after a short time and although there was grog—for no ship's Captain dared run short of rum—a man could be flogged for drunkenness which was the only way they could escape from misery into unreality.

One thing Conrad swore to himself was that as long as Delora was on board, there would be no flogging on the *Invincible*.

However hardened he might be to the standard punishment which was carried out with the "cat-o'-nine-tails," he made every effort not to order it to take place on any ship he commanded.

He knew that seamen expected it as a deterrent, but strangely enough it appeared to have little effect.

At the same time, he wondered how anyone so exquisite and so in-

nocent of the world as Delora could exist for weeks on a ship filled
with men of all sorts and descriptions without being shocked and
disgusted by some of the things she would see or hear.

He found himself wanting to protect her and to ensure that none
of the seamier side of Naval life impinged on her consciousness, but
how he was to do so, he had no idea.

The dinner came to an end and Conrad realising that some of his
young officers had to be on duty at 4 a.m. rose to take Delora
back to her cabin.

As they climbed the companionway onto the quarter-deck she
said:

"That was the most exciting evening I have ever spent. Thank
you! Thank you, Cousin Conrad, for being so kind to me. I am so
very glad it was your ship that was chosen to carry me to Antigua."

"I am glad too," Conrad said quietly. "But I cannot promise you
such excitements every night. My officers and men have a great deal
of work to do."

"I am aware of that," Delora replied, "and I will try not to be a
nuisance, but please . . you will come and see me as . . often as you
. . can?"

There was an insistence in her voice which told Conrad without
more words that she was afraid of being left alone to think inevitably
of what lay ahead.

"I promise I will come as often as possible," he replied, "but I am
hoping that Mrs. Melhuish will soon be better so that you will have
somebody to talk to."

"I doubt it," Delora replied. "She is groaning and complaining
about the movement of the ship before it has even begun to be
rough!"

Conrad laughed.

"Let me commend you on having found your 'sea legs' so quickly.
Not everybody is so fortunate."

"I was not being unkind," Delora said quickly. "In fact, I would
never be unkind to Mrs. Melhuish, but even her best friend would
not say she is a good traveller!"

"Which I am sure you intend to be," Conrad said. "Good-night,
Cousin Delora, and may I say in all sincerity that I am delighted to
have you aboard."

"You were hating the idea when I first arrived!"

He was startled.

"How did you know that?"

"I could hear it in your voice and feel it when I shook your hand," she explained. "I was so afraid we were going to carry on the family feud all by ourselves in the middle of the ocean."

"That is something we certainly will not do!" Conrad said firmly.

He opened the door of her cabin as he spoke and saw Abigail waiting for her inside.

The maid stepped tactfully back into the shadows beside the bed as Delora held out her hand.

"Good-night, Cousin Conrad," she said. "Thank you so very, very much."

He felt her fingers cling to his for a moment. Then as he went from the cabin he heard her cry out to her maid:

"Oh, Abigail, I have had such a glorious evening! It has been fantastic!"

*

The following day Conrad rose when eight bells sounded at 4 a.m. and settled down to the serious work of getting the crew into shape.

The gun-crews loaded and reloaded their guns, many of them finding difficulty getting used to the new carronade which worked on a recoil roller.

Other seamen were practising the numeral signal code, while Deakin was sending the new men up aloft one after the other until they were no longer afraid of the height or the movement when they reached the top of the mast.

There were also new midshipmen who had come to sea for the first time, white-faced and nervous. They moved about afraid of doing the wrong thing and still more afraid of doing nothing at all.

Conrad spoke to them kindly, learning their names, recalling how he had felt many years ago on his first ship, and how secretly, although he had been ashamed of his weakness, he had sobbed himself to sleep night after night because he was home-sick.

He was so busy that it was not until five o'clock in the afternoon when he remembered Delora and his promise to go and see her.

He had, in fact, been aware that braving the cold wind and the sleet which was carried on it in sudden gusts she had come out onto the quarter-deck and walked around it, obviously enjoying the weather as no-one else did.

He had a feeling that she would like to be higher still on the Poop where he spent a great deal of his time.

But she was wise enough not to go there until she was invited, and he told himself that would certainly have to wait until they encountered better weather.

He went to her cabin and when he knocked on the door found her sitting on the sofa curled up and reading a book.

At his appearance she threw it down and jumped to her feet.

"You have come to see me!" she cried, "I am so glad! I was hoping you would remember your promise!"

"I have been too busy until this moment to remember anything but the work I have to do," Conrad replied.

"Now you are here, would you like a cup of tea? We have some with us and I am sure you would enjoy it."

"That would be delightful," Conrad replied.

Abigail who had been sitting in the further part of the cabin now left to make the tea and as soon as they were alone Conrad said:

"You are all right? You have everything you want?"

"Everything except being able to talk to you."

He smiled.

"I am here now."

"I am so glad! Please . . can I dine with you tonight?"

Conrad was surprised that she should invite herself before he invited her. Then as he wondered whether to have another dinner party so quickly would be a mistake, he thought of a compromise.

"Instead of my inviting you to my cabin," he said, "may I suggest that you invite me to yours?"

"Could I do that? Would it be correct?"

"I am not certain it would be correct either for me to dine with you or for you to dine with me, as you have no chaperon," Conrad replied. "But what we can ask ourselves quite legitimately is who is to know, and who is to care what we do when we are between two opposite points on the compass and outside anybody's jurisdiction except my own?"

Delora clapped her hands together.

"Of course! A Captain's ship is his Kingdom. I read that some-where, and he has complete and absolute command over everyone who sails with him."

Then with a mischievous little smile she added:

"Please, Captain Horn, will you order me to give you dinner? It would be particularly exciting if tonight we could dine alone so that I could talk to you."

Just for a moment Conrad hesitated.

He had a feeling that a *tête-à-tête* dinner was something slightly reprehensible from a social point of view, even though Delora was his cousin.

Then he told himself he was being needlessly worried about the conventions and, in view of what awaited her in Antigua, anything she did aboard ship would pale into insignificance beside the behav-iour of her brother and her future husband.

"I should be delighted to accept Your Ladyship's invitation!" he said formally, and liked the little chuckle of laughter she gave.

*

Two hours later Conrad entered Delora's cabin to find the table laid and lit with candles instead of the lantern hanging above it, and he realised from her appearance she had made every effort.

The gown she wore tonight was a very pale blue, but instead of flowers there were two little bows in her hair and round her neck was a string of pearls which he was to learn later had belonged to her mother.

He realised as he greeted her with a formal bow while she curtsied that she was so excited that she gave a little jump for joy and said as if she could keep it a secret no longer:

"I have planned a very special dinner for you tonight, and I shall be very disappointed if you do not enjoy it."

"A special dinner?" Conrad enquired.

"Lord Rowell told me when he knew I was coming on your ship it would be wise to bring some delicacies with me to augment what he warned me might be a very prosaic and unimaginative ship's menu."

"That is certainly a polite word for it after we have been at sea for some weeks," Conrad remarked. "But at the moment we have fresh chicken, lamb and pork aboard, and unless the Chef ruins them in cooking, they should be palatable."

"I was enjoying myself so much last night that I did not notice what I was eating," Delora said, "but I must not spoil the surprise by telling you what I have for you tonight."

It was certainly a surprise, Conrad thought, to eat pâté together with ox-tongue and a goose, both of which Delora told him came from the Home Farm.

"Have you never been to the family house?" she enquired curiously.

Conrad shook his head.

"My father would have had a fit if I had even suggested such a thing! When I was a small boy and heard him ranting against your grandfather and his cousin, I used to imagine it was something like hell, all black with the inhabitants enveloped in flames which flared from within them because they were so wicked!"

Delora's laughter rang out.

"The very opposite is the truth. It is a beautiful house and I know because you have good taste that you would love it."

"How do you know I have good taste?"

"I think it is part of your character and your personality," she replied, "just as I know you are kind and generous, brave and truthful."

Conrad held up his hands in dismay.

"Stop! Stop!" he objected. "You are giving me a halo and making me into a hero when I assure you I deserve neither. I am simply a man dedicated to his profession who has been extremely lucky. Beyond that I am nothing else."

"Now you are being modest," Delora said teasingly. "You forget I have read everything they said about you in the *Times* and the *Morning Post* and I saw the way your officers looked at you last night. Whether you like it or not, they think you are wonderful!"

She paused before she added:

"As I do!"

She spoke spontaneously as if it came to her lips without really thinking what she was saying.

Then as she met Conrad's eyes it was impossible to look away and he saw the colour rise slowly, very slowly up her cheeks.

It was like watching the dawn break over the horizon as he had done so often in his life, and he thought it would be impossible for any woman to be so lovely, and at the same time unspoilt.

As if she was suddenly aware that he was staring at her there was a strange expression on her face to which he was afraid to put a name, and he pushed back his chair from the table.

"Thank you, Cousin Delora," he said. "You should find yourself something to do while you are at sea, such as painting, unless you prefer sewing."

"What I really want to do," Delora replied, "is to walk about the ship and watch you and your seamen at work. Today I was afraid to leave the deck outside my cabin, while I longed to join you overhead on what I believe you call the Poop deck."

"You have to await an invitation from the Captain."

"And will you invite me?"

"That remains to be seen. As you must realise, we are a battle-ship and there is little time for frivolities."

He deliberately made his voice sound scathing.

"Are you saying," Delora asked in a low voice, "that you have changed your mind . . and now wish I was . . not on . . board?"

There was something so wistful and hurt in her tone that instinctively Conrad said quickly:

"No, of course not! I like having you here! You know I want you to be happy. It is just. . ."

It was his turn to find it difficult to finish the sentence but Delora did it for him.

". . . it is just that you do not wish to be too . . involved with me. That is the truth . . is it not?"

He was surprised that she was so perceptive.

At the same time he felt he was deliberately being unkind and he knew without being told that she desperately needed his help and comfort.

He did not answer, and after a moment she said:

"I knew as soon as I saw you that you were everything I had . . hoped you would be . . and when you . . talked to me yesterday I felt . . or rather I sensed that you would help me when I was so . . so frightened, that I wanted to . . die!"

"You must not feel like that," Conrad said almost sharply, as if he was talking to a terrified midshipman.

"I cannot help it because it is the truth," Delora said, "and you did say that we would forget what lay ahead and you wanted me to be happy while we were between yesterday and tomorrow."

"That is of course what I want," Conrad agreed, feeling as if he was being driven into a corner. "At the same time, for your sake I have to be sensible."

"By that you mean not being . . involved," Delora said logically.

"Not exactly," he objected. "I am trying to do what is best for you."

He knew as he spoke that what he was really saying was that whatever happened this child must not rely too much on him, because inevitably when the moment came, he would be obliged to fail her.

More important still she must not in any circumstances fall in love with him.

He did not think it was likely to happen because she was so much younger not only in years, but he was sure in every other way.

But he would not have been human if he had not been aware that because of his looks, his fame, and because he himself had never given his heart lightly, women were often bowled over the moment they met him.

Until he had known Nadine and been more or less faithful to her because she supplied a need in his life which every sailor recognised, there had been a number of women who had pursued him.

While they had tried by every wile and allure known to the feminine mind to inveigle him into the position of a supplicant, he had always turned the tables on them.

They had become involved with him but he had remained wholehearted and to a certain extent uncommitted.

He had accepted the favours that were offered him. At the same time, he had known that they meant nothing serious but were as delightful as the flowers on a dinner-table which had begun to fade by the time the dawn broke.

Any *affaire de coeur* in which he had been involved had been with

a woman well able to look after herself and who knew that if she
played with fire, it was easy to get burnt.

Delora was different, so different, Conrad thought, that he wanted
to think of her as the child she had appeared to be when he had first
seen her.

He was, however, already aware that her intelligent mind had nothing childlike about it, and he knew too that feelings were awakening
in her like a rose coming into bloom.

It only needed love to turn her from a girl into a woman.

It suddenly struck him that nothing could be more exciting, more
thrilling or more enthralling than to awaken her to a realisation of
what love could be.

Then shocked by the idea he told himself that must never happen!

It would be wrong, absolutely wrong in every way, to abuse the
trust she had given him and in his position as a relative to make her
aware of him as a man.

Besides, apart from anything else, she was promised in marriage
and it was not his place to question the character or the behaviour of
her future husband.

Even as he thought it, he felt himself rebelling violently as the idea
of anything so exquisite and so pure being touched—perhaps be-
smirched was a better word—by a monster like Grammell.

As he recalled the man he had last heard mouthing obscenities
which the roughest seaman would have been ashamed to use, Conrad
felt his hands twitch as if they were ready to choke the life out of the
man who could debase not only the name he bore, but the class from
which he had come.

Then strangely, surprisingly, because he was not aware that Delora
could read his mind, he heard her say in a whisper:

"If you . . feel like that about . . him . . how do you think I . .
feel?"

CHAPTER FOUR

STANDING ON the Poop deck from which he could observe the sea occasionally spraying over the bow, Conrad was acutely aware of a small figure moving about on the deck below.

They were now ten days out from Portsmouth, and the Atlantic had been at first tempestuous but was now settling down to an uncomfortable deep swell.

There had been no sign of Mrs. Melhuish and Delora reported that she had no intention of leaving her cabin until they were in calm waters.

"Which will be never!" Delora laughed, "because she dislikes the sea and she is praying only to reach dry land."

This had meant that Conrad spent a great deal more time with his cousin than he would have done otherwise.

He was aware, with a sensibility he had not expected in himself, how when she was alone her thoughts dwelt on what was waiting for her at the end of the voyage.

He saw when he came into her cabin that for the first moment the fear was vividly there in her eyes before his very presence dispersed it.

When he turned his head to look up at the masts he could see her wrapped in a blue cloak that was lined with ermine and trimmed with the same soft white fur round the hood.

It framed her face giving her an ethereal spiritual appearance until she smiled, when Conrad had found there was a hint of mischief in the soft curves of her mouth.

"She is lovely! Absolutely lovely!" he would tell himself in the dark watches of the night. "How can I hand her over to a beast like Grammell?"

Vaguely out of the mists of time memories had come to him of other things he had heard about the present Governor of Antigua, things so revolting, so distasteful to any decent man that Conrad was disturbed even to think of them.

Nevertheless he could not banish them from his mind, and when he was obliged to think of them in relation to Delora he wondered if the best thing he could do would be to throw her overboard before they reached Antigua.

At least she would die a clean death in the sea.

Those were his thoughts at night. In the day-time he told himself he was being absurd and hysterical and tried to go on pretending it was not really any of his business.

There was no doubt, apart from her fear of the future, that Delora was enjoying herself.

By now every young Lieutenant thought himself to be in love with her and even the seamen's eyes followed her whenever she was on deck.

Conrad made a pretence of looking at the main mast, but he knew in reality that his eyes wandered downwards to where Delora was walking round the three boats secured on the quarter-deck, and moving with an unmistakable grace despite the fact that the ship was rolling quite considerably.

Conrad had already warned her a dozen times not to go out on deck if it was rough, but she had laughed at him and told him she was a country girl.

"I am used to fresh air," she said, "and if the spray makes me wet I have plenty of gowns to change into."

"It is your health I am worrying about," Conrad protested. "These North winds bite into one, and I do not want you to go down with pneumonia."

"I will do my best not to inconvenience you, Captain!"

She spoke with a smile on her lips, and although he wanted to be firm with her he smiled back and knew she would get her own way.

He was aware now that the wind was growing stronger and the ship began to come alive with a creaking of timber and a harping in the rigging.

He saw that the gusts were whipping Delora's skirts around her and she was holding on to her cloak with both hands.

"She should go to her cabin," Conrad said beneath his breath.

At that moment there came a hail from the crow's nest.

"Sail ho! Deck, there, a sail ahead!"

"A sail!"

Conrad gazed upwards.

The look-out was clinging to his perch being swung backwards and forwards by the swell.

He saw one of the midshipmen standing beside him and ordered:

"Up you go, Harris! Take a glass with you and tell me what you can see."

The midshipman hurried to obey him and a few minutes later the Captain heard his voice calling down to him through the wind:

"I think she's a Frenchie, Sir. I can see the cut of her tops'ls."

Conrad drew in his breath.

"Man the braces, there!" he shouted, and as Deakin joined him on the Poop, added:

"Beat to quarters, if you please, Mr. Deakin and clear for action!"

As the drum rolled the hands came pouring up to man the guns on the quarter-deck and Conrad walked down from the Poop to where Delora was standing staring excitedly out to sea.

"Your place is below, Delora," he said. "Take Abigail with you, and you will stay in a lower cabin until the action is over."

"Oh, please. . ." she began, but Conrad was in no mood for argument. He called to the nearest Lieutenant.

"Mr. Latham—conduct Her Ladyship and her maid to my cabin and see that they are safe before you leave them!"

"Aye, aye, Sir!" the Lieutenant replied, delighted at the order.

Deliberately, because he was worried about her, Conrad tried not to look at Delora as she left him.

Nevertheless he saw her smile and wave her hand as Mr. Latham led the way to her own cabin to collect Abigail.

For several minutes the ship was in a turmoil of activity as the men began the drill they had been practising almost every hour of the day since they left Portsmouth.

The guns were run out and manned, the decks were sanded, the hoses rigged to the pumps and fire-extinguishers.

Conrad looked up at the sail and said harshly:

"I'll have two reefs taken in those tops'ls, Commander!"

Now he could see the ship they were approaching quite clearly, and she was unmistakably a Frenchman.

She was flying a red, white and blue flag and Conrad glanced up overhead to make certain the White Ensign fluttered in the breeze.

Then he heard Deakin say quietly beside him:

"She's opened fire, Sir!"

It was a mistake, as every English Captain knew, to open fire at long range. The sound did not reach them and the puff of smoke was blown away by the wind.

Conrad had always believed that the first broadside should be saved up for use at the exact moment when it could do the maximum harm.

Then as the ships drew a little closer a strange thing happened.

There was no more firing, and the French ship altered course.

Conrad waited, then as she turned to starboard he realised what was happening.

She, by now, had seen the size of the *Invincible* and was running away!

"Mr. Deakin," he asked, "what distance do you think there is between our two ships?"

"Over half of a mile, Sir."

"Thank you," Conrad said.

He gave the order for more sail, then watched the ship ahead doing the same thing.

He knew now it was a French Man-o'-War not much smaller than the *Invincible* but older, and it had doubtless been at sea for a long time.

That would account for her not being anxious to do battle with anything except ships smaller than herself whom she could easily out-gun.

"We'll overhaul her, Sir, if only the wind holds!" Deakin said excitedly.

It seemed as if it had every intention of doing so, for the *Invincible* under full sail, was pitching and tossing unpleasantly, but at the same time, she was riding the sea in a manner which Conrad had hoped she would be able to achieve in an emergency.

He drew nearer and nearer to the French ship and now Conrad gave the order for which every man aboard was waiting.

"Cock your locks!" he commanded. "Take your aim—fire!"

The roar of the broadside coincided exactly with that of the French ship. Conrad heard the sound of their shot as it passed overhead, fortunately without striking a mast.

It was obvious the French knew they could not go on running and must fight to save themselves.

The *Invincible* was enveloped in smoke, and Conrad could hear his First Lieutenant's voice, high with excitement, giving orders.

The guns bellowed, the crews sponged and rammed.

"Fire as you will!"

Conrad heard the order, and the more expert gun-crews got their shots off quicker than the others.

He realised the enemy's returns were now falling short as great fountains of spray rose above the side of the ship and splashed onto the deck.

Then he saw a main mast on the French ship fall and heard the cheer of his seamen as they saw the sails and rigging trailing over the side.

The Frenchman was now drifting helplessly before the gale.

It was only a question of a few more minutes before the battle was over.

Boats were lowered to pick up survivors but when Conrad was about to send a boarding party there was a sudden cry which he had expected.

"Fire! Fire!"

Flames leapt up from the sides of the French ship and ran along her decks.

Old ships, because their timbers were dry, burnt quickly, and in a few minutes the whole vessel was ablaze.

Conrad could see men throwing themselves into the sea and he knew there were many more trapped below decks for whom there would be no escape.

When the survivors were brought aboard there were pitifully few of them and no officers.

He learnt that the ship was returning to France after being away for three years.

There was no doubt she had been responsible for the loss of a great many small British craft, and she had filled her holds with cargo the weight of which had made her effort to escape more difficult.

The prisoners were sent below and Conrad now enquired as to his own losses.

"One of a gun-crew killed, Sir," Deakin informed him, "not through enemy action but from the explosion of his own gun."

Conrad's lips tightened, but he said nothing. This was a hazard all ships encountered sooner or later especially when the guns were new.

"Another man had his arm broken by the recoil of his gun, and two others were wounded by splinters when a shot scraped the upper deck."

"Did it do any damage?" Conrad enquired.

"Little, Sir, that can't be repaired and re-painted."

"Thank you, Commander."

It was only then that Conrad remembered Delora and wondered if she had been afraid.

He was about to send Deakin to enquire, then thought he had best go himself.

By now, it was growing dusk and the wind had turned to rain.

Leaving Deakin in charge of clearing up the decks Conrad went below where the six cabins, of which he occupied one, were safer than what was normally the Captain's cabin on the quarter-deck.

Going to the cabin where he knew Delora would be, he met Abigail coming towards the companionway.

"Is it all over, Sir?" she asked in what he thought was an admirably calm voice.

"Yes, Abigail," he replied. "Is your mistress safe?"

"She'd like to see you, Sir. I was just about to make her a cup of tea."

Conrad smiled, feeling sure that like most English servants Abigail thought a cup of tea was a panacea for all ills.

"I am sure a cup of tea is what we all need," he said.

He knew that what the men were expecting was a tot of rum all round and was sure it was something that Deakin would not overlook.

He opened the door of his cabin and as he did so, saw that as the lantern had not been lit, it was in semi-darkness.

For a moment there was silence and he thought perhaps Delora was not there. Then even as the thought flashed through his mind there was a little cry and she flung herself against him.

"You are . . safe! You have not been . . hurt?"

The words seemed to burst from her lips, and as the ship suddenly lurched he instinctively put his arms around her to hold her steady.

It was then as he felt the trembling of her slight body against him he was aware that her frightened little voice had died away and her face was turned up to his.

Without conscious volition, without thought, but obeying an impulse stronger than will, his lips found hers.

He knew as he touched her mouth that it was exactly as he had thought it would be in his dreams, soft, sweet, innocent and a wonder he had never known in his life before.

Because he was no longer himself but a stranger over whom he had no control, his arms tightened and he felt her quiver with an unmistakable rapture that matched his own.

He kissed her possessively, demandingly, and at the same time reverently because she was different in a way which for the moment he could not explain even to himself.

Only when the movement of the ship forced him to raise his head did Conrad come back to sanity.

"Forgive me," he said almost inaudibly.

He was horrified at what he had done but for the moment he was not certain what he should do about it.

"I . . love you?"

The words were hardly above a whisper but he heard them.

"I know . . now that I have loved you from the first . . moment I saw you when I knew you were . . the man I had . . prayed would come to help me . . to save me!"

With a superhuman effort Conrad took his arms from Delora leaving her to hold onto the nearest chair which was battened down to the deck.

He walked away from her across the cabin to stand at the porthole looking out into the gathering darkness outside, as if there he could find an answer to the pounding of his heart and the questions which already besieged his mind.

He did not speak, but he knew that Delora moved with difficulty to an arm-chair and sat down.

Her head was turned towards him and although it was too dark to see clearly he knew that her eyes seeking his face would be wide and questioning.

At last Conrad found his voice.

"You must forget what happened just now, Delora!" he said. "It was something which would never have occurred except, I suppose, I was elated by our victory."

There was silence, then Delora asked in a very small voice:

"A-are you . . saying that you are . . sorry you kissed me?"

"It is something which should not have happened."

"But it . . did happen . . and I know now that I . . love you."

"That is something you should not say."

"But it is . . true."

"If it is, then it is extremely regrettable and you must do your best to convince yourself that it is only an illusion—something which is due to the fact that you are having an unusual experience in the middle of a war, and that strange things do often occur at such times which are best forgotten."

Again there was silence until Delora said, and now there was no mistaking there was a little sob in her voice:

"So . . you do not like . . kissing m-me! To me it was the most . . wonderful thing that ever happened!"

He realised she was perilously near to tears and he said quickly:

"Of course I liked kissing you, but I am ashamed of my lack of control. It is something of which any Captain would be ashamed."

"I do not think you . . kissed me as a . . Captain," Delora said, "but as . . a man."

This was so palpably true that Conrad had no answer.

As if he was afraid of what might be said next, he turned to the door remarking:

"I have a lot to do."

"No . . please . . there is . . something I must . . say to you."

Because he could not ignore her appeal, he moved towards her and sat down in a chair near to hers.

She put out her hands towards him and he took them because it would have been unkind to refuse to do so.

He felt her fingers tremble as he held them, but he forced himself not to kiss the softness of her skin as he longed to do.

He felt her hold onto him as if he was a lifeline that she could not relinquish. Then she said softly in a different voice than she had used before:

"I love you . . and even if you do not love me . . I shall go on loving you . . all my life . . until I . . die."

"Delora, you must not say such things."

"But they are true . . and because I love you . . I will do anything you . . want . . but please . . go on . . liking me even though I am your . . relation."

"*Liking* you. . . !"

The two words burst from Conrad's lips. Then as he too was afraid of what he should say next, Delora bent forward in her chair and held his hands against her breast.

"I think," she said in a whisper, "that even . . though you are . . fighting against it, you do . . love me a . . little."

Because they were practically in darkness and because the softness, the sweetness of her voice seemed almost to mesmerise him, while the nearness and the touch of her made his heart beat painfully, Conrad could no longer resist her.

"I love you! Of course I love you!" he said harshly. "But you know as well as I do that this is something which should never have happened."

"But it *has* happened," she said, "and, oh . . my wonderful cousin, it is what I have . . prayed for."

"But, my sweet, there is nothing we can do about our love," Conrad protested. "I am bound to carry out my orders and deliver you safely to the Governor and your brother in Antigua. That I have fallen in love with someone who is in my charge is against my own code of honour, apart from anyone else's."

"When I was so terribly . . afraid that you might be . . killed or . . wounded in battle," Delora answered, "I knew that if you . . died I would . . want to . . die too."

"You are not to talk like that," Conrad said automatically.

As he spoke he was not quite certain how it happened, but she had moved from her chair into his and was in his arms, and he was kissing her as he had before, only more insistently.

He kissed her until he forgot everything but the magic of her lips, the softness and fragrance of her, and the wildness of his own love.

He could no longer think clearly, he only knew that Delora was everything that was his ideal.

There had always been a secret shrine in his heart in which was hidden the woman he wanted as his own, but whom he had thought never to find.

Now, as in the last few days he had learned of the quickness of her mind, the beauty of her character, and the strength of her personality, it was all a part of his love.

Beside which, she was so utterly desirable and it was difficult to believe that he had ever wanted any other woman.

He took his lips from Delora's and she whispered:

"Tell me that you love me . . tell me just once . . and I promise I will not bother you again."

"Do you really think it is a bother?" Conrad asked. "I love you, my precious little Delora, more than I can put into words, and much more than I can dare to contemplate."

His hand touched her cheek as he said:

"I think you are a dream and not real, a dream of perfection that draws a man like a star which is always out of reach."

As he knew she was going to say she was not out of reach but close beside him, it seemed superfluous to put it into words and Conrad was kissing her again.

It may have been a few minutes or a few centuries later they heard Abigail's voice outside and moved apart.

Conrad rose to his feet and was opening the lantern as Abigail came in followed by a steward carrying the tray on which were the tea-things.

As if she could not trust him she carried the tea-pot in her hands and quickly, for fear the movement of the ship might cause her to stumble, set it down on the table.

"Still in the dark, M'Lady?" she asked sharply.

"I am having trouble with this lantern," Conrad replied as if she had spoken to him. "See what you can do with it, Briggs."

"Aye, aye, Sir!"

The steward set the tray down on the table.

"When you have had your tea, Cousin Delora," Conrad said in a commendably ordinary voice, "you will be able to return to your own cabin."

He left as he spoke and wondered as he did so, if things would ever be the same as they had been when he went, after the battle, to look for Delora.

Fortunately for his peace of mind there was still a great deal of work waiting for him and a number of officers who wished to see him on one pretext or another.

Although he longed to do so, he did not see Delora again that evening and in consequence found it hard to sleep, thinking perhaps she was lonely without him.

"What am I to do now?" he asked himself in the darkness of his cabin as the *Invincible* sailed on through the night, creaking and groaning as if she too was in pain.

As he faced a new dawn he decided he must take a tight hold on himself and the kindest thing he could do, where Delora was concerned, was to convince her she was not really in love with him and what she felt was nothing but a school-girl's infatuation.

"After all, she has known very few men in her life," he told himself. "How can she be sure that this is the love that is real and lasting which at the moment she believes it to be?"

Then he told himself he would be belittling something that was so beautiful, so unearthly, that to spoil anything so perfect would be committing a vandalism of which he should be deeply ashamed.

But that only brought him back to his original question.

What could he do?

He was still asking himself the same thing when he went up on the Poop deck, vividly conscious that Delora, in the cabin immediately below him, was lying in the big bed with its curved oak posts and blue curtains in which, when she disembarked at Antigua, he would sleep alone.

He knew when he did so, he would be haunted, as he would be at all other times in his life because in the space of only a few days she had entwined herself around his heart, so that he would never be free again.

Then he asked if it was really only an acquaintance of ten days that had made him feel as he did now.

He was certain in his own mind that fate had meant them for each other and perhaps they had known love together in other centuries. When he had seen her first standing in his cabin, although he had been afraid to admit it, perhaps they had recognised each other across eternity.

Deep in his thoughts he was suddenly aware that a midshipman stood at his elbow.

"What is it, Campbell?"

"If you please, Sir, Lady Delora wishes to speak to you immediately."

Conrad frowned.

He knew it would cause comment in the ship that Delora was sending for him so early in the morning and he decided he must warn her against such impulsive actions.

"Inform Her Ladyship," he said to the midshipman, "that I will be with her at the first available opportunity."

"Aye, aye, Sir!"

The boy hurried away and Conrad deliberately had a long conversation with the man at the helm and the boatswain, before finally going down to the cabin where he knew Delora was waiting for him.

He knocked and when he heard her voice telling him to come in he entered, with what he hoped was a slightly stern expression on his face.

He was, however, conscious that his heart was beating a little faster at the knowledge that he would see her and there was a throbbing in his temples which had been there, he thought, ever since he had kissed her.

Then when he saw the expression on her face he knew the reason she had sent for him was no ordinary one.

"What is the matter?"

For a moment it was hard for her to speak. Then she said:

"M-Mrs. Melhuish . . died last n-night! Abigail found her a little . . while ago . . when she went to call her."

"She is dead? How is it possible?" Conrad asked.

"She always said she had a . . weak heart," Delora replied, "but . . I am afraid because she had so many aches and p-pains I never believed her. Now I feel guilty that I did not . . sit with her when the battle was taking place."

"You did what I ordered you to do."

"Yes, I know," Delora agreed, "but I did ask Abigail what we should do about Mrs. Melhuish and she replied that it would be an unkindness to move her when she was feeling so unwell."

"I am sure Abigail was right," Conrad said consolingly. "Wait here. I will go and see what is happening."

He went from the cabin to the one occupied by Mrs. Melhuish.

It was very small and it had been intended for Barnet, but it was more comfortable than the accommodation a Captain's steward would expect in an older ship.

As he entered he found Abigail had already laid out the elderly lady, and with her eyes closed and her hands crossed on her breast she looked at peace.

"I am sorry about this, Abigail," Conrad said.

"It can't be helped, Sir," Abigail replied. "She was a lady who was always ailing."

"This means that Her Ladyship will be alone," Conrad said, as if he was following his own thoughts.

"No more than she was while Mrs. Melhuish was ill, and anyway she was no companion for a young girl."

"But Her Ladyship should be chaperoned," Conrad insisted.

"It's no use fretting, Sir," Abigail said in the tone of a Nanny speaking to a rather recalcitrant child. "What's happened has happened, and nothing can undo it. Her Ladyship will be all right with people to talk to. That's what she's been missing living with only a lot of old servants and no companion of her own age."

"But surely there must have been other young people in the neighbourhood?" Conrad asked.

"The neighbours who were the right type of people to be friends with Her Ladyship didn't approve of His Lordship."

The way Abigail spoke told Conrad all too clearly what she herself thought of the Earl and, as if he knew nothing could be gained by furthering this conversation he said:

"I will instruct the ship's carpenter to make a coffin for Mrs. Melhuish. I feel the sooner she is buried the better for Her Ladyship. There is no use in dwelling on these tragedies."

"No, indeed, Sir," Abigail agreed, "and it would be a real kindness if Her Ladyship's not left alone too long with her thoughts."

Conrad did not reply but he knew as he walked away that it would be impossible to see only a little of Delora as he had half-intended to do.

Nothing could make her more miserable than she was already and the mere fact that Delora had spoken out so frankly made him aware that she too was afraid and apprehensive of the future.

"This is a hell of a mess!" he muttered to himself.

Then as the morning progressed and he went through his duties smoothly like a well-oiled machine, he knew that his mind, like his heart, was with the small, frightened girl alone in the Captain's cabin.

*

Mrs. Melhuish was buried at sea that evening.

A small contingent of the Marines stood to attention while Conrad read the Burial Service because there was no Chaplain aboard.

There should have been one, but on the day they sailed Conrad was told that the Chaplain who had been posted to the *Invincible* was too ill to join them and there had been no time before they sailed to find a replacement.

Actually Conrad had been rather pleased.

His experience in the past of ship's Chaplains had not always been pleasant. Far too often they were men who could not make a success of their calling on shore and who for want of being offered a Parish chose to go to sea.

It was very rare to find one who could help and encourage the cabin-boys and midshipmen to get over their home-sickness, or to comfort men who were desperately unhappy at leaving their wives and families.

In fact a number of Chaplains were only too happy to sit drinking the voyage away or else wanting to deliver long, depressing sermons on Sundays until their time was strictly limited on Captain's orders.

Delora thought that Conrad read the Service more movingly than any Chaplain could have done.

She felt tears come into her eyes not only because she was sorry at Mrs. Melhuish's death, but because she loved Conrad so overwhelmingly that even to look at him and hear his voice made her feel emotional.

"I love you!" she said in her heart as he said the last prayer.

Then she was praying, praying desperately that she need not leave him but be with him always.

"Please, God, please . . let us be together. Let me love him . . let me look after him . . and keep him safe."

She felt as if her prayers winged out over the rolling sea and up into the grey sky, and because it was so intense she felt almost as if a cloud would open and a shaft of sunlight would tell her that God had heard her prayer.

But instead there was only the grey clouds, the indefinite horizon and the emptiness of the sea.

As the coffin went over the side and into the water the Marines presented arms while Conrad and the other officers saluted.

Now it was over and Mrs. Melhuish was no longer with them.

Delora felt the tears blind her eyes, then Conrad was beside her leading her back to her cabin.

They went inside and he shut the door.

"It was very upsetting for you, Delora," he said quietly.

"I am not really crying for her," Delora replied, with a handkerchief to her eyes, "but because . . death seems so . . final. If she had lived there might have been many more . . things for her to . . do and . . see."

"That is something we feel when we are young," Conrad said, "but to the old there is peace and rest, and perhaps they ask nothing more."

Delora gave him a sad little smile and took off her cape.

"You have an answer for everything," she said. "You are . . so wise."

Her eyes met his, then she added very softly:

"And so . . marvellous!"

"If you say such things to me," Conrad said, "all my good resolutions as to our future behaviour will fly away. You have to help me to behave in the way I should—but it will not be easy."

"And who will be impressed?" Delora asked. "The sea, the stars, or my future husband who is marrying me for my money?"

The last words were spoken with such bitterness that Conrad was startled.

Then as if he could not help it he moved towards her and put his arms around her.

"Whatever happens," he said, "you are not to let it spoil you and you will face it with courage. But now, now at this moment, and until the voyage ends you must be happy, and I never wish to hear you speak in that tone again."

Then he drew her closer and she hid her face against his shoulder, and when he had finished speaking, she did not move.

Then she looked up at him and he saw that the bitterness had gone from her eyes. Instead, and he knew it was because she was in his arms, there was a light that shone as if it came from her heart.

"Is that an order, Captain?" she enquired, and her lips were smiling.

CHAPTER FIVE

To DELORA the days seemed to fly by on wings and everything was touched with the magic of sunlight even though the skies were dull and grey.

But soon the conditions changed so dramatically that it seemed as if one day they were labouring over leaden seas into a south-westerly gale with waves running as high as the yard arms, and the next there were blue skies and gentle breezes from the south-east.

The sea was blue, as blue as Delora's eyes, and there were flying fish and porpoises performing their antics with the grace of ballerinas.

It was all an enchantment that rested on the fact that Conrad was there and Delora could see him, hear his voice and, when they were alone, touch him.

Her love for him was like a light that glowed within her and made her a hundred times more lovely than she had been before.

It was as if her happiness and his infected the whole ship.

The men sang and whistled as they worked and in the evenings there was the sound of the hornpipe coming from the lower decks.

Delora had not asked again that the men should play for her for the simple reason that Conrad had said there were no musical geniuses aboard, but their voices ringing out as they climbed the mast-head or scrubbed down the decks were somehow very uplifting.

Conrad seemed to relax in the happiness of the atmosphere: he gave dinner-parties in his cabin and when his officers were not entertaining Delora, he dined with her alone.

Sometimes his conscience pricked him, but as she had said: who was there to be impressed or scandalised by their behaviour? All too soon they would reach Antigua, then he had sworn to himself that he would never see her again.

He knew he could not bear to know that she bore another man's name and, more unbearable, that she should be married to Grammell and that he and her despicable brother were rubbing their hands together with the anticipation of handling her fortune.

When he thought of it the agony was so intense that he would rise in the middle of the night to walk up and down the deck, knowing that only by exercising his body would he somehow be able to control the torment of his soul.

When he was alone with Delora it was a joy and a wonder which he told himself he would remember until he died.

"Tell me about yourself," she would ask in her soft voice, "what were you like when you were a little boy? And when did you first know that you wanted to go to sea?"

Conrad responded by telling her things he had never told any other woman, and the picture he drew for her of his childhood and his growing up made her not only love him the more, but know that she wanted to have a son who would be like him.

It was impossible to suppress the thought that if she did have a child by the man who was waiting to marry her, it might be as horrifying as he was, and she felt herself shiver at the idea.

Because they both loved each other too much to inflict unnecessary suffering, they tactfully did not speak of what would happen when they reached Antigua.

It was, nevertheless there in their minds and it was in the darkness of their eyes, and when Conrad saw Delora shiver and her lips droop pathetically, he would pull her into his arms and kiss her until she could think of nothing and nobody but him.

"Perhaps I have made a mistake," she said one night.

Dinner was finished and they were sitting on the sofa, their hands linked together.

"What sort of mistake?" he asked.

"Perhaps . . because the world is round . . we shall go on travelling without sighting land . . and sail and sail into infinite space."

Conrad laughed.

"We must find land soon. Our stores are becoming depleted and we need vegetables, fruit and most of all fresh water."

"Abigail insists on boiling everything I drink."

"That is very wise of her," Conrad commended, "but even so, I shall be glad when we can refill the water-butts, and when you see fruit growing on the trees and a profusion of flowers everywhere you look, you will know that you are in the West Indies."

There was silence and he knew what else was waiting for them in the West Indies and so he took Delora in his arms.

Then they could only whisper of themselves, and everything else was of no importance.

Each day grew warmer and Delora no longer walked about in her fur-lined cloak but appeared in attractive muslin gowns and soon needed a sunshade to protect herself from the heat of the sun.

It was a day when everything seemed to be golden, and Conrad on the Poop deck was vividly aware of Delora on the deck below him, so lovely in her summer attire that she might have been dressed for a garden-party.

He could not help looking at her and as if the magnetism of his eyes drew hers, she looked up at him with a smile that illuminated her small face.

For a moment they were as close as if they were in each other's arms and Conrad could almost feel her heart beating in unison with his.

Then, like a voice from another sphere he heard the look-out call: "Sails ho! And Oi thinks Oi heard gun-fire!"

Conrad sent a midshipman up the masthead and a few minutes later he called:

"I think there are several ships ahead, Sir, but I can't be sure."

Deakin appeared at Conrad's side to ask:

"Shall I clear for action, Sir?"

"Yes, Commander," Conrad replied, "and have the guns loaded and run out too, if you please."

There was enough wind to keep the *Invincible* steady on her course and a short while later Conrad could see through a glass what was happening.

There was a small convoy of four or five merchantmen all flying the British flag and attacking them were two Privateers.

They were, without exception, the largest and finest ships of their type Conrad had ever seen at sea, and he was certain they were newly built, strongly armed and the merchantmen had no chance against them.

As they drew nearer he could see that the British ships were huddled together, each ship closer to its neighbour than any merchant captain could be induced to steer unless activated by fear.

Boarding nettings had been set up on their decks and they were running out their guns.

But Conrad knew any defence they could offer would be feeble, though the fact that they could defend themselves at all was a help.

He knew long before they were within range what his problem would be. It was that if the *Invincible* opened fire on the Privateers it would be impossible not to damage the merchant ships at the same time.

As if the Privateers were well aware of this they were working to windward so as to have the merchantmen between them and the *Invincible*.

With their sharp, black hulls and steeply raked masts they were, even though they were the enemy, a beautiful sight which any seaman would be forced to admire.

There would be at least one hundred and fifty men aboard each ship and with the wind on their quarters, the white water foaming at their bows, lying over in the breeze, they were a picture of malignant efficiency.

Conrad knew that to attack them as he wanted to do, he had somehow to get between them and the convoy. Then as if they were aware of his intention they changed course zooming in on the nearest merchantman and he saw the flash of their guns.

Conrad was astute enough to realise it would not be their intention to sink the merchantmen. What they wanted was their cargo, and if possible, the ships themselves to send to the nearest American Port as a prize capture.

He was quite certain the superior guns of the Privateers and the manner in which they were intimidating the convoy would have a bad effect on the morale of the crews of the merchant ships.

He stared at the enemy, calculating their speed, observing their course.

The Privateer to starboard would arrive at the convoy first and he would have a minute or two in hand to deal with the second Privateer if he disposed of this one.

"Starboard and two points!" he called.

"Starboard and two points!" echoed the Quarter master.

The *Invincible* swung round and managing to hold the wind swept between the Privateer and the nearest merchantman.

There was very little space to spare, but the *Invincible* managed it, and the Captain of the merchantman keeping his head, moved his ship as swiftly as he could out of the way.

"Stand to your guns!" Conrad bellowed. "Commander, give the Privateer a broadside as we pass her!"

There was the resounding explosion of the guns which appeared all to fire at the same moment.

Then as Conrad saw the Privateer's masts falling and felt a cheer rise in his throat, a red hot coal from Hell struck him in the leg and the world disintegrated into a sudden darkness.

*

Conrad came back to consciousness to hear voices raised and he wondered why they should make so much damned noise when his head felt as if it was splitting open and something heavy appeared to be holding him down on a hard surface.

Then through a mist which gradually evolved from black into crimson, he heard a voice he recognised, saying:

"I must insist, My Lady, on doing my duty. I'm the Surgeon, and it's my decision whether I do or do not amputate!"

"I will not allow you, whatever you may say, to remove Captain Horn's leg without his permission!"

The voice was soft but firm, and as Conrad realised who was speaking he opened his eyes.

He tried to ask what the devil was going on, but for the moment the words would not come to his lips.

Then as he saw a number of heads and shoulders above him he realised that he was lying on the amputation table on the upper deck and with a sudden tug of his heart, he wondered where he had been wounded.

Now he could see Delora bending over him and he heard her say:

"You are awake! Can you hear me?"

"I—can—hear—you."

His voice started weak, but grew a little stronger.

"Listen, Cousin Conrad, this is important," Delora said. "The Surgeon wishes to amputate your leg. But you have only been hit by

grape-shot, and I know that Abigail and I can treat it so that you will
be able to walk again."

"That's extremely unlikely, Captain," the Surgeon intervened,
"and if gangrene sets in, you know as well as I do, Sir, that you'll
die!"

"Please, Conrad, please let us try to save it," Delora pleaded.

It seemed to Conrad that it was his head which was wounded and
everything seemed far away so that it was difficult to concentrate.

Then as he forced himself to do so, he knew that Delora was
speaking sense. He had always loathed the ship's Surgeons who
chopped the men up as if they were nothing but ox-meat.

"I am—in your—hands," he said to Delora.

His voice was weak and as if the effort of speaking had been too
much for him, he closed his eyes, but he heard her give a little cry as
she said to the Surgeon on the other side of the table:

"You have your orders. I will nurse Captain Horn, and you can
see to anyone else who needs your attention."

"Your Ladyship'll live to rue this day!" the Surgeon replied disa-
greeably.

He walked away but he left his instruments behind and as Abigail
picked up a probe Delora said:

"Have you the laudanum with you?"

"It's here, M'Lady."

"Then I will give it to him if he regains consciousness, but in the
meantime see if you can remove the grape-shot."

*

It was a long time afterwards that Conrad was to learn that fortunately it was a shot from one of the smaller guns on the Privateer
that had hit him.

The force of the shot had thrown him to the deck, and as it did so,
he hit his head against the navigating instruments which had ren-
dered him unconscious.

He had been carried down to the amputation table on the upper
deck and while the Surgeon was attending to another wounded man,
Barnet had run to tell Delora what had happened.

It was a strict and inviolable rule that the wounded should take

their turn, the first brought down was the first to be dressed. No
favour was shown to any man, be he officer or swabber.

The fact that Conrad had to wait saved him from having his leg
chopped off the moment the Surgeon sighted him.

By the time Delora and Abigail arrived Barnet had cut away
Conrad's white breeches and they could see the mess which had been
made by the grape-shot.

They were, however, obviously only flesh wounds in his thigh, and
though unpleasantly deep, the bone was intact and unbroken.

The wounds were also all above the knee which apparently was
not injured, and Abigail said at once that if they could get the grape-
shot out and prevent it from festering there was every chance they
could save the whole leg.

Delora was well aware of how Conrad would feel if he was crippled.

She had seen many legless men in the last few years, men who had
been wounded at sea or in the Army, hobbling about with wooden
stumps or struggling on crutches.

"We must save his leg . . we must, Abigail!" she cried.

"I think it's possible, M'Lady," Abigail replied in her slow, calm
voice, "but it'll mean probing deep and hurting him a great deal."

Delora had remembered that when Lord Nelson's arm had been
amputated the only thing he had been given to help him after the operation had been performed, was opium.

She knew that Mrs. Melhuish frequently took small doses of laudanum to relieve the pain of an aching head, and she sent Barnet
running to the dead woman's cabin to see if it was still there.

He returned with a bottle which was three-quarters full and as
Abigail took it from him, she thought that at least Conrad would not
have to suffer the agonies of men who were given nothing more than
a tot of rum or a leather pad on which to bite during the operation.

It was at that moment that the Surgeon, having finished with his
first patient came to the amputation table.

He was rubbing a knife with a blood-stained rag, saying as he did
so:

"Your Ladyship had best return to your cabin. This is not the sort
of sight you'd wish to see."

It was then that the argument started and when the Surgeon

walked away in a temper, Abigail began to probe in the torn and
bleeding flesh.

It was not a pretty sight, but Delora watched Conrad's face and
when he began to show signs of consciousness she made him swallow
several spoonfuls of laudanum and he slipped away into a dark
slumber.

*

It was not until the middle of the night that Conrad opened his
eyes again and for a moment he could not think where he was or
what had happened.

He was certainly in a strange bed, and by the light of the lantern
he could see it had carved oak posts.

Then he knew there was somebody beside him and found it was
Abigail.

She put a hand on his forehead, found it was hot and wet with
sweat, and lifting his head so that he could drink, put something
sweet and cool to his lips.

As his head rested again on the pillow, he remembered the argument on the upper deck and asked:

"My—leg?"

"You still have it," Abigail replied, "so go to sleep, Sir. That's
what you need—sleep!"

He thought later there must have been something in the drink she
had given him, for he fell asleep immediately.

When next he awoke, the cabin was bright with sunshine and it
haloed Delora's head with gold as he looked up into her face.

"Can you hear me, Conrad?" she asked.

He tried to smile at her and was conscious as he did so, that he
felt very hot and there was something heavy on his forehead.

She took it away and replaced it with a cloth that was cool and
moist.

His whole body seemed to be burning, and he knew that he had a
fever and hoped as Delora was beside him, it was not infectious.
Then he drifted away again into a grey "No-man's-land" where he
need no longer think or wonder why he was so hot.

It was a few days before he could think clearly and the first thing he realised was that he was in the Captain's cabin which he had given up to Delora.

"Why am I here?" he demanded.

"Her Ladyship insisted, Sir," Abigail replied, "and it's more convenient for us to nurse you here than if you were on the deck below."

"Where is Her Ladyship sleeping?" Conrad demanded.

"In Mrs. Melhuish's cabin, and she's comfortable enough. There's no need to be worrying yourself about anything except getting well and proving to that butcher who calls himself a Surgeon that we were right and he was wrong!"

Conrad wanted to laugh at the asperity in Abigail's voice.

In the days that followed his leg was so painful, especially when it was being dressed, that he sometimes thought it would have been best if he had lost it.

But that was only a passing thought when the pain was almost unbearable.

He refused to take any more laudanum, even when Abigail cleaned the wound with spirit which was brandy.

He was aware that this was saving him from gangrene, and he was interested to see that Abigail's dressings, which she changed twice daily, were applied with honey.

"As soon as we reach land I'll find some herbs which will cure you more quickly than anything that Surgeon can suggest," she said in her tart manner.

Conrad tried to smile but he was concentrating his whole willpower in a determined effort to justify Delora's faith that he would walk again without any support.

As soon as his head was free of the mists caused both by his fall and the laudanum, he had sent for the First Lieutenant to find out what had happened.

"We sank the first Privateer," Deakin said gleefully, "and the second with Watkinson in command, is on its way to Plymouth."

"A prize the Admiralty will undoubtedly welcome!" Conrad exclaimed, "because there is no doubt that the American ship-builders can teach us quite a lot we do not know about fast ships."

"I have never seen a better designed craft for the work for which it was required," Deakin replied, "and as the Navy will pay for it, that'll mean a nice sum in your pocket, Sir."

"And in yours, Deakin," Conrad replied.

They both grinned knowing that prize-money was divided in proportion amongst the Captain and the crew of the vessel that captured her.

"How many casualties?"

"Two men killed outright, Brown and Higgins, and twelve wounded."

Conrad frowned but Deakin quickly spoke of something else.

It was then Conrad asked the question which had been hovering in the forefront of his mind during the night.

"How many days before we reach Antigua?"

"Another nine or ten," the First Lieutenant replied. "I'm trying to keep her on a steady keel, Sir, since you've been ill, and it's always wise to go slower when a ship has a certain amount of damage."

"Damage?" Conrad questioned sharply.

"It's nothing very serious, but it'll undoubtedly take several weeks in a dock-yard before we're fit to fight another battle."

Conrad was not certain whether he was glad or sorry that he would have to stay in Antigua.

He had made up his mind that the moment he had set Delora ashore and replenished his stores he would put as many miles between himself and her as was possible.

He knew he could not endure the misery of seeing her with a man whose real interest lay in her fortune.

Delora must have asked the same question as he had, for after Deakin had gone, she had come and sat on the side of his bed and slipped her hand into his.

"We still have more than a week together," she said softly.

"I suppose I should thank you for keeping me alive and a whole man," Conrad answered, "but at the moment I am asking myself if I would not be better dead."

"While there is . . life there is . . hope," Delora said softly, "and because I believe not only in prayer . . but that God is merciful . . I still have . . hope."

Conrad drew in his breath.

"My precious, has there ever been anyone as perfect as you?"

"Or as brave and wonderful as you?" she replied.

She told him how first the officers, then almost every member of the crew, had come the first night after the battle to the cabin to ask how he was and re-assure themselves that he was still alive.

"So many of them said they could not lose you because there had never been a Captain like you."

There was a pause before Delora went on:

"It was not only because they admire you for your bravery and your victories, but because you are kind and treat them as men rather than animals."

She knew her words pleased Conrad and because he wanted to hear about his men, she told him little bits of gossip to keep him amused.

"If only we had better food to give him!" Abigail grumbled, as she stewed the salted beef until it could be made into a broth, and ransacked the ship's stores for anything she thought would give Conrad more strength.

She refused to allow him to be bled as was usual, when he had a fever, and the Surgeon had gone about muttering that the Captain's days were numbered.

One man had died while his arm was being amputated and another who had his foot removed because of a splinter which had inserted itself under the skin during the engagement, had died after three days of agony.

Delora refused to tell Conrad about it and warned both Deakin and Barnet not to do so.

"It will only upset him," she said, "and he will feel guilty that we saved his leg while we were unable to stop the Surgeon from doing his worst on those other wretched men."

"It is always taken for granted that a man who has been wounded must lose the limb that is injured, there being no other way of keeping him alive," Commander Deakin said.

"There are other ways, as you see now," Delora replied, "and perhaps when Conrad returns to England he will be able to show himself to the Admiralty as an example of what can be done if only we had a little more knowledge."

"I doubt if anyone in the Admiralty would listen," Deakin said grimly. "They hate new ideas and innovations. If we could find somebody to speak about it in Parliament, that would be a different thing."

"I am sure Conrad would know somebody," Delora said confidently.

She wondered as she spoke, whether there would be any use asking her brother to support such a contention in the House of Lords.

Then when she remembered Denzil's utter indifference to anything which did not concern his own comfort or amusement she knew what a foolish idea it was.

"In a few days I shall see him," she thought.

The idea was so horrifying that the moment it was possible, she ran to the Captain's cabin, determined not to waste a minute of time when she might be with Conrad.

Abigail and Barnet had just finished dressing his leg and he was lying back against the pillows rather white-faced, his lips set in a hard line.

As Delora came towards him looking like spring itself he smiled at her and forgot his own sufferings.

"Did you sleep well?" she asked.

"I lay and thought about you," he replied.

Barnet and Abigail had left the cabin, to dispose of the soiled dressings and to fetch Conrad a cup of tea.

"It is going to be hot today," Delora said. "Shall we carry you up on deck so that you can be in the sunshine?"

Conrad considered for a moment, then he said:

"I think Abigail will insist that I rest as much as possible because when we dock I must go ashore."

"Where . . will you . . stay?"

It was the first time they had discussed what they would do once they had arrived and he heard the fear in Delora's voice.

"I hope I shall be able to stay in Admiral Nelson's house which is by the edge of the dockyard."

There was a little pause, then Delora asked in a very small voice:

"And how . . far away will . . I be?"

Conrad took both her hands in his.

"I do not know, my precious," he said. "Government House is at St. John's, several miles away. But there is another house which stands on a hill just above the dockyard."

He saw Delora's eyes looking at him intently, and he went on:

"It is called Clarence House, and it was built in 1787 for Prince William, Duke of Clarence. He lived in Antigua when he commanded the *Pegasus*."

"You think I might stay there?"

"It is only an idea I had because somebody told me the Governor used it as a country house, and I think it unlikely that you will move into Government House until you are actually married."

At the last word Delora gave a little cry and bent her head so that her forehead was resting against Conrad's hands as he covered hers.

"How . . can I . . bear it? How can I . . marry anyone but . . you?"

He could hardly hear the words as they tumbled from her lips and yet he knew only too well what she was saying.

His fingers tightened until hers were bloodless, and though he desperately wanted to comfort her, he knew there was nothing he could say, nothing he could do.

Then as they heard the door open and Abigail come back into the cabin, Delora sprang to her feet and walked to a port-hole so that she could hide her tears.

*

A week later they had their last dinner together by candlelight as they had dined the first evening when they had been alone.

The menu was a very different one, but it would not have mattered if they had been served ambrosia and nectar because they could think of nothing but themselves and their love.

Either Conrad or Delora would start to speak, then as their eyes met, the words would die away and they could only look at each other as heart spoke to heart and soul to soul.

"You will not . . forget me?" Delora asked later when the food had been taken away.

As soon as it had gone she sat beside Conrad on the bed on his uninjured side and he put his arm around her so that she could lay her head against his shoulder.

He kissed her forehead but not her lips, and she knew that for the moment both of them were trying not to be too emotional for fear that their feelings would sweep away the last vestiges of control.

"You know that would be impossible," Conrad answered in a low voice. "You know too that wherever I am, even if there is a whole world between us, I shall feel that you are with me, guiding me, helping me and loving me as you are now."

"That is what . . I feel," Delora said, "but, darling, if only I could . . die I should be . . with you, then there would be no more problems."

There was something in the way she spoke which made Conrad say sharply:

"You told me that while there is life there is hope. So let us both believe that one day fate will be kind and we shall be together in this world."

She drew a little closer to him and he knew that she was thinking that Lord Grammell was an old man and perhaps they would not have to wait so very long.

But to Conrad it was an agony worse than anything he had endured from the wound in his leg, to wonder what would happen to Delora until Grammell died.

He had not been with her without realising how innocent she was not only of the world but the ways of men. She had no idea of the depths of depravity to which men like Grammell and her brother could sink in their search for what they called "pleasure."

The thought of her being shocked and appalled by what she would learn at the hands of these creatures turned Conrad into a would-be murderer, and he thought he should be man enough to destroy them both before they could hurt anyone as sensitive and spiritual as Delora.

He knew there was nothing he could say which could prepare her for the ordeal which lay ahead, and like her he could only pray for a miracle, but what it could be, he had not the slightest idea.

Delora stayed with Conrad until he knew that he must be unselfish and force her to rest.

"You must go to bed, my lovely darling," he said.

"Do you . . really want me to . . leave you?"

"You know I never want you to do that," he replied. "I want you with me always and for ever, but we have, both of us, to try and do what is right."

She turned very gently so as not to hurt him, and put her arms round his neck.

"I love you with all my heart, because I cannot . . help it," she said, "but I also love you with my mind and soul because you are everything that is wise, noble and good. Whatever happens to me, I shall try to behave as you would . . wish me to do, so that you will be . . proud of me."

She spoke so simply and sincerely that Conrad felt the tears prick his eyes.

He told himself it was because he was so weak from his wound, but he knew there was no other woman of his acquaintance, or perhaps in the world, who would behave so courageously at this particular moment.

He held her very close against him and when he kissed her it was not with the passion they had known so often before, but with a love that for the moment was not human, but wholly divine and sacred.

He felt her cling to him and knew that if he could die to save her he would do so.

At the same time he must live and somehow give her the inner strength he had always had himself so that she would not kill herself.

He was aware the idea was vaguely at the back of her mind and because he was afraid that would happen, he said:

"Believe, my darling, and pray. Pray that one day we shall find happiness and a new life together."

He felt her arms tighten around his neck and he went on:

"The darkest hour is always before the dawn, and that is what we are going through now. I have a feeling that we both know the dawn will come. Promise me that you will not allow yourself to despair but will go on believing."

"I believe . . in you," Delora answered. "Will you swear to me on everything you hold sacred that you believe we have a chance, a real chance of being together one day?"

Conrad was still for a moment, then he said:

"Sometimes when I have been in a battle in which all the odds have been stacked against me, when it seemed impossible for me not to be defeated and perhaps annihilated, I have known in a strange way that I cannot explain, that I shall be victorious."

"And . . you feel that now? You really . . feel it?" Delora enquired.

"I swear to you not only on all I hold sacred, but on you, who are more holy to me than anything else in Heaven or earth, that I know in my heart and in my mind that one day we will be together."

Delora gave a little cry.

"Oh, Conrad, darling, I will believe that too, and we will both pray that it may be soon!"

"Pray God let it be soon, very soon!" Conrad said quietly before he kissed her again.

CHAPTER SIX

THERE WAS very little wind and anyway Deakin did not press the *Invincible* during the night.

This was not only in consideration for his Captain's comfort, but also because he had not told Conrad how much damage had actually been done by the Privateers to the lower deck of the *Invincible*.

Damage to the lower decks of a ship was always dangerous because when she changed course or the sea was rough, it was easy to ship water.

They therefore sailed slowly through the smooth sea and in the morning Delora learned that they would dock about noon.

She went to see Conrad as soon as Abigail had finished dressing his wounds, and found him sitting up in bed while Barnet had already arranged what clothes he would wear on a chair.

She looked at them doubtfully and said:

"Are you wise to dress?"

"As far as I am able to do so," Conrad replied, "I intend to arrive in style."

He smiled as he spoke, but Delora knew he was serious in that he intended to show her brother and Lord Grammell that he had some authority although whether it would be any use as far as she was concerned, they neither of them had any idea.

She walked towards the bed and he put his hand out towards her, saying as he did so:

"You look very beautiful this morning, my darling."

She held onto him as if she was drowning in the despair of her own thoughts. Then she said:

"I have . . something to ask you."

"What is it, my precious?"

"Will you be as . . nice as possible to Denzil and . . try not to let him see your . . real feelings for him?"

Conrad was surprised but he questioned in a quiet voice:

"Why are you asking me to do this?"

"Because Abigail feels it is important that she should go on dressing your wound, and I do not want Denzil to refuse to allow her to do so."

"Do you think he might do that?"

Delora hesitated a moment before she said:

"You must know that he hates you!"

Conrad raised his eye-brows.

"I cannot conceive of any reason why he should do so, unless of course, you are referring to the family feud."

"There is a much more personal reason than that."

"I have no idea what it can be."

"Have you forgotten that you are the heir presumptive to the title until Denzil has a son?"

If she had intended to startle Conrad, she had certainly succeeded.

For a moment he stared at her incredulously. Then he asked:

"Is that the truth?"

"But of course it is!" Delora replied. "I thought you must be aware of it."

"I had not the slightest idea!" Conrad said. "To begin with, just as I did not know of your existence, I had no idea how many children your father had. He might have had six sons."

"He had an only son and he was one himself," Delora answered, "and so far Denzil's wife, Charlotte, who is a pleasant woman, has only three daughters."

She paused before she said in a low voice:

"She was very ill with the last one, and because Denzil was so angry with her because the baby was not a boy, the doctors insisted that she should have rest and quiet. That is one of the reasons why he came to Antigua."

Everything Conrad had heard about his Cousin Denzil made him dislike him more than he did already, but for Delora's sake he did not say so.

As he did not speak, after a moment she said:

"I want to be able to see you . . I must see you after we arrive . . so please . . Conrad, darling . . be nice to Denzil . . and we can only hope that he will make no objection to our meeting . . or to Abigail nursing you."

Because she did not want to worry him, she added quickly:

"Of course she has told Barnet exactly what to do if Denzil takes me away to another part of the island, but I am praying that we shall be in the house that you spoke of . . and . . near to . . you."

Conrad was not sure if this would be a joy or an agony.

He could only wait, as he knew Delora was waiting, apprehensively, for them to reach the dock-yard where he anticipated that Denzil would greet them.

While he was being dressed, Delora went up on deck and had her first glimpse of the heavily wooded islands.

As they sailed through a sea more blue than she had imagined any sea could be, she could see the green bays which Conrad had told her were all round the island with their white and gold sand beaches.

Because she was interested he had informed her that the trees were red and white cedars and mahogany, while along the shore coconut palms and mangoes grew.

As they drew nearer to the land she could see, as she expected, the flaming blooms of the red poinsettias and patches of other brilliant flowers that she had read about.

Then she had her first sight of what the First Lieutenant told her was called the English harbour with Nelson's Dock-yard and a fine building just above it, which she was to learn later, was Clarence House.

Only when the *Invincible* was letting down her anchor did Delora feel suddenly afraid of the man who was waiting for her on the shore, and felt her lips were dry with the fear she had almost forgotten during her last weeks of happiness.

Then as the seamen hurried about taking in the sails, she saw a boat put out from the shore and knew who would be in it.

She turned to one of the officers standing near her.

"Will you tell the Captain, Mr. Lloyd," she asked, "that I think the Earl of Scawthorn is approaching us?"

The Lieutenant sent a midshipman with the message, and just as the boat reached the ship and a rope-ladder was let down, Conrad was brought on deck.

He was carried in a chair which Barnet had made for him in which his legs were supported by a rest and covered with a rug.

He was wearing his uniform coat with his decorations, his China silk scarf was tied immaculately round his neck and his gold lace hat was on his dark head.

He looked almost well except that much of the tan had faded from his cheeks and his face was thinner from the amount of blood he had lost and also the pain he had endured.

Those who were close to him like Delora and Abigail were aware what a stupendous effort it had been to make himself ready to receive the man he loathed and despised.

Denzil was piped aboard, the Marines presented arms, the officers saluted, and Delora stepped forward to curtsy before Denzil kissed her cheek.

"So—you are here!"

There was something gloating, she thought, in the way he said the words, and she knew that his eyes with the deep lines of debauchery beneath them, were flicking over her, taking in every detail of her appearance, as if she was a horse he was putting up for a sale.

With an effort she said:

"Yes I am here . . but it has been a somewhat . . adventurous voyage."

"We had news yesterday that you had been in action," the Earl answered.

"The Captain will tell you about it," Delora said quickly. "I do not know whether you are aware, Denzil, but he is our cousin, Conrad Horn."

"So I have learned from an Admiralty communique which told me in which ship you were travelling."

Delora knew from the note in his voice that he had not been pleased at the information.

He walked across the deck to where Conrad was waiting for him.

"So we meet after many years of animosity, Cousin," Denzil said. "And I see that you are somewhat the worse for wear."

Delora drew in her breath at the jeering way in which he spoke, but Conrad put out his hand.

"Welcome aboard the *Invincible*! I can only regret I am not in the position to offer you any extensive hospitality."

"There is no necessity for that," the Earl replied. "You have brought me what you were asked to bring, and I imagined you would then be glad to return to the battle area off the coast of France."

"Apparently our enemies are to be found not only in European waters."

As Conrad spoke he saw there was an undoubted scowl on the Earl's forehead and there was a look in his eyes which instantly made him suspicious.

He had known that when Nelson was in Antigua he had found the Governor was far too lax in his treatment of the Americans who ever since, after the Declaration of Independence, were no longer entitled to the rights possessed by British citizens.

As Colonists they had enjoyed a very prosperous trade with the West Indies, and they could not see why now they should be debarred after they had become what was, to all intents and purposes, a foreign power.

Nelson had protested and acting as he saw fit, he had seized many of the American trading ships.

He had incurred so much displeasure that as he said himself: "I was persecuted from one island to another, so that I could not leave my ship."

Conrad had often thought that, when everybody applauded and recounted Nelson's physical courage, the moral courage he had displayed in the West Indies when he was in conflict with his Senior Officer showed him in a dazzling light unlit by cannon or thundering sails.

Nelson had won and the Governor having had his attention drawn to the Navigation Act, had finally been forced to take action.

Now Conrad was suspicious after what the First Lord had said that the new Privateers were ready to recompense in one way or another, a Governor who was prepared to turn a blind eye to their activities.

All this flashed through his mind, but he merely said blandly and disarmingly:

"I am afraid not only the *Invincible* needs some repairs but so do I."

"Then of course you must take things easy until you are completely well again," the Earl answered.

As he spoke Conrad thought he was pleased at the idea that if he was laid up he would certainly not be able to go snooping around, pushing his nose into places where he was not wanted.

"Cousin Conrad has been very ill indeed," Delora said quickly, "and I think we should find somewhere ashore where he can stay while the ship is being repaired."

"Yes, of course," Denzil agreed, as if he had just thought of it. "I imagine he will find the Admiral's House which is empty at the moment, the best place to accommodate him."

"I should be extremely grateful if that could be arranged," Conrad said, as he knew he was expected to say.

"I know Lord Grammell, who is at present in St. John's," Denzil said, "would wish me to make proper arrangements for you, and I will therefore take Delora ashore with me and inform them at the Admiral's House to expect you."

"That is exceedingly kind of you," Conrad replied, "and will you both be travelling to St. John's?"

He was aware as he spoke, that Delora drew in her breath.

"As it happens," the Earl answered, "the Governor has put Clarence House at my disposal, and I intend that my sister and I should stay there while we arrange her marriage."

Without looking at Delora, Conrad was aware of the relief in her eyes, and now the Earl, as if he had nothing more to say to the cousin he disliked, remarked sharply to his sister:

"We had best be going ashore. Your luggage can follow."

"Yes, of course," Delora said, "and would you wish that Abigail comes with us, or shall she follow later?"

"Abigail?" her brother repeated.

Then as if for the first time he was aware there should have been another woman aboard, he enquired:

"Where is Mrs. Melhuish? I ordered her to come with you."

"I have not had time to tell you, Denzil," Delora replied, "but Mrs. Melhuish died during the first battle we had in the Atlantic."

This was obviously something the Earl had not expected, and there was a momentary pause before he remarked:

"She always was a tiresome woman and I cannot imagine anything more inconvenient than for her to die at that particular moment."

"She could not . . help it," Delora murmured.

She was acutely conscious that the Lieutenants, as well as the Marines standing round them, were listening to their conversation, and she thought they would be shocked that her brother should speak in such an unfeeling manner about somebody who had died when she was merely doing her duty.

As if his mind was on something other than Mrs. Melhuish's death, the Earl said almost as if he spoke to himself:

"I suppose as you had Abigail with you, you were properly looked after?"

He shot a suspicious glance at Conrad as he spoke, who knowing exactly what he was thinking, wished that he could knock him down.

How dare anyone even imagine that if Delora was alone on the ship he or any other man would have taken advantage of her position?

Then even as he felt his anger rise, he knew this was the sort of behaviour that might be expected of Denzil and he was not likely to give any other man credit for being decent and chivalrous.

As if in answer to the unpleasantness of the Earl's suspicions, Abigail appeared at that moment on deck.

In her black dress with her plain bonnet and her greying hair she looked, Conrad thought, the embodiment of respectability and propriety.

She walked towards Denzil and dropped him a small curtsy.

"Good-day, M'Lord."

"I hope you have been looking after your mistress properly after the untimely death of Mrs. Melhuish," the Earl said sharply.

"Her Ladyship has been in my care, M'Lord, as she has been ever since she was born!" Abigail retorted.

It was an answer with which it was impossible for the Earl to find fault, and he walked away to the side of the ship saying as he did so:

"Come along! There is no point in wasting time here when there is a great deal to do ashore."

Delora ignored the urgency in his tone. She curtsied to Conrad and held out her hand.

"Thank you for all your kindness," she said, "and for the very happy time I have had in this magnificent ship which has proved herself worthy of her name."

It was difficult to say the words she had rehearsed to herself before she left her cabin, and only as she finished did she raise her eyes to Conrad's and feel her heart turn over in her breast.

Then she shook hands with the First Lieutenant who had joined them on deck and all the Lieutenants.

Only when she had finished and heard her brother shout at her from the boat below, did she turn back to Mr. Deakin to say:

"You will be very careful how you take him ashore? His wounds must not start bleeding again."

"I promise you we will look after him," he replied.

Then at another shout from the Earl she hurriedly climbed down into the boat and a moment later it was pulling away from the ship.

*

Clarence House was not a large building but a very attractive one, set on the hill which overlooked the dock-yard.

It was different from any house that Delora had ever been in before and the view over the green bays and sea was breath-taking.

She was concerned at the moment only with what plans her brother had for her, and he did not delay in telling her what they were.

"I have sent a message to the Governor to tell him of your arrival," he said when she joined him in the comfortable Drawing-Room. "He will undoubtedly arrive this evening to stay here. That is why I have given you the small bed-room for the present. You will share the largest one with him as soon as you are married."

Delora felt the colour rise in her cheeks and her brother went on:

"I was not quite certain of the actual day of your arrival, but there is no point in delaying your wedding. The sooner we can send evidence of it to those damned Trustees in New York, the quicker they will be forced to hand over your money."

"Why do you need it so badly?" Delora asked. "I always thought Papa was a very rich man."

"He was!" Denzil replied, "but things have become much more expensive since the war."

She knew as he spoke, that was not the real reason why he needed money, and she was sure that it was his wild extravagances that had brought him to the point where he must "sell" his own sister to replenish his pockets.

But there was no point in saying so and making him disagreeable, so she merely said:

"As you know, Denzil, I have no wish to marry a man I have never seen. I think it would be wise if Lord Grammell and I got to know each other, before our marriage takes place."

Denzil poured himself another drink from the decanter that was standing beside his chair.

"Grammell knows all about you he wishes to know," he replied, "and that is that you are rich! It is damned expensive being a Governor, even in an out-of-the-way hole like this, although I dare say you will enjoy the power it will give you, once you are his wife."

"Lord Grammell may know all he wishes to know about me," Delora said, "but I know nothing about him, except that he is a very old man."

"Are you making difficulties?" Denzil asked aggressively. "Well, let me make this clear to you, Delora—you will marry who I tell you to marry and when I tell you to do so. If not, I will make things so unpleasant that you will rue the day you were ever born!"

He spoke so ferociously that without being aware of it, she took a step further away from him.

She had forgotten when she had been with Conrad, how frightening her brother could be, and she thought now, as he glared at her with his eyes too close together, that there was something about him which made her feel that he was not quite sane.

"I suppose," he went on, "because you have been flaunting yourself about on a ship before all those men, you have got new ideas of getting your own way. Well, let me make this clear, you will do what I say or I will beat you into submission! You are a damned lucky girl to have the chance of marrying a Governor whatever he may be like, and you will show your gratitude by being pleasant to him."

Denzil shouted the last words at her, then swallowed the wine that was in his glass, in one gulp before he went on, working himself up into a rage that she thought was even worse than those with which he had frightened her in the past.

"How dare you argue with me!" he stormed. "How dare you discuss—suggest—you—an unfledged chick with no knowledge of the world—to whom you should or should not be married! It is I who will decide those things for you, and all you have to do is to obey me. And make no mistake, I intend to be obeyed! Do you hear?"

He roared the question at her and as if she could bear no more,

Delora turned and ran from the room back to the bedroom where she had left her bonnet when she first arrived.

As she rushed she found to her relief that Abigail was there. She flung herself against the old maid, holding onto her, as she said:

"Oh, Abigail . . thank God you . . are here!" and burst into tears.

*

It was after an uncomfortable luncheon, with Denzil grumbling and finding fault with the food which Delora found delicious after the restricted rations in the ship, that she went to lie down. When she did so, Abigail said:

"His Lordship will expect you to rest for at least two hours, M'Lady, as I hear he does himself. I'm going to slip down to the Admiral's House to see how the Captain is."

"Oh, Abigail, can you do that?" Delora cried. "I intended to ask His Lordship if you might continue to look after the Captain, but he never gave me a chance, and I know, because he is angry with me, he would not agree to any suggestion I might make. In fact, he would be glad to refuse me."

"Now don't you worry, M'Lady," Abigail said. "It's best to say nothing to His Lordship. You've upset yourself enough as it is, and if the Captain heard about it, he'd be worried about you."

"Do not tell him . . please do not tell him!" Delora begged. "There is nothing he can do . . and I do not wish him to quarrel with His Lordship."

"I'll say nothing," Abigail promised, and Delora knew she understood.

She felt as Abigail left her, that the old maid was the only thing left in her life which was solid and secure.

When two hours later Abigail came into her room, she sat up eagerly in her bed to ask:

"How is he?"

"He's a brave gentleman," Abigail replied in a low voice. "I've made him comfortable and his wounds, believe it or not, are better than I dared to hope they would be."

"Oh, Abigail, I am so thankful!" Delora cried.

"Of course, the Captain was asking about you, M'Lady."

"What did you tell him?"

"I told him you were being very brave."

"Did he ask . . when I was to be . . married?"

"I couldn't tell him what I didn't know myself."

Abigail busied herself getting Delora dressed in one of her pretty summer gowns, thinking as she did so, she had never known a gentleman suffer so intensely as the Captain, not physically, but mentally.

"It's a pity," Abigail told herself, "they can't be man and wife as nature intended."

She knew that to say such things would not help either Conrad or Delora whom she had worshipped ever since she was a baby.

"Look after her," Conrad had said, "and if it is humanly possible, help her to bear what lies ahead of her."

Abigail had heard the agony in his voice and knew he was thinking of what marriage to a man like Lord Grammell would mean.

Even in the short time he had been at the Admiral's House people had talked to Conrad of the excesses and the outrageous behaviour of the Governor.

Other English Captains with ships in the harbour as well as officials in charge of the dock-yard had called at the Admiral's House as soon as Conrad had been brought ashore.

Deakin had entertained them while Barnet said fiercely that the Captain had done enough for one day and in fact, no-one was going to talk to him until he was stretched out in bed, which was a place he should never have left anyway.

It was only reluctantly, after Conrad in defiance of his usual very abstemious habits had drunk a glass of claret, that Barnet allowed his visitors, one by one, to have a few minutes with him.

The first was the Commander of a Brig who had got passed over in seniority even though he was older than Conrad. They had known each other for some years.

"It is good to see you, Horn, and your reputation has preceded you. There is not a crew that comes out to this island which is not talking about you and your exploits. Nelson himself was not admired more."

"You are making me embarrassed," Conrad protested, "but I am glad to see you, Forester. How long have you been here?"

"Nearly two months," Commander Forester replied. "My ship was practically sunk by a Privateer, but I was saved by an English ship which towed us into port. It will be another month at least before I can get to sea again."

"In the meantime it is a pleasant island in which to have a holiday," Conrad remarked.

"It could be, if it were not for the Governor!"

"Surely he does not interfere with you, or the dock-yard for that matter?"

"No, but I will tell you something that will make your hair stand on end. . . !" Commander Forester replied.

What he related made Conrad feel physically sick, not only with revulsion, but in fear for Delora.

When his other visitors told him almost the same thing with various elaborations, he swore that somehow, but God knew how, he must save her, but he had no idea how he could do so.

That night he cursed his wounds for making him immobile, and yet at the same time he could not help being aware that if the *Invincible* or himself had not been wounded he might at this very moment, be making ready to sail away without realising the unbearable conditions in which he was leaving Delora.

*

His Excellency the Governor of Antigua, the Right Honourable Lord Grammell, arrived at Clarence House at five o'clock that afternoon.

He came there from St. John's in an open carriage drawn by four horses and escorted by a troop of Cavalry.

He ignored the surly looks that he received as he drove along the beautiful road bordered on each side by trees and flowers, nor did he notice the exquisite view that was visible from every incline the horses reached or the red blossoms of the Flameboyant which were a vivid contrast to the verdant green of the other trees.

He was, in fact, thinking with satisfaction of the amount of money he would receive on his marriage to the Earl of Scawthorn's sister.

"A good chap, Scawthorn!" he told himself with satisfaction. "Since he has been here he has doubled the rate those Yankees have to pay me for trading on the island."

The sun was still warm and as he neared Clarence House Lord Grammell thought of the wine that would be waiting for him.

He could never go for long without a drink, and he took the precaution of ensuring that every Captain who wished to ask him a favour brought with him a case of wine as an introductory opening to their conversation.

His escort turned in at the drive of Clarence House and the carriage came to a stop outside the stone steps which led up to the front door.

Lord Grammell negotiated the steps with difficulty owing to the fact that in the hot climate he took no exercise and his weight had increased since his arrival in Antigua.

He was panting as the sentries came to attention and he passed them without making any acknowledgement of their presence.

Denzil was waiting for him in the cool of the hall.

"It is good to see Your Excellency," he said formally because he knew His Lordship enjoyed all the traditional pomp of his position.

"She has arrived—good! I was waiting for your message," Lord Grammell said.

"And looking forward to meeting Your Lordship," Denzil replied suavely.

As they entered the Drawing-Room the Governor said:

"You have told her we are to be married at once?"

"Yes, of course," Denzil replied.

He held out a large glass of wine as he spoke, which Lord Grammell took from him and drank thirstily. Then he lowered himself carefully into an arm-chair and asked:

"What is all this I hear about a new two-decker in the harbour? And the Captain injured?"

"I expect you have been told he is a cousin of mine," Denzil replied. "Tiresome chap! It is a pity he was not killed!"

"Tiresome? Why tiresome?" the Governor's voice was sharp.

"It is all right," Denzil replied. "He is wounded and will be confined to a chair for some time."

"Thank God for that!"

"I was thinking," the Earl said, "it would be wise to be pleasant to him, not that it does not go against the grain to have to do so."

"Why do you think that is necessary?"

"Well, he is inclined to be an interfering fellow like Nelson. You remember the trouble they had here with him?"

"I do because the damned idiots on this island never stop croaking about it," the Governor said savagely.

Then in another tone of voice he asked:

"You really think this cousin of yours will make trouble?"

"He will if he gets to know too much. What I suggest is that we make ourselves agreeable."

"In what way?"

"By sending him presents of wine, entertaining him to dinner if he is well enough. Anything to keep him from being nosey."

The Governor thought for a moment, then he said:

"You are right! Of course you are right! I will leave all the arrangements to you. And now let me see this little filly you have told me about."

*

Delora had been sitting in her bedroom with Abigail waiting for the summons that she knew would come soon after she had heard the Governor arrive.

There was no need to tell the old maid she was frightened, and when a servant knocked on the door to inform her that her presence was required in the Drawing-Room, she gave a little cry that was almost inaudible, and yet to Abigail it was a scream for help.

"Now you behave as the Captain expects you to, M'Lady," she said.

She knew she could not say anything that was more likely to give Delora the courage to face the man who was waiting for her.

She saw her chin go up and knew that her beauty would appeal to any man, even to one about whom Abigail had already heard so much that she too felt like screaming.

Delora went through the door with her shoulders back and when she entered the Drawing-Room, while she felt everything was swimming before her eyes, she appeared quite composed, although her face was very pale.

Both Denzil and the Governor were sprawling in arm-chairs with glasses in their hands, and as Delora came into the room there was a perceptible pause before either of them moved.

Then with an effort Lord Grammell struggled to his feet and Denzil followed him.

"Present her!" he said almost sharply to Denzil, who his sister realised, was drunk, but making an effort to oblige.

"Lemme pres-ent, Your Exshellency," he said, slurring his words, "my sister, Lady Delora Horn, who's delighted—yes, delighted, to make your acquaintance."

Delora curtsied, then as she raised her head, it was only her breeding and the thought of what Conrad expected of her that prevented her from crying out aloud.

Never, she thought, had she seen a more repulsive man in her whole life.

His huge red and bloated face, a body puffed out and swollen with disease, a bulbous nose and thick sensuous lips made Lord Grammell look in appearance the monster he actually was.

His head was bald and the fat hand he outstretched towards Delora felt wet and sticky with the heat.

"My bride-to-be!" he announced in a thick voice. "Welcome to Antigua, pretty lady! We will deal well together, you and I!"

His sharp eyes half-hidden by rolls of flesh seemed to Delora to look not only at her face but at her body, and she felt almost as if he undressed her.

Then as if with an effort at gallantry he raised her hand to his lips, and as she felt them touch her skin it was as if she shrank from the proximity of a reptile, and one that was so poisonous that her instinct was to run away.

But she stayed her ground, her eyes very large in her face. Then having inspected her again, the Governor said:

"Sit down, sit down! You must tell me about yourself and your voyage here. Have a glass of wine."

"N-no . . thank you," Delora managed to say, thinking even to herself that her voice sounded strange.

"Nonsense!" the Governor replied. "You need a drink! We all need a drink! What do you say, Scawthorn?"

"Of course!" the Earl replied.

He clapped his hands together, the door opened instantly and a servant came into the room.

He was a black man and elderly, and Delora suspected he had been at Clarence House for many years.

"Wine!" Denzil ordered briefly. "Why the devil are you so slow with it?"

"It's here, M'Lord," the servant replied as another man came into the room carrying a bottle wrapped in a white napkin.

"Fill up His Excellency's glass!" Denzil ordered, "and bring another one for Her Ladyship."

The glass appeared, the wine was poured into it and Delora held it, not liking to refuse to drink it, but knowing she did not need it and feeling somehow that if she drank with these two men who had already had too much, she would become like them.

"I hear you were engaged in a battle on your way here," the Governor said.

"Yes . . My Lord . . but one of the Privateers that was preying on four merchantmen was sunk . . and the other has been taken as a prize."

"A Privateer sunk? Why was I not told of this?" Lord Grammell asked angrily.

He looked across at Denzil as he spoke and as if he realised that the information his sister had imparted was important he sat forward in his chair.

"Who sunk a Privateer?" he asked in drunken stupidity.

"The *Invincible* of course," Delora replied, "although they were very large ships, new and with better guns than anything the First Lieutenant had ever seen before."

"And you say one was taken as a prize?" the Governor asked.

"Yes, Your Excellency. A crew from the *Invincible* was put aboard and she was sent back to England."

"You are noting that, I suppose, Scawthorn?" Lord Grammell said.

"There is nothing we can do," Denzil replied.

"No, but it is unfortunate. I suppose the *Invincible* is bigger than anything we have had in these waters for a long time."

"Much bigger," Denzil agreed, "and swifter!"

The Governor made an exasperated sound and sat back in his chair.

Delora looked from one to the other in perplexity.

She did not understand, but she felt perceptibly that what they had said was important and she must tell Conrad about it.

Then she wondered frantically, desperately, if there would be any chance of her seeing him, and if so—when?

Aloud she broke the silence by asking tentatively and in a very small voice:

"W-will Your . . Excellency tell me . . when you were . . anticipating we should be . . m-married?"

"This is delicious, Barnet!" Conrad said, sipping from the long glass that he had just been handed.

"It's mango juice, Sir."

"Then I could drink a bucketful of it."

Sitting on the terrace outside the house with the sea lapping only a few feet from him and the sun shining through the leaves of the big trees, Conrad felt a surge of well-being sweep over him.

He knew it was due not only to the fruit, vegetables and fresh food he had eaten since he had arrived, but also that Abigail had been satisfied with his wounds when she had dressed them very early this morning.

She had crept out of Clarence House before anyone was awake and when she took off the old dressings she had exclaimed with pleasure when she saw how cleanly the flesh was healing and that the inflammation had gone.

"You are a good nurse, Abigail," Conrad said.

"And you're a strong man, Sir," Abigail replied. "Another without your strength would have taken far longer to heal."

Then as if she had been too encouraging she said quickly:

"Now don't you go doing anything stupid, Sir. There's Her Ladyship worrying herself sick about you and the best you can do for her is to take things easy."

"That is rather difficult at the moment."

Conrad knew he did not have to elaborate to Abigail what he was feeling, and as if she knew what he wanted to ask her without having to put it into words, she said:

"His Lordship's intent on the wedding taking place in a few days."

"What does Lady Delora say to that?" Conrad asked harshly.

"What can she say?" Abigail replied. "She's always been frightened of His Lordship ever since she was a small child, and when he gets into one of his rages it's no use talking to him. He won't listen!"

She could feel the tension in Conrad's body as he wondered despairingly what he could do to help Delora or at least prevent this monstrous marriage from taking place.

Then because they were not questions he could ask Abigail he enquired:

"What is Her Ladyship doing today?"

"I think, Sir, she'll have a headache after being so long at sea, and we've already planned that I'll tell His Lordship after breakfast that she requires rest and quiet."

Conrad gave a sigh of relief.

"That is wise."

Yet he knew that if it did not suit his Cousin Denzil he would not allow Delora to rest but would force her to see Grammell and make herself pleasant, if that was what the Governor required.

Abigail had finished his dressings and she gave Barnet instructions as to what was to be done that evening if she could not get away to tend to Conrad herself.

"The Captain's to have plenty of fruit-juice," she said. "That's what he needs after a voyage where everything began to taste like ashes in our mouths!"

Conrad laughed.

"You are not very complimentary, Abigail. We did our best on the *Invincible*."

"I'm not saying, Sir, that you weren't obliging, and so were them as served under you, but I know what your body needs now, and it's up to Mr. Barnet to see that you gets it."

"I am sure Barnet will do that," Conrad smiled, and Barnet had been bringing him glasses of fruit-juice all the morning.

Because Conrad loathed being in bed and also wished to discipline himself by getting onto his feet as quickly as possible, he insisted on being partially dressed and taken outside on the terrace so that he could not only be in the sunshine, but look at the sea.

The house which Nelson had occupied when he was in Antigua was very attractive with long French windows opening out of every room on the ground floor.

There was a terrace which was shadowed with cedar trees while huge clumps of hibiscus and poinsettia were patches of colour that somehow reminded Conrad of Delora.

He was sitting reading the newspapers, which were a month old but which he still found interesting, when he heard a carriage draw up outside.

With a little sigh he thought that more visitors had called to see him and he had hoped, after the crowd there had been yesterday, that he would have a little respite.

Then as he heard footsteps coming from the house he turned his head and to his surprise he saw a grossly fat man who he knew without being told, was the Governor, and behind him Denzil.

"His Excellency the Governor, Sir!" Barnet announced, "and the Earl of Scawthorn!"

Conrad forced a smile to his lips.

"You must forgive me, Your Excellency, for being unable to rise and greet you."

"No, no, of course not," Lord Grammell replied. "You must not exert yourself, but your cousin and I thought we should call and enquire after your well-being."

"That is exceedingly gracious of you, My Lord," Conrad replied politely. "Good-morning, Denzil."

"Good-morning, Conrad! I am delighted to see you in better health than I expected."

"I am better, but it will take time," Conrad replied.

"Of course, of course!" the Governor exclaimed. "One cannot hurry nature. You must take things easily, Horn, like these damned niggers manage to do. They never exert themselves in the heat—they make sure of that!"

Conrad was not obliged to reply because Barnet, without being told, came from the house followed by a servant carrying a tray with glasses and drinks.

He had not thought that anyone would wish to drink wine so early in the morning, but the Governor apparently had no qualms about doing so while Denzil preferred rum.

They sat talking and Conrad had the impression that the Governor was anxious for the *Invincible* not to be repaired too quickly.

"You will find things very slow here," he said in his thick voice. "However much you take a whip to the niggers they will not work. I get complaints all the time about their indolence, but what can I do about it?"

"What indeed?" Conrad echoed as he had no wish to make himself disagreeable.

At the same time he thought it would be impossible for any man to look so revoltingly debauched, so gross and unpleasant.

The Governor drank three glasses of wine before he came to what Conrad was sure was the point of his visit.

"Now listen, Horn," he said, "your cousin and I have a treat in store for you this afternoon, something I do not suppose you have seen before, even with your vast experience of visits to ports all over the world."

"What is it?" Conrad enquired.

Lord Grammell put his finger up to his bulbous nose.

"That would be telling!" he said. "It shall be a surprise! If you do not feel well enough to see it this afternoon, we could postpone it until tomorrow."

"I feel well enough to do anything unless I have to travel any great distance," Conrad answered.

"There is no question of that," the Governor said. "Where we are taking you is only a hundred yards or so from here. My men will carry you in the chair you are sitting in now."

"You are making me curious, Your Excellency."

"It will give you something to think about until we collect you at four o'clock," the Governor said. "In this climate we all need a *siesta* after luncheon. Is that not so, Scawthorn?"

"Yes, indeed," Denzil replied. "You will find, Cousin, the place is like the dead between two and four."

"A good way of describing it. Like the dead! Oh, well, that is what one person will be today anyway."

He laughed again and Conrad wondered what he was talking about.

Then when his visitors had gone he wondered where they could be taking him and what he had to see.

He was puzzled by the Governor's remark about one person being dead, but could hardly imagine it would apply to himself.

At the same time, he was extremely suspicious at these overtures of friendship that were being made to him not only by the Governor but also by his Cousin.

He had not forgotten that Delora had said that Denzil hated him because he was his heir.

Even so, he could hardly imagine that they were plotting to murder him, although he had learned by this time they had plenty of good reasons for doing so.

The Captains of the other ships in the dock-yard and the Naval Personnel living in Antigua had made it perfectly clear in one way or another what they suspected the Governor was doing.

They also said how ashamed they felt of his behaviour when the British were at war with the French.

Only the decisive defeat of Napoleon could bring peace to a world that was heartily sick of battles, and death, privation and suffering.

"Once you get the *Invincible* back to sea, Captain," an officer had said, "then you will have the chance of clearing up much of the treachery that is taking place around these shores. It prevents food from reaching England which I believe is vitally needed."

"It is indeed!" Conrad replied.

His visitor had dropped his voice even lower than it was already.

"They say because the English cannot pay the Governor as much as he wants they are not given the best stores when they come here to replenish their ships. In fact, they are often sent away without enough meat for the voyage ahead of them."

Conrad felt his anger rising knowing that it was very easy for the Governor to say there were not enough cattle, sheep and pigs for a ship's requirements.

But if it sailed with empty holds, the men who were manning it suffered quite unnecessarily, once they were at sea, to the detriment not only of their health, but of discipline and fighting ability.

Having seen Grammell he realised how much he had deteriorated physically in the years that had passed since they had met at a Board of Enquiry. He could believe every story that was told about him, and a great many more besides.

Yet he told himself that for Delora's sake he must not antagonise either the Governor or Denzil, and he hoped by agreeing to anything they suggested that he would perhaps be asked to Clarence House where he could see her if only across a dining-room table.

The mere thought of her having even to talk to this monster, let

alone do anything else, made him clench his hands together and long
to hit something.

Then there was Barnet's voice announcing another visitor who
came eagerly from the house with an outstretched hand to greet him.

*

Surprisingly, after a good luncheon Conrad slept during the *siesta*.

He had expected to lie awake thinking of Delora. But he was more
tired than he had realised, and when Barnet woke him he felt
refreshed and knew that whatever the condition of his leg, his mind
was alert and active.

"What I want to discover," he told himself, "is exactly what
Grammell and Denzil are up to."

He had already thought of ways by which he could send a secret
report to the Admiralty if he found, as Nelson had done, that they
were breaking the British Navigation Act.

He knew the difficulties of enforcing laws made in England when
they were so far away, but it had been strictly laid down that "the
function of His Majesty's Ships of War was to protect the commerce
of the nation," which in its turn meant ensuring that foreigners did
not trade in areas where they were forbidden.

"I must manage to stop the Privateers somehow," Conrad thought
optimistically, "but with the Governor encouraging them and taking
bribes from them, it is not going to be easy."

He hoped his feelings towards Lord Grammell did not show when
a little after four o'clock the open carriage in which he and Denzil
were driving accompanied by their usual escort of Cavalry clattered
up to the front door of the Admiral's House.

Denzil informed Barnet that they were driving on a little way
down the road to the prison and four soldiers had been given orders
to carry Captain Horn there.

When Conrad heard where he was being taken he was surprised,
but he said nothing and putting his cocked hat on his head, he allowed the soldiers to lift him.

Barnet, fussing like an anxious hen, gave them incessant instructions as to how careful they were to be, especially in carrying the
support on which his leg rested.

He walked beside the chair, watching anxiously every step while

Conrad looked about him interested to see how Antigua had altered since he had last been in these waters nearly fifteen years ago.

The prison was a small building which in peacetime did not have many inmates.

It was built surrounding a court-yard in the middle where he was carried to find the Governor and Denzil already there, seated on a platform against one side of it, which had an iron railing in front of it.

On Denzil's instructions the soldiers set Conrad down on the platform beside them, and while they did so, the Governor was in deep conversation with a man whose uniform proclaimed him to be a Prison officer.

Beside the soldiers who had carried Conrad, there were four others armed with muskets standing on either side of the platform.

As Conrad stared out onto a patch of beaten-down sand he wondered what exactly was about to happen.

Then suddenly there was the baying of bloodhounds and when the heavy doors on the other side of the court-yard were opened Conrad could see six large dogs all jumping about behind iron bars.

He remembered he had heard that in the Southern States of America plantation-owners hunted any slaves who had tried to escape, with bloodhounds.

He could not believe that on an island the size of Antigua this was necessary, because if a slave ran away, where would he run to?

At the same time, the presence of the dogs made him uneasy and he looked at the Governor as if for an explanation.

His Lordship, having finished his conversation, turned his head.

"Those are my dogs, Horn," he said. "I brought them with me from England. They have given me a lot of sport one way or another, but I am getting too old now to follow them on a horse. However, they can still provide me with some amusement, and that is what you are going to see this afternoon."

"See what?" Conrad asked.

Before the Governor could reply the prison-officers brought into the centre of the court-yard a negro heavily chained.

He was an enormous man, over six foot tall, with a magnificent body with highly developed muscles that made him look like a young Samson.

He was chained not only around his wrists but also his ankles. As he proceeded further Conrad could see that he had been flogged until his back was criss-crossed with weals, most of them raw and bleeding.

"You see that man?" the Governor asked. "The strongest creature I have seen in my life! He can lift a tree out of the ground and smash it across his knees!"

"What crime has he committed?" Conrad asked.

"Oh, the usual ones," the Governor replied blandly, "disobedience, fighting and whoring. Well, those are things he will not do again!"

"Why not?"

Already Conrad felt a cold suspicion of what was going to occur.

"Flogging has only made him more defiant than he was already," the Governor replied, "and so he is going to be taught a lesson that he will not forget because he will not be alive to do so."

Conrad drew in his breath.

"My little pets," the Governor continued, mouthing the words above the baying of the dogs, "have not been fed for forty-eight hours. They are hungry, Horn, and hungry animals can be very ferocious!"

Conrad felt the words of protest come to his lips, but he had lost the Governor's attention for Denzil was saying something on the other side of him.

"Yes, yes, of course," Lord Grammell said, rising to his feet.

Then when both he and Denzil were standing he said to Conrad:

"Your cousin suggests we have a closer look at this man's muscles. They are amazing—absolutely amazing! He ought really to be stuffed and put into a Museum!"

Lord Grammell walked down from the platform as he spoke and a soldier opened a door in the iron railing which Conrad realised now was a protection against the dogs.

There was nothing he could do, but sit on the platform, tense and with tight lips and watch while the Governor and his cousin walked up to the huge negro who was standing quite still, staring at the bloodhounds.

As the Governor moved, two soldiers with muskets in their hands

walked after him and as they stood to one side, Conrad could see by
the expressions on their faces, they were admiring the negro in the
same way that their master was doing.

Lord Grammell and Denzil were laughing together. Then the Governor gave an order and the chains were unlocked and taken away
first from the negro's feet, then from his arms.

He was told to throw out the latter, then bring them in slowly so
that the huge biceps above the elbow swelled in a manner that was
quite remarkable.

Denzil said something which was undoubtedly obscene and the
Governor laughed uproariously.

Conrad thought, watching the two men, that the expression on
their faces was so revolting that it was even worse than the torture
they envisaged for the man towering over them.

He was wondering what would happen if he shouted out that the
whole idea was an outrage and something to which no man, black or
white, should be subjected, in a civilised world.

Then as he felt that even for Delora's sake he would not be able to
control the words which were rising to his lips, the negro made a
sudden movement.

On the Governor's orders he had stretched out his arms once again
so that he could bend them in slowly, making his muscles rise as he
did so.

Then unexpectedly with a swiftness which was extraordinary in so
large a man, he brought his arms back and as he did so, he reached
out and clasped his great hands around the throats of the two men
taunting him.

The movement was so quick that before Conrad or anyone else
could grasp what had happened, he had bashed the Governor's and
Denzil's faces against each other, not once but half-a-dozen times.

There was the sound of flesh slapping against flesh, of bones
breaking while the force of the negro's movements made the blood
spurt out over his victims' and his own body.

Then after what seemed an interminable time the bemused soldiers
raised their muskets and shot the negro in the back. He fell forward
crushing the bodies of his torturers beneath him.

His fingers were so firmly locked around their throats that it was
to take several men a long time to force them apart. . .

*

Conrad signed the paper that lay in front of him and having sealed it with a wafer, handed it to the Naval Officer standing at his side.

"You will, Commander Beemish, carry this to the First Lord," Conrad said, "and inform His Lordship that I would be most grateful if he would convey its contents to the Foreign Secretary, Viscount Castlereagh."

"I will carry out your orders, My Lord," Commander Beemish replied. "My ambition is to reach England in under twenty days."

"With the new American frigate you captured yesterday I have no doubt you will succeed," Conrad replied with a smile.

Commander Beemish grinned.

"It is very fortunate, My Lord, that she came into St. John's harbour at just the right moment, having of course, no expectation that the Governor was dead."

"Of course not," Conrad agreed. "At the same time, I have learned from the prisoners you took captive, that they have sunk or captured no less than six of our merchantmen in the last month!"

His voice was serious as he said:

"You know as well as I do, Beemish, that cannot be allowed to continue."

"No, of course not, My Lord."

"I have written fully to the First Lord telling him of the situation here," Conrad said, "and so that you shall be aware of what the report contains, I will tell you that I have been requested by the authorities in St. John's and by the Naval Personnel on Antigua, to act as Governor until a replacement for Lord Grammell can be sent from England."

"There is no need for them to be in a hurry," Commander Beemish replied. "When we heard you had agreed to do what was asked, every man in the dock-yard, including the crew of the *Invincible,* cheered themselves hoarse!"

"Thank you," Conrad said simply.

"And may I, My Lord," the Commander went on, "add my good wishes and say that I am as glad as everybody else that the nightmare is over."

Conrad was silent for a moment. Then he said:

"I think, Beemish, you will agree with me that in the best interests of Britain it would be wise not to say too much of what has been happening. They will have a pretty shrewd idea, but I can promise them that as long as I am here, things will be cleared up and rapidly!"

"We all of us know that, My Lord."

The Commander held out his hand and Conrad shook it.

"Good luck, Commander!" he said, "and I hope you enjoy your voyage. I only wish I was coming with you."

He spoke almost wistfully. Then as the Commander left, Barnet came in to say:

"There's another visitor waiting to see you, M'Lord!"

The way he spoke brought a light to Conrad's eyes, and without waiting to be announced, Delora came running into the room.

She hardly waited until Barnet had shut the door before her arms were around Conrad's neck and her cheek was against his.

"I thought you would never be free!" she said. "I am so jealous of all these people who take up so much of your time!"

"I am clearing the deck, my darling," Conrad answered, "so that when we get married in two days time, I shall be able to have a honeymoon with you alone, without suffering from a guilty conscience."

"Alone? Do you really mean alone?" Delora asked. "Can we do that?"

"Am I, or am I not, at the moment, the Governor of this island?" Conrad asked.

Delora gave a little chuckle before she replied:

"You have become very important all of a sudden and I think, now you are an Earl and also a Governor, I am going to miss the brave but otherwise unimportant Captain, whom I used to dine with alone on board the *Invincible*."

"I am important only because you love me," Conrad said, "and because although I can hardly believe it is true, you are going to be my wife!"

Delora gave a little cry.

"I, too, find it difficult to believe," she said. "Sometimes I wake up at night thinking the miracle has not happened, and I am to marry that horrible, ghastly old man!"

Conrad put his fingers against her lips.

"We agreed we would not talk about him," he said. "As the Commander has just told me, the nightmare is over. Not only is Antigua free, but so are we, and we must not waste our minds and thoughts dwelling on what is past."

"No, you are right," Delora agreed. "All I want to think about, darling, wonderful Conrad, is you!"

He smiled at her, realising as he did so, that she had a new loveliness because she was so happy, and because although it seemed incredible they could now be married, as they believed God had always meant them to be.

Conrad, in his usual decisive and authoritative way, had cut through all the red tape and the conventions that might have prevented their wedding taking place at what was certainly unprecedented speed.

One thing that had made it easy was that he had discovered that although it was known in England that he was taking Delora to Antigua to marry the Governor, it had not been announced on the island.

This made it easy for him to say that he and Delora had come to Antigua so that they could be married with the permission of her brother who was to have given her away.

The only thing that might have delayed their wedding was that Delora was in mourning, but he evaded criticism on this account by saying that it was imperative for her to be properly chaperoned.

The day after the Governor and Denzil had died, Conrad had arranged for Delora to stay with the wife of the Naval Officer in charge of the dock-yard.

She and Abigail had moved into their small house which was less than a hundred yards from where Conrad was.

Delora was so delighted at being nearer to him that she did not feel cramped, even though he was aware that her hosts were put to quite a lot of inconvenience to house her.

This provided another urgent reason why they should be married as quickly as possible, and he could think of no more attractive place for them to have a honeymoon, than at Clarence House.

Delora had already described to him how beautifully it was furnished, and he knew that in his new position of authority he could give the order that they were to receive no visitors and that those who insisted on seeing him should be turned away at the gates, and they could find the flower-filled garden, the waving palms and flowery trees a Paradise all their own.

Although his injured leg was still lifted high on a stool beneath the writing-desk, he was feeling so well and so strong, he no longer thought of himself as an invalid. Now he said to Delora teasingly:

"You are quite certain you want to marry me? You realise I have never asked you formally."

Delora gave a little laugh. Then she replied softly:

"I think actually I asked you! I know when Abigail came into my room to tell me that Denzil and the Governor were dead I exclaimed:

"'Now I can marry Conrad!'"

She bent forward as she spoke to kiss his cheek and he knew it was because she did not want him to see the tears of happiness that had welled up into her eyes.

There was no need to tell her that he had thought exactly the same thing, for he had no wish to speak of the horror of the mutilated blood-stained bodies lying in the court-yard of the prison or what they had looked like before they had been hastily buried that evening as was the custom in the tropics.

Now, as Delora had said shyly when she had come to see him the following day, all their dreams had come true.

"I suppose really," she said tentatively, "I ought to be worrying about your wounds and insisting on waiting until you are really well before I become your wife."

"Abigail has said that I am well enough to be married," Conrad answered, "and you know perfectly well that we cannot argue with her!"

"I do not want to do so," Delora replied, "but I do not want to hurt you in any way. If you want me to, my darling, I will wait just as I was prepared to wait for years and years until we could be together as you promised we would be."

"We are not going to wait one second longer than we need," Conrad said firmly. "I would have married you tomorrow only I had first to see the Bishop. He intends to have the Cathedral massed with flowers, and apparently everybody on the island wishes to be present."

"I would really . . like to marry you . . alone . . or perhaps . . aboard the *Invincible*."

"That is what I too, would have liked," Conrad agreed, "perhaps even more than you would, because every woman enjoys a wedding. But I thought I should give Antigua something to think about, besides the behaviour of her last Governor, and when they have seen you, my beautiful, they will talk of nothing else!"

"I love you!" Delora replied, "because you are not only so wonderful in every way, but you are so wise too. Oh, Conrad, will you go on loving me and wanting me, even when you leave me to go back to sea!"

There was a moment's silence. Then Conrad said:

"I have been facing facts, my darling, and I know that while in about six months time I may be well enough to undertake an arduous sea-voyage, I think it is unlikely I shall do so."

He saw a sudden excitement creep into Delora's expression, and because he knew exactly what she was thinking, he said:

"First, I have a great deal to do at home in putting our affairs in order. I know from what you have told me and what I have heard, that Denzil neglected the family estates which must be restored to their past prosperity."

"And then?" Delora questioned.

"Then I have the feeling, and I am almost sure I am not wrong, that the war will soon be over. We have to all intents and purposes, beaten Napoleon at sea. There now remains only a decisive battle to beat him on land and I believe the Duke of Wellington will do that!"

Delora gave a little cry of happiness.

"Then you can leave the Navy and stay with me? It is the most wonderful, perfect thing that could ever happen. But darling, suppose I . . bore you?"

"You could never do that," Conrad replied, "but I have no intention of settling down so that I have nothing to do, except spend money whether it is yours or mine. I have a feeling there will always be a job waiting for me at the Admiralty, and apart from that I want to take my place in the House of Lords and fight for an improvement, not only in the ships that we must have to protect our shores, but in the treatment of our seamen."

"No-one could do it better than you," Delora cried.

"I have seen the appalling conditions in which men are prepared to fight and die for their country," Conrad went on, "and I am absolutely determined that something should be done for them."

"And for the treatment they receive when they are wounded," Delora said quickly.

"Naturally that is in my mind," Conrad agreed, "but I am afraid I cannot arrange that there should be two women called Delora and Abigail aboard every ship in the future!"

"But you can try to arrange that the Surgeons are more capable and are prepared to use other methods than the knife?"

"I shall never forget that it was you and Abigail who saved my leg," Conrad replied. "And I am prepared to dedicate a very large part of my life in the future to trying to see that other men are cared for as I have been."

"You will let me . . help you?"

"You know I cannot do all these things without your love and without your inspiration."

"That is what I want you to say," Delora answered.

She pressed herself closer to him and she knew that no man could be so magnificent in every way, no man could make her feel when his lips touched hers, as if he carried her up into the sky and she was no longer human, but part of the divine.

She thought for one brief second of her unhappiness and fear when she had embarked on board the *Invincible,* which seemed now a century ago. . .

Then it had been cold and dark and because she knew where the ship must carry her, it made her feel as if she was journeying to an unutterable hell.

Yet from the very moment she saw Conrad coming into the cabin she had felt as if he was enveloped by a light like a Knight going into battle and her whole life had been changed.

"I love you," she said now, as he raised his head. "I love you, and I pray every moment of the day that I shall make you the sort of wife you want, and one who is . . worthy of you."

"You are not to talk like that, my darling one," he answered. "You are so perfect that I thank God that I am the most fortunate man in the world, because you love me."

His lips were on hers again and he kissed her until the room vanished and they were both part of the sea and the sky.

Then she felt a warm wave that yet was a flame of fire, rising in her breasts which was so exciting and yet at the same time, part of the Glory of God.

She knew Conrad felt the same, and as he drew her closer and his heart beat against hers, the flame grew into a burning fire and yet she was not afraid.

His lips were fierce, passionate, demanding and she wanted to give him what he wanted, only she did not exactly know what it was.

She only knew she wanted him to go on kissing her. She wanted to be closer and still closer, to belong to him, so that they became one person and nothing could divide them.

Conrad released her lips to put his cheek against hers. Then holding her very tightly in his arms, he said in a strange voice:

"You excite me to madness, my darling, little love, but I promise that when we are married, I will be very gentle with you. I could never bear you to be frightened of me as you would have been with the man I brought you here to marry."

"I could never be afraid of you," Delora replied, "and, darling, wonderful Conrad, I know that because I am very . . ignorant you have a great deal to teach me about . . love. I want to learn . . I want to love you . . as you want me to and whatever we do . . it will be a part of God . . and part of . . Paradise."

Her words made Conrad draw in his breath.

Then he was kissing her again, kissing her passionately, but at the same time, with a reverence that he had never given another woman.

Delora had filled the shrine in his heart that had always been empty.

Now he knew she would be there always and for ever, and he would worship her because she had brought him the true, pure love for which all men seek as they voyage over the difficult, unpredictable and often tempestuous sea of life.

"I worship you," he said against her lips.

Then there was no further need for words.